DARING BRIDE

Other books by Jane Peart

The Brides of Montclair Series

Valiant Bride
Ransomed Bride
Fortune's Bride
Folly's Bride
Yankee Bride/Rebel Bride
Gallant Bride
Shadow Bride
Destiny's Bride
Jubilee Bride
Mirror Bride
Hero's Bride
Senator's Bride

The Westward Dreams Series

Runaway Heart
Promise of the Valley
Where Tomorrow Waits
A Distant Dawn

The American Quilt Series

The Pattern
The Pledge
The Promise

Brides of Montclair 13

DARING BRIDE

MONTCLAIR at the CROSSROADS 1932–1939

By best-selling author

JANE PEART

ZondervanPublishingHouse
Grand Rapids, Michigan

A Division of HarperCollinsPublishers

Daring Bride

Requests for information should be addressed to:

ZondervanPublishingHouse
Grand Rapids, Michigan 49530

Library of Congress Cataloging-in-Publication Data

Peart, Jane.
Daring Bride : Montclair at the crossroads, 1932-1939 / Jane Peart.
p. cm.
ISBN: 0-310-20209-4
I. Title. II. Series: Peart, Jane. Brides of Montclair series ; bk. 13.
PS3566.E238D37 1997
813'.54—dc21 97-12008
CIP

Printed in the United States of America

---

97 98 99 00 01 02 03 04 /❖ DH/ 10 9 8 7 6 5 4 3 2 1

Mayfield, Virginia
Fall 1932

THE ELDERLY WOMAN standing at the gates to Montclair was elegant if not fashionable. Her ensemble was identical to the style originated by the British monarch Queen Mary, from the creamy beige silk turban, the coat, collared and cuffed in pale lynx, to the French-heeled kid pumps. Although Garnet considered it flattering to have her resemblance to the sovereign of her adopted country commented upon, she maintained a distinctive style of her own. Never one to imitate, she refused to follow slavishly the current trend of hemlines, wearing hers long enough to complete her dignified appearance, short enough to show off her still-lovely ankles.

Today Garnet Devlin's thoughts were less on appearance than on the earlier part of her long life. Looking through the ornate scrolls of iron lace toward the house, memories flowed over her.

A sudden rise in the wind rippled the ruff of fur collar. Although the afternoon was not cold, Garnet shivered. Foolish to dwell in the past. It was the *present* that demanded her attention. She was back in the United States, in her native Virginia, to see her grandchildren.

She was on her way to Cameron Hall, her childhood home, a few miles further along the country road. Her nephew Scott and his English wife, Jill, now lived there, and she was to stay with them during her visit. It had only been on impulse that Garnet had told her driver to stop at the entrance to Montclair.

She had delayed long enough. She started to turn back to

the Chrysler limousine, which she had rented in Richmond, when something caught her eye—a small sign posted to the left of the gate.

Riding Instruction, Beginners through Jumping
Quality Horses, English Saddle
Also Pony Classes, Ages 5–8
Cara Montrose, Instructor
Experienced, Enthusiastic, Patient
Inquiries Welcome—Phone: 2375

A frown drew her arched brows together. What in the world was this? Cara teaching riding? She would certainly have to ask Scott about this. Were Kip and Cara's finances that bad that she was reduced to being a riding instructor? Things must have come to a pretty pass at Montclair if that was the case.

Garnet pursed her lips thoughtfully. Well, she'd soon get to the bottom of this. She walked back to the car, and the chauffeur assisted her into the backseat. She leaned back against the cushioned seat as the car started. Good thing she had made the effort to come. There were things here she must see about.

Her concern for the youngest of her grandchildren, Bryanne Montrose, was the main reason she had made this trip. A letter from Brynie's older sister, Lynette Maynard, the wife of a state senator, had prompted this visit. From what Garnet had gathered, Bryanne was still mourning for the young Irishman she had loved. On a visit to his family in Ireland during the time in which that beautiful country had been plagued by the strife they called the Troubles, Sean had been killed. It had been a case of mistaken identity. He had been shot in a street battle, caught in the crossfire between the Sein Fein, the revolutionary underground army, and the British militia. He had died instantly.

It was heartbreaking, to be sure. But Bryanne had grieved long enough. Life was for the living. Garnet had learned that from her own tragic experiences. She must make Bryanne realize that she was still young, that life held a great deal more for her than sorrow. Surely she would listen to reason from her grandmother, who, after all, had raised her from the time she was five years old until she was eighteen.

Garnet pressed her lips together firmly. She also intended to have a talk with Cara regarding this nonsense about horseback riding lessons. A surge of energy flowed through her. Yes, indeed, coming back had been a good idea. There was a great deal for her to do during this visit. There were problems to solve, things to set straight, steps to be taken. She felt rejuvenated.

chapter 1

Montclair

THE OLD BRASS knocker on the paneled front door needed polishing, Cara thought, glancing at it as she swept the windblown leaves off the wide veranda. She made a face. One more thing to do before the family began to arrive for Aunt Garnet's party. Another reminder of how she'd neglected keeping Montclair to its old level of perfection. But they never used the front entrance anymore. Hardly ever had what you'd call company.

Recently they had all been so busy. Kip at the airfield as an instructor, she giving riding lessons, trying to keep up the stables with little help and less money.

With Aunt Garnet's visit, she now had to get busy, get things in order. Especially since she had volunteered to host the birthday dinner party at Montclair. Cara shook her head ruefully. Another one of those reckless impulses that had got her into trouble most of her life. But Garnet had come here as the bride of Bryce Montrose, her first husband, and it somehow seemed appropriate to have the party here.

Thank goodness Kitty would be here to help. Of course, Kitty would notice every single thing that needed doing! Kitty was as opposite Cara as a twin sister could be.

With a final swoop of the broom, Cara went inside. Looking

around herself and seeing the house through her sister's eyes, Cara realized that it badly needed a great deal of attention.

When she had first come here after marrying Kip in Paris five years ago, she had had the best of intentions. She remembered the dismay and discouragement she felt when she had opened the door of Montclair. But she shouldn't have been surprised. Kip and Luc had lived here alone after Mattie, their longtime housekeeper, retired.

The house had become a repository of museum-quality pieces alongside wicker sets that needed both repairing and repainting. Fan-backed Victorian chairs with curved legs and shredded velvet upholstery were set opposite worn leather Morris recliners. Priceless mahogany Duncan Phyfe tables bore white circles where glasses had been carelessly placed. Fine portraits hung slightly askew, their elaborate gold frames covered with dust.

Cara had had her work cut out for her. Not that keeping a perfect house or entertaining was something she had wanted to spend the rest of her life doing. But some semblance of order had to be made of that chaos to be able to have a home where children could live and grow up in some sort of normal fashion.

She had been sure there would be children besides Nicole, the little French orphan she had brought back to Virginia, and Luc, Kip's son by his first marriage. Cara had wanted a whole houseful of little Montroses running about. However, there hadn't been the slightest sign that this dream would be fulfilled, and by now Cara had given up hope. After all, she was nearly forty. She had started to wonder if they should think of adoption....

Well, that decision was for a less hectic day. First things first.

Cara made a slow walk through the downstairs, but her mind couldn't seem to stay in one place. She kept thinking of Paris and how it had been for them. Lost in thoughts of the past, she did not hear the back door open or Kip's footsteps. He had left his boots outside and was in his stocking feet. He came up behind where she was standing, encircled her waist, and kissed her cheek.

Startled, she twisted around and pushed him a little away, saying, "You scared me, sneaking up on me like that!"

"I live here!" he said in mock protest. "Can't I walk into my own house, kiss my own wife?"

Trying to recover her composure, she asked, "Where's Luc?"

"With Niki. They're feeding the ducks," he told her and released her.

"You'd better shower and change," she said. "I'm not sure when Kitty will get here."

Kip started toward the stairway and then turned back, "Oh, by the way, Beau and Tim are coming for supper."

Cara bit back the words she had almost flung at him—*Why didn't you let me know?* It was, after all, Kip's home. He could invite whomever he wanted here. She just wished . . . Then she remembered she'd put in a roast earlier. Having dinner guests just meant cutting up more vegetables, potatoes.

Beau Chartyrs and Tim Pratney were fellow flyers, friends of long standing. Tim had been with Kip in the Lafayette Esquadrille, the squad of American volunteers who had flown for France in the war. The two of them had been among the very few survivors of that group. They shared memories, a love of flying, a friendship that was bonded in steel, a camaraderie that would last a lifetime.

That's OK, isn't it?" Kip asked.

"Sure," Cara said over her shoulder as she headed for the kitchen.

She took some potatoes to the sink and began scrubbing

them, her mind still occupied with Aunt Garnet's coming visit. For as long as she could remember, the old lady had caused ripples. Garnet had never got over being the prettiest belle in Mayfield, a pampered daughter and wife used to having her own way. She still liked to have her way, even if it meant manipulating other people's lives. Poor Bryanne. She was probably in for it this time.

Kitty Traherne took the turn off the highway, drove through Main Street, then onto the familiar country road. Her neck felt tight and her back ached. The drive from Williamsburg was long and depressing. So much of what had been quaint and picturesque about the countryside seemed to have vanished. Of course, Rockefeller money was restoring Williamsburg to its Colonial beginnings, or so it was rumored. But Mayfield looked dreary, its buildings drab, run-down. The depression had taken its toll, and there was no northern multimillionaire interested in a small, out-of-the-way, rural Virginia town of no particular significance.

It was late afternoon when Kitty started up the winding road that led to Montclair. Halfway up she drew to a stop. A turn to the right would take her to Eden Cottage. So many memories of Richard and their life together there swept over her, memories she still did not feel strong enough to face. Someday perhaps she could go back there to live, but not yet.

The last few weeks, spent traveling, speaking, signing Richard's poetry books, relating to people almost constantly, had been exhausting. Now, with Aunt Garnet's arrival, there was the family reunion to face. What Kitty really wanted, really needed, was time to herself, time to think, to pray, to plan. Where did she go from here?

With a sigh, she turned on the ignition, shifted, and drove

the rest of the way up to the house. There she braked and got out of the car, just as the front door opened and Cara came running down the steps, calling, "Kitty! Wonderful. I was beginning to wonder, but here you are. Come in. Welcome back to Montclair!"

"There's so much to talk about, so much to catch up on," Cara said, curling up at the bottom of the bed in the room Kitty would be using while she was here. "Did you know Aunt Garnet has arrived?"

"Yes. I thought she was here. I had dinner with her at her hotel in New York before she left for Richmond." She paused. "You heard about Evalee, didn't you?"

"No, what about our dear cousin?" Cara asked sarcastically. Evalee Bondurant had never been one of her favorite relatives.

"She's married," Kitty told her. "To a Russian count."

"You're kidding!" exclaimed Cara, astonished, sitting up straight.

"No, it's true. Aunt Garnet can fill you in on the details. She attended the wedding."

"Where?"

"In Paris. You knew that Aunt Dru and Evalee were over there. They'd been to visit Leonora and Lalage, then went on to France. And that's where the romance happened."

"Ah, Paris!" Cara affected a dreamy expression. "But really, a *count*? That sounds like something Evalee would do."

"An impoverished count, I'm afraid. One of the many White Russian émigrés that fled when the Bolshevik revolution took place."

Cara shook her head. "Hmmm. Then our luxury-loving cousin won't be living in a palace, after all."

"More likely a garret, I suspect. They're all refugees, lucky to get out with their lives."

Just then a knock came at the door. "Tante, I want to see Aunt Kitty," came a child's voice.

The sisters exchanged glances. "Niki, and probably Luc too," Cara said, then raised her voice. "OK, come on in."

The door opened and in rushed a little girl, small-boned, with dark, curly hair and huge, sparkling brown eyes. She flung herself into the arms Kitty held out to her. A tall boy followed more slowly and stood waiting for the enthusiastic hugs and greetings between his aunt and adopted sister to be over. Then he stepped up and thrust out his hand to Kitty. Over his head Kitty's eyes met Cara's amused ones. Luc, at twelve, was giving notice that he was too old for sissy stuff like kisses.

"Oh, I almost forgot," Cara said. "Some friends of Kip's will be here for dinner."

"Had I better change?" Kitty asked.

"Heavens, no!" Cara got up and moved to the bedroom door. "They're just some of his flying buddies. Practically family," she flung over her shoulder as she went out of the room, not waiting for Kitty's reaction to this additional information. Cara knew how Kitty felt about Kip's continuing interest in flying. She called it his protracted "daredevil ace" obsession, something he should have got over by this time. Cara just hoped her twin wouldn't let her own distaste for any reminder of the war spoil what could be a pleasant evening.

chapter 2

A FEW MILES away, over at Cameron Hall, Garnet was regaling Scott and Jill with her account of Evalee's wedding.

"Wouldn't you guess, she wanted as elegant a wedding gown and as lavish a reception as if her family were still in Charleston society! Of course, Dru was beside herself. Who wouldn't be, if a daughter was determined to marry a man whose background, religion, and outlook were so foreign? Would you believe the child had only known him two weeks?"

Garnet looked at each of them in turn, expecting an affirmative response, then continued. "Naturally, as soon as I heard about it, I went to Paris. Dru needed family support, and I intended to give it to her."

"What's the guy's name?" asked Scott.

"Andre Oblenskov. I think that's the way it's pronounced."

"And what was he like?" This was from Jill.

"Charming, I must say! Looks like a movie star. Has eyes like Rudolph Valentino." Garnet's own eyes twinkled in the telling. "It's not hard to understand how someone as romantic and irresponsible as Evalee would fall for him. Of course, she's been spoiled all her life, stubborn, self-centered. Randall doted upon her, never denied her anything. No wonder!" Garnet threw out her hands in a helpless gesture.

"Tell us about the wedding," urged Jill.

"Well, my dear, it was like nothing you or I ever saw, I can say that. I felt I was witnessing a play. It was very strange indeed. It took place in a small Russian Orthodox church. They were married by a dark-bearded priest dressed in elegant robes, embroidered and trimmed in gold braid. Of course, Dru and I didn't understand a word he said, but actually it was quite beautiful. At the end of the ceremony, he held two golden crowns over their heads and made a sign of the cross over them as he blessed them."

"And what did Evalee wear?"

"I declare, she did look every inch the countess she was becoming—in name, at least. White satin and a diamond tiara."

"Diamond?" Scott asked. "I thought you said the groom was penniless."

"Oh, he is. So are they all. But it seems the only thing they managed to take out of the country was their jewels. One of Andre's aunties, Countess Vera, confided to me that they all had sewn them into their corsets when escaping." Suddenly Garnet began to chuckle.

"What's funny, Aunt Garnet?" Scott asked.

"I was just thinking of the discussion Dru and I had before the wedding. Knowing the financial situation of Andre's family, we decided to dress simply and not wear any jewelry. But when we got to the church, we saw that even though their gowns were rather out of style, we were completely outshone by the Oblenskov ladies, who were aglitter with diamonds, sapphires, emeralds."

"Does Evalee seem happy?" was Jill's next question.

"She should be, if all the many toasts wishing them a long and happy marriage have anything to do with it," Garnet said.

Then she added, "I don't think I ever saw a young couple more in love."

After that the conversation went on to other things, but Garnet's description of Evalee's wedding had made Jill pensive.

She knew what it was to be suddenly bereft of everything, just as the Oblenskovs were. The world war had also wiped out her former life. She hoped that in spite of differences in background, religion, and nationality, Andre and Evalee had found true love and would have a long, happy life together.

"It's disgraceful," Garnet was saying to Scott. "Hasn't she any sense of the propriety of such a thing? The Montrose name is one of the oldest in this county. And to *advertise* to give riding lessons! It's a wonder Kip has allowed it."

"Kip allow it?" Scott echoed her statement sarcastically. "No one tells Cara what to do. She's as self-willed as ever, Aunt Garnet. Even mother and father learned that."

"Well, nevertheless, I intend to have a talk with her and give her my opinion."

"I'd leave it alone, Aunt Garnet. It won't be appreciated," advised Scott.

"It's my duty, Scott. Since your mother chose to move to California, there's no one to direct your sister."

Scott rolled his eyes upward. "Take my word for it, Aunt Garnet, you'll be wasting your breath—besides making Cara angry."

Garnet ignored him placidly. "Now, about Bryanne. . . ."

At this point Jill rose and excused herself, saying she had to check with the cook in the kitchen about dinner, and left the room.

She should have known, having worked for Garnet Devlin as a companion-governess to Bryanne before her marriage to Scott. Garnet always stirred things up. Talk about a storm brewing! Confronting Cara was sowing a whirlwind. And Garnet would probably reap a whirlwind.

However, Jill was determined to try to prevent Garnet from intimidating Bryanne. That is, if she could.

That night at the dinner table at Montclair, Nicole felt anxious. Uncle Kip's flyer friends often ate meals with them. Usually it didn't make any difference. They practically ignored her and Luc, except for some teasing remarks when they first came to the table. Most of all, the men just talked to each other, swapping airplane stories, detailing exciting moments of near misses, describing close calls as if they were fun.

Niki shot a quick glance at Cara. Tante always pretended interest, laughed at the right times, but sometimes Niki had seen a glaze come over her eyes, a faraway look. Niki, who knew her so well, suspected she was thinking of something else. The ponies, perhaps. She was probably thinking about the riding students that were having a difficult time, and what methods she might use to help them. Tante was wonderful with kids. Too bad she and Uncle Kip hadn't had some of their own. Maybe then Tante wouldn't be so protective, so possessive.

But what worried Niki tonight was that Aunt Kitty was here. Niki knew Kitty hated talk of flying because it reminded her of the war. Niki knew all about Kitty's story. She had been a nurse in France at the battlefields. She had fallen in love with a soldier, and he had been horribly wounded. They had lived in the darling little cottage in the woods until he died. Niki thought it was terribly romantic but very sad. She wished Uncle Kip would remember that and talk about something different. Niki wasn't sure what else he was really interested in except planes and flying.

She looked over at Luc. He liked to hear his father and his

friends tell stories. He made model planes and had them hanging from the ceiling in his bedroom. Niki tried to catch his eye but he was listening to the men.

Niki's glance shifted to Tante and she felt a small jolt of alarm. Tante looked nervous and was darting quick looks toward her sister. Aunt Kitty had grown very pale. She was crumbling her roll to pieces and wasn't eating. Niki felt her stomach tighten.

Suddenly Aunt Kitty burst out, "Didn't you men have enough of this kind of talk in the war? Or are you still living your glory days, when you were the knights of the air?" She shook her head. Her eyes were bright with anger. Niki had never seen her like this. "I can't understand how you could have forgotten your friends who were shot down and died in fiery crashes—or worse, lived for a few agonizing weeks afterward."

Kip looked startled at first, then flushed a deep red. His jaw clenched. "Kitty, listen—," he began, but she wouldn't let him stop her.

"No, Kip, *you* listen! And your friends should hear this, too! I saw men brought into the hospital with third-degree burns over half their bodies. Can you even imagine what excruciating pain that is? They were in shock, screaming for somebody to put them out of their agony. I can't forget that. And you shouldn't be able to, either. How can you take the risks you take every time you go up in a plane? Don't you care about your wife and children?"

"Kitty, please," Cara said in a low voice. "We have guests."

But Kitty whirled around and demanded. "And how about you, Cara? You drove an ambulance. You were with me when we loaded mortally wounded men into ambulances. How can you let Kip do this?"

"It's not war, Kitty," Kip said. "We're planning for the future of aeronautics."

"Future? That's a laugh. I've been to Europe, just a year ago. I don't think Germany and Italy are building their factories and making airplanes for fun. I think they're planning for another war."

"That's ridiculous, Kitty," argued Kip. "You don't know what you're talking about. You've been taken in by all these isolationists. People that are paranoid about—"

"Paranoid? You're the ones who are crazy." Kitty pushed back her chair and got up. "I can't listen to any more of this."

An audible sob caught in her throat and she rushed out of the dining room. A stunned silence followed her departure. No one moved or said anything for a full minute.

Beau and Tim looked down at their plates. Then Kip broke the uneasy pall that had fallen over the table. "You'll have to forgive Kitty. She was, as she said, a field nurse. Lost her husband . . ." His voice trailed off. His lips were pressed together tightly. He glanced at Cara, and the look that passed between them was cold. The two other men murmured something.

Then Cara spoke. "Niki, you and Luc please clear the table. Then you can go upstairs and listen to your radio or read until bedtime."

Luc did his part of the job in a slapdash manner, piling the plates on the drain board haphazardly. Then he went back into the dining room, where the men were hotly debating the need for America to build up an air force.

Feeling sick and unhappy about the scene, Niki used the back stairway from the kitchen to her bedroom. As she passed the guest room, she heard raised voices. She halted. She couldn't help overhearing. Tante and Aunt Kitty were having a terrible quarrel.

Frightened yet fascinated, she unabashedly listened.

"I'm sorry if I embarrassed you, Cara, but I don't understand how you can sit by and let Kip do this."

"Do what? He's doing what he does best. He's an experienced, skilled pilot. He's teaching young men to fly."

"For *what*? To go off to war, kill other young men, and be killed? Is that something to be proud of?"

"That's not fair, Kitty. There's no war. Kip and men like Beau and Tim see a great future in the air. They're thinking of starting a mail service with trained pilots and—"

"Do you really believe that, Cara?" Kitty demanded. "Anyone with a brain can see what's ahead if those strutting egomaniacs in Italy and Germany have their way. What they did in Ethiopia was barbaric . . . ." She looked at her twin. "Or don't you read the papers? Are you so isolated in your cocoon in rural Virginia, occupied with your ponies and your children, that you don't pay attention to what's happening in the rest of the world? If you did, you'd know how dangerous what Kip and the others are doing is."

Cara was insulted. "I told you, Kitty, they're simply instructors—"

"I can't believe you can't see it! Kip's never got over being a hero, an ace."

"That's not only unfair, it's unkind," Cara retorted. At first all she had wanted to do was calm Kitty down, but now she was angry.

"Just wait and see. The bugles blow and he's off, ready for the glory of it all." Kitty's hands were clenched, the knuckles white. "Oh, I cannot believe that someone—*anyone*—who's seen the horrors of war firsthand could ever have any part in it." She shivered and hugged her arms close to her body, as though she were physically cold. "For you to stand by and encourage him . . ." She looked at her sister aghast. "If it weren't for the last terrible war, my life—and yours too, Cara—would be so different. My darling Richard—and Owen—would not have had to die."

"Kitty—," began Cara, frustrated.

"Don't!" Kitty put both hands over her ears, turned away. "Don't say any more. I don't want to hear it." She whirled around, faced her sister, trembling. "What does it take to get through to you? I'm shocked that you aren't as incensed as I am. Don't you see where all this is leading? Don't you read anything but *Horse Digest*?"

Niki heard Tante respond in an angry voice, then loud footsteps on the uncarpeted floor. Afraid of being caught eavesdropping, she ran down the hall to her own room. Shakily she let out the breath she hadn't realized she had been holding. It was scary and awful to hear the twin sisters talk to each other like that.

Kitty was too distressed to sleep. She had always hated any kind of confrontation, avoided it—often to her own regret at being perhaps too passive. But to quarrel so with her twin! She and Cara had differed often on many things, but this was the worst argument of their lives.

She loved Cara even as herself. It was a physical pain to be apart from her physically, emotionally, and spiritually. But there was no way she could reconcile their opposite viewpoints on this most vital matter. She would have to—as she had had to do once before—separate from her sister, follow her own direction no matter what....

Kitty closed her eyes and pressed clenched fists against her mouth, reliving the horror she could usually keep at bay. Wasted pain, men who needn't have died. Lives, bodies, minds, souls, wrecked. The world would plunge headlong back into it all, unless someone cried, *"Stop the insanity!"*

She had to try. Even if she was the only voice lifted up against the battle cries of those using patriotism to justify killing. She remembered Richard's long agony after the parades, the flag waving, the medals. She had sat up nights with him, holding him as he fought against begging for the relief of the narcotic that she had the power to give. They had wept together, prayed together. She had to tell others—for Richard's sake and for the sake of all those she had seen suffer and die in the human slaughter—that there was no glory in war.

Kitty shuddered. Pain and anger, if turned inward, festered. You had to deal with emotional wounds. What could she do? One thing she knew—she couldn't stay here much longer. She didn't want to face Kip in the morning. Or talk to Cara. They'd already said too much. They had said things they would probably both be sorry for later—but of that she wasn't sure. Her own words had been her heart's cry. She knew her feelings wouldn't change.

She dreaded facing Kip. But she had to stay until after Aunt Garnet's birthday party. It would be too awkward, too awful, to leave before then. To let everyone know the rift that had come between her sister and her.

Kitty heard the grandfather clock downstairs strike five. She reached for her robe, wrapped it around herself, and went to the window. The early-morning sky was lavender streaked with pink. In the distance, half hidden by the dense foliage of the trees leading to it, she could see the faint outline of the little house. Eden Cottage. She hadn't lived there since Richard's death, couldn't bear to. She had rented it a few times but mostly it stood empty. Slowly the thought came. While she was in

Mayfield, she would move out to Eden Cottage. That way she could avoid another confrontation with Cara or Kip. Yes, that's what she would do. It would give her the space she needed, the time to think, to plan what she could do.

chapter 3

Arbordale, Virginia
Avalon

ALTHOUGH BRYANNE MONTROSE did not have the cameo beauty people admired in her sister, Lynette Maynard, she was very attractive. Her features were just irregular enough to make her face interesting. She had lovely blue eyes, a sweet, generous mouth, and shiny red-gold hair worn in a fashionable "page-boy" style. At the moment, her expression was all concentration as her hands moved quickly in the clay. At a knock on the studio door, her eyebrows drew together in a frown. Without looking away from the figure of the child she was molding, she called, "Come in!"

"How's it going, little Sis?"

She turned to look at her tall brother as he entered. Gareth was handsome in a rugged sort of way. Dressed in a denim work shirt, worn corduroys, and boots, he could easily have been taken for an ordinary workman. He set down a tray with a coffee pot and two mugs and came to stand behind her.

"Oh, I don't know. I'm about to smash it all down and start over!" she replied, half joking, half serious. Spotting the tray, she exclaimed, "Oh, great! Just what I needed. Thanks!"

"A little sustenance to stimulate the creative artist," he said, smiling, and he filled both mugs.

"I don't know about that," she sighed. "Creative? Not really. I'm using Mama's sketches, you know. Oh, good. I didn't realize I was hungry." She reached for one of the oatmeal-raisin cookies on the plate.

"You've been out here working for hours." Gareth handed her a steaming mug, then studied the model on the pedestal. "I think it's good. In fact, very good, Brynie."

Bryanne sat back on the high stool and looked critically at it. "Do you truly think so? Mama's sketches are so delicate, but when I try to translate them into clay, they look so chunky, so—"

"It's funny that Mama never painted. She drew so well."

"Imagine us finding these after . . ." Bryanne shook her head. "I mean, Papa didn't even know she made so many drawings of us when we were children."

"She always wanted him to be the center, the star." Gareth's smile was a bit rueful. "She didn't want to take anything away from him. She did her tapestries. That was a safe place for her to indulge her creativity."

"I guess you're right," Bryanne said, nodding. She took a bite of her cookie and asked, "What were you doing all day?"

"Mulching, hoeing, getting the ground ready for spring."

"Farmer Jones!" she teased.

He grinned. "I guess you could call me that."

Bryanne smiled. She adored her older brother, admired him for being such an individual. He had resisted all the family's pleas, suggestions, and entreaties to finish college, to go into law or medicine. Instead, he had opted to live at their family home, Avalon, which stood on a small island near Arbordale, a town located fifteen miles from Mayfield. He had restored the house after it had stood empty for years. Ever since their mother had lost her life in the *Titanic* disaster, their father, Jeff Montrose, had abandoned it.

On his own, Gareth had studied botany. He had learned how to grow fruits and vegetables, how to take care of the trees and the fertile land on the island. Now he had a thriving landscape gardening business. He was doing what he wanted, what he loved best, in the place he loved best. Of course, they both loved Avalon—it was the place where they had experienced a magical childhood.

Gareth finished his coffee, replaced his mug on the tray, and said to Bryanne, "You'd better clean up here, go home, and get ready. Grandmother's party at Montclair is this evening."

"Oh, I nearly forgot," Bryanne gasped. At her brother's skeptical look she amended, "Not about Grandmother! Who could forget her?" She dimpled mischievously. "It's just that when I'm working, everything gets forgotten. Time just disappears. But truthfully, I'm not especially looking forward to this evening. She'll probably come at me again about going back to Birchfields with her."

"And you don't want to."

"It's not that I don't love her, Gareth, you know that. And I know she's getting old and is probably lonely in that big house all alone. But . . ." She paused. "When I'm with her, I become a child again. At least in her eyes. She can't help it. After all, I was only five when Mama died and Grandmother took over. But I'm not a child anymore." Her eyes suddenly became brilliant with tears. Gareth knew she was thinking about Sean. An understanding silence fell between them.

Then Bryanne said seriously, "I'm happy working here in the studio. I'm developing a talent I wasn't even sure I had. I'm finding myself. Do you understand?" She looked beseechingly at her brother. "Of course *you* do. I appreciate the way you've encouraged and supported me, Gareth. And Grandmother Blythe has, too. I don't think Lynette supports me, not really. She'd like me to be more social. She's always giving these little dinner parties and inviting eligible young men to meet me!" Bryanne threw out her hands in a helpless gesture, then laughed. "You see how it is, don't you? The only way I'm going to be able to be myself is here, where I'm left alone and not bothered."

Gareth looked at his younger sister affectionately for a moment, then said, "Well, at the risk of bothering you, I do have to remind you that we're due at Montclair at seven and it's after five now. So—"

"Yes, you're right. I'd better go." Bryanne got down off her stool. She went over to the stationary sink and wet and wrung out a cloth, then draped it over the model of the little child cuddling a small bunny. Then she wiped her clay-dried hands on her smock. "I'll leave this now. Tomorrow it may look better to me. Tomorrow's another day."

From the library window, Jill Cameron saw Bryanne's small red sports roadster round the drive and stop, watched as the slender, pretty young woman got out and walked toward the house.

How graceful she was, Jill marveled, thinking of the chunky, awkward child she had loved. From the very first time she had seen Bryanne, when Jill had gone with Garnet to the girls' boarding school so she and Bryanne could meet, Jill's heart had gone out to the motherless young girl so full of life, so eager to be loved. Once Jill had accepted Garnet's offer to become Bryanne's companion-governess, she and Bryanne had been inseparable. Jill couldn't have loved her more if she had been her own. Even after Jill's own two children were born, Bryanne claimed a special place in her heart.

She had wept with her over the neglect Bryanne's artist father, Geoffrey Montrose, had shown her, and again when the news of Sean's tragic, unnecessary death had come. She had worried about Bryanne's months of heartbroken sorrow over the loss of her first love. Jill had been awed by the gradual development of her dormant creativity, the deepening of her spirituality. She had come to appreciate and care ever more deeply for this lovely young woman who had known tragedy and yet had made something beautiful of her life.

Jill was aware of the constant, if loving, pressure that Bryanne's older sister, Lynette, was putting on Bryanne to bring her into a more active social life, and she dreaded Garnet's insistence that Bryanne abandon her reclusive existence. Jill realized, as no one else seemed to, that in order for art to come into its fullest, it must have time. Times of aloneness, quietness, in order to achieve its potential, like a butterfly that must remain hidden in its chrysalis before emerging in all its beauty.

Jill had tried to explain this to her husband, Scott, since Bryanne had come to live with them at Cameron Hall. "She needs to be left alone. She is not dramatizing herself or being dangerously melancholy."

In the months after Sean's death, Jill had seen Bryanne heal herself. Bryanne had wandered through the gardens, spending hours in the gazebo, sometimes reading, sometimes dreaming. She had ridden her horse through the surrounding woods, letting the tranquillity of nature envelop her with its own magic powers.

Jill knew that Bryanne had passed through the valley and had begun to approach a new plateau when she decided to take some classes at the university. That's when her interest in sculpting began. She came to the attention of her instructor, who encouraged her to submit one of her figures in a student exhibit. There it received an honorable mention. That was all Bryanne needed to openly pursue an urge to create that, before, she had been too shy to declare.

Jill knew, more than anyone else except perhaps Gareth, that Bryanne had lived under the shadow of her famous father for so long that she had not dared to show the slightest artistic ability, afraid that she would be compared or critiqued by him or his admirers.

With his usual self-absorption and indifference, Jeff Montrose had not seemed to take note of the emerging artist in his daughter. He had moved to Taos, New Mexico, after Faith's death, and at that point Bryanne had been able to forge ahead. Gareth offered her the use of Jeff's old studio at Avalon, since Jeff rarely came back to Virginia. It was at the studio where Bryanne seemed to flower. Her new contentment and self-acceptance gave her a radiance that Jill rejoiced to see.

As for love or romance, something Lynette worried a great deal about for her sister, Jill was certain that when the time was right, that too would come. When she imagined this for Bryanne, Jill was reminded of a sleeping princess slowly awakening to her own indwelling nature, awaiting the kiss of a prince who would bring her fulfillment and completion.

No one should try to—or for that matter, could—bring this about until the time was right. The phrase "God is never too early, never too late; God's timing is always perfect," Jill prayed for Bryanne.

At the front door she greeted Bryanne. "Good day?"

"I think so. I hope so, or people will start telling me I'm wasting my time," Bryanne replied with a little shrug.

"Don't worry about other people. Follow your heart. You're

doing fine," Jill said encouragingly. "I can't wait to see your next piece."

Bryanne gave her an impulsive hug. "Thanks, Jill. You're great. And so is Gareth. My cheering squad." Then she asked, "Where's Grandmother?"

"Scott already took her over to Montclair. It seems she wanted to have a private talk with Cara before all the rest of us gathered."

The two women exchanged a look, and then Bryanne laughed, saying, "Poor Aunt Cara. She's probably in for it."

"I wouldn't worry. Cara can hold her own."

Bryanne started toward the stairway. "Well, I'm off to take a long, leisurely bath and unwind a little before the party."

"Wait, Brynie," Jill said. "You got a letter today." She picked up an envelope lying on the hall table and handed it to her.

A puzzled frown creased Bryanne's forehead as she took it. Noting the New Mexico postmark, she lifted her eyes and met Jill's. "It's from father."

Jill nodded. "I thought so." Then, realizing Bryanne would want to read this rare communication in privacy, Jill started down the hall toward the back of the house, saying tactfully, "I have to go round up the children. We have to leave for Montclair soon. Do you want to ride with us or take your own car?"

"I think I'll drive over on my own, thanks," Bryanne said over her shoulder as she went up the stairs.

"All right. See you later at Montclair."

As soon as she got to her own room, Bryanne tore open the envelope and read the single sheet written in Jeff Montrose's spiky, almost illegible handwriting.

My Dear Daughter,

Just a short note to tell you I am planning to go to

Scotland next summer to visit my late brother Jonathan's widow. I've never met their children, Fraser and Fiona, and thought this as good a time as any to do so. Phoebe manages her family's inn in a small town, Kilgaren. It is a part of the world I've not seen, and I shall probably stay there for several weeks, hoping to do some painting as well. If these plans work out and time allows, I intend to make a short stop in Mayfield to see your sister and brother and you. I will let you know my traveling dates so the three of you can make appropriate arrangements for us to be together.

Ever your devoted father,
Jeff Montrose.

The signature was a flourishing scribble, familiar to collectors of his paintings.

Still holding the letter, Bryanne sat down on the edge of the bed. It was one of the few, hastily written communications she had had from her father over the years. He'd let so many years go by that she sometimes wondered if he even remembered she existed. Did he even know that his youngest daughter was artistically talented?

Bryanne thought of the time the three of them had gone to Taos on impulse. It had been Gareth's idea and Lynette had quickly agreed. Bryanne had just graduated from Miss Drummond's Academy, and her father had been noticeably absent from the ceremony. In an uncharacteristic burst of resentment, Lynette had said to the other two, "he can't just ignore us as he did when we were children. He can't claim bereavement at this point. Mama's been gone over twenty years." A telegram had been dispatched, arrangements and train reservations made.

It had not been too satisfactory a time. Their father had been awkward around these three strange adults, having missed most of their childhood. But Bryanne had found Taos beautiful. In fact, she had fallen in love with it—the endless sky, the colors of the hills, the expanse of the desert, all so different from Virginia and the English countryside where she had grown up.

Her father's house was a sprawling California-Spanish style with a tile roof, second-story veranda, terra-cotta tile floors, and a large, gracious courtyard with a fountain in the middle. Twisting paths lead down to a swimming pool in a natural setting of rocks and succulent plants and cacti.

His studio was separate from the house, having large windows with magnificent views. Bryanne had longed to ask him if she could stay and watch him paint. But he rose at dawn and secluded himself there until noon. He joined them for lunch on the patio, and the afternoons were spent driving around in his convertible, the evenings filled with the arrival of the circle of artist friends—writers, dramatists, actors—he had made in his winter stays there.

It had been a fascinating, heady time for Bryanne. Lynette had expressed disappointment that they had never had any time alone with Jeff. But Gareth had been philosophic, saying, "It's too late for him to learn how to be a father now." Bryanne, never having really known her father as a parent, was in awe of him as an artist, and she longed to have him talk about his work. She wanted to get to know him, learn from him.

They had left at the end of the week. Bryanne had felt sad that this opportunity had slipped away in social events and superficial conversation. She still didn't feel she knew her famous father, and felt an emptiness in her heart that she was afraid would never go away.

And now this letter. It came at a time of decision in her own life. Again she felt pulled. Knowing how strong Garnet was, Bryanne had already begun to build strength to resist what *she* was suggesting. To go back to England with her grandmother was to become a child again. Garnet was a benevolent tyrant, Bryanne thought, smiling.

Scotland. She had a romantic image of the country. Rockbound coast, fields of heather, picturesque crofter's cottages. Why couldn't she accompany her father there, meet her Scottish aunt and her cousins? Perhaps such a trip would be her chance to really get close to a father she had missed, longed for, most of her life.

Bryanne folded the letter and replaced it in the envelope. It was something she would have to consider, think about, certainly pray about. But now she had to hurry, bathe, dress for the family birthday party at Montclair.

chapter 4

Montclair

IN THE MASTER bedroom, Cara stood in front of the full-length mirror, surveying herself. The dress was ages old and probably hopelessly out of fashion. She didn't keep up with such things anymore. But its design was classic, the color good with her hair and her eyes. She wished she could ask Kitty about it. . . .

As that thought flashed through her mind almost unconsciously, Cara was stricken anew with what had happened. Last night had been bad enough with the scene at the dinner table, followed by their awful quarrel. This morning was even worse. Kitty had moved out to Eden Cottage.

Kip had been livid about Kitty's outspokenness in front of his guests. "Who does she think she is, anyhow?" he'd demanded when Beau and Tim left after dinner. "She hasn't a clue about what's really going on in aviation. Why does she have to bring the war into it? The rest of us have moved on. Kitty's wallowing in the past." He had flung himself down in the sagging leather chair in their bedroom and looked to Cara for some explanation.

"What can I say? Except that she's still grieving over Richard."

"It's all that poetry stuff. Going to colleges and reading it, influencing all those young people with her pacifist notions."

"Kip, it's Kitty's choice. It's her life."

"Well, it's a poor way of living it, that's all I have to say," Kip had grumbled.

Cara regarded her reflection in the mirror of her dressing table and sighed. People used to call the sisters "mirror twins," like two sides of the same coin. Kitty had always seemed so much more everything—smarter, sweeter, better. Being around her sometimes seemed to bring out Cara's perverse traits, her dark side—selfish, self-willed, stubborn. And that made Kitty's nature shine all the brighter.

Why can't you be more like Kitty? That's what their mother, Blythe, used to sometimes ask in despair at some of Cara's wild, rebellious ways.

Well, I'm not like Kitty. Never have been, never will be! Cara put down her hairbrush and got up. Her reaction made her feel guilty. She felt cross and not ready to play the hostess tonight at the festive family party. She'd be glad when all the fuss of Aunt Garnet's visit was over.

Just then she heard the sound of tires on the gravel driveway beneath her bedroom window. She went to look out and, to her dismay, saw Scott assisting Aunt Garnet out of his car. Too early! There were still a half dozen last-minute things to attend to. Why had Scott brought Aunt Garnet this soon? She would want to supervise everything. And she'd notice that Kitty wasn't here. Then there'd be explanations to make and any number of other things to account for. . . . Well, there was no help for it. She'd have to go downstairs and see to everything.

As she hurried down the steps, the melodious chimes of the majestic grandfather clock rang out. This clock had stood in the front hall at Montclair as long as Cara could remember.

Brought from Scotland by Clair Fraser, for whom Montclair was built but who had never lived here, it had an inscription carved in Gothic letters on the lower panel.

> The clock of life is wound but once,
> And no man has the power
> To tell just where the hands will stop
> At late or early hour.
>
> To lose one's wealth is sad indeed;
> To lose one's health is more
> To lose one's soul is such a loss
> As no man can restore.
>
> The present only is our own
> Live, love, and toil with a will
> Place no faith in "Tomorrow"
> For the clock may then be still.

By the time it counted out the last stroke, Cara had reached the front door, put on a bright smile, and opened it. "Good evening! Happy birthday, Aunt Garnet. Welcome."

While Scott went with Kip to view the new foal in the barn, Cara ushered Garnet into the small parlor. Without preamble Garnet said, "I'm glad to have this chance to speak to you alone, Cara, to tell you how shocked I was to see that sign at the gate. Yes, shocked is the word for it! Advertising riding lessons! My dear, don't you have any idea how that looks? As if you and Kip were destitute. That's a terrible image for the family. A *Montrose* taking paying students! Why, it's outrageous, and you must stop it at once."

Already upset from last night's dinner table scene and her quarrel with her twin, Cara was hard put to check her indignation. However, in deference to her inbred respect for her elders, she tried to keep her voice even as she replied, "I need the money, Aunt Garnet, and I intend to keep on giving lessons."

Garnet's eyebrows rose in alarm. "Don't you care what people say?"

"No, I don't care what people say. I never have and I don't intend to start now. And," Cara added pointedly, "if family history is correct, neither have *you,* Aunt Garnet."

Garnet regarded her niece with astonishment and pique. The arrow had hit the mark, however. She knew exactly to what Cara was referring. Outwardly maintaining her dignity, Garnet said smoothly, "It is only for your own good, my dear, that I'm even bringing this up. You've put Kip's pride on the line. If I know anything about the Montrose men, their pride is their most cherished possession. If they lose that, if that is undermined . . . Remember, I was married to one, and I certainly know what I'm talking about."

"That was then, this is now, Aunt Garnet. Things have changed. Women—even *southern* women—don't have to kowtow to their husbands anymore. We have our own pride, our own independence." Cara smiled and, trying to soften her words with some humor, added, "Remember, we now have the vote!"

Garnet sniffed. "A rather hollow victory, I say, after what women in England went through to get it there—making public spectacles of themselves, being arrested and put in jail, being force-fed, and all the rest." From the expression on her niece's face, Garnet saw she wasn't getting anywhere and switched tactics. "Besides, that's not what I'm talking about. Mayfield is a small town. Reputations are gained and lost in a single round of gossip. If people think that Kip is hard up and that you are in financial difficulties, just think how it will affect Luc and even Nicole—later on, when you want Luc to succeed at whatever he plans to do, and if you want Niki to be asked to join the Legacy Ladies' League."

At this Cara could not help laughing. "Aunt Garnet, do you really believe that those snobbish women on the admittance board of the Legacy Ladies' League would invite an adopted French orphan to become one of their elite members? If so, I think I know Mayfield society even better than you do."

Garnet rose, adjusting her lace shawl, and said, "Well, Cara dear, I've said what I came to say. Naturally, you will have to do what you think is best for you and your family. But with your own mother so far away, I felt it was my duty to at least speak to you."

Cara went over to Garnet and kissed her cheek. "Let's not argue, Aunt Garnet. Kip and I are happy the way things are. Luc and Niki are growing up to be fine, responsible youngsters. I believe we're instilling the important values in them. So please don't worry about us, OK?" She gave her aunt a hug. "Come on, it's your birthday. I want it to be a lovely party. Let's go in the drawing room. I think I hear voices. Maybe some of the others have arrived."

Although Garnet submitted to her niece's hug, she in no way agreed with Cara's explanation. If Cara wouldn't listen, she would talk to Kip. After all, if he was any kind of man, he wouldn't want his wife announcing their financial woes to the whole county. Surely he had proper pride in the name Montrose. Yes, Kip was the one to address in this matter.

On the way over to Montclair, the ten-year-old Cameron twins were squabbling in the backseat of Jill's rather ancient station wagon.

"I can't wait to see Luc and Niki!" Scotty declared, bouncing up and down impatiently.

"You just saw Niki this morning at pony class," jeered her brother, Stewart.

"I don't care. We have a secret and I want to talk to her about it. So there!" Scotty stuck out her tongue.

"That's enough, you two!" Jill said sharply. "I want you to be properly behaved tonight, understand? No fighting."

Glancing into her rearview mirror, Jill thought incongruously that they looked like two little angels, scrubbed and shiny, with russet-red curls, round faces sprinkled with golden freckles, beautiful amber-brown eyes. Stewart wore an Eton-collared white shirt and tie, Scotty a starched, smocked dress.

Her children were special, even though both were inclined to be headstrong, self-willed, and needful of a firm hand—discipline that their easygoing father did not wield very often. She had to be the disciplinarian, Jill thought regretfully. Scott was either too distracted or concerned about the future of the *Mayfield Messenger*, the newspaper he owned and edited. In the face of the ongoing economic morass that had hit the county hard, times were tough, and the paper was barely meeting its payroll and its ink and paper bills.

"We *do* have a secret," Scotty continued in a loud whisper. "And we're not going to tell you and Luc."

"Who cares about you girls' silly ol' secret?" Stewart retorted, folding his arms across his chest. "So there!"

"Didn't you two hear me?" Jill demanded in her sternest voice. "I'm not going to warn you again. Best behavior, or else."

The two in the back moved to opposite sides of the seat and subsided. Jill suppressed a smile. What a handful. How mischievous. But how darling. She loved them fiercely. She had been so happy to have twins, a boy and a girl! Scott had been thrilled to have a man child to carry on the proud Cameron name.

As they turned into the Montclair gates, Jill was reminded—as she was every time—of the strange, special connection she had here. Her maiden name was Marsh, and when she left England and came to Virginia, she had discovered that she was a descendant of the first bride to live at Montclair, Noramary Marsh.

It always struck Jill as an interesting turn of the wheel of life that she should follow her ancestress to Virginia, marry a Virginian, and live happily ever after! At least, she hoped Noramary had been as happy at Montclair as she herself was at Cameron Hall.

"Shhh." Niki put her forefinger up to her mouth as she and Scotty crept along the upper hall. From downstairs, where the older members of both families were gathered in the drawing room before dinner, they could hear the murmur of adult voices, the clink of glasses, and bursts of laughter.

"I'm not making any noise!" protested her cousin. "It's these old floors. They creak."

At the end of the hallway, they opened the door into what was the old nursery, and darted inside, closing the door quietly behind them. It was nearly dark, and only the last lingering light of evening filtered through the long, narrow windows. The room was wrapped in shadows, haunted by the ghosts of children who had once slept and played here. It was almost empty now—the toys that had earlier been the delight and amusement of those long-ago little ones had since been removed or had fallen to pieces. The rocking horse, its leather body now worn down to the wood structure underneath, its mane tangled and wispy, its glass eyes missing, stood alone and motionless in a dusty corner. A large dollhouse, devoid of the handcrafted furniture that used to elegantly decorate its many now-empty rooms, remained abandoned, deserted by its doll-family residents.

Niki and Scotty considered themselves too old now for dolls and were much more interested in exploring and other adventurous games. The secret room no one else seemed to know about, which they had found in the nursery, had been an enormous discovery. They slid open the small door and crept into the hidden enclosure, excited at the prospect of perhaps coming upon an old trunk filled with gold or some other fabulous treasure.

Niki was randomly shining the flashlight, pilfered from Luc's Boy Scout belongings, around in the darkness, when its beam landed on a battered cardboard box, tied with rotting twine, pushed back under the eaves. Both girls drew long breaths.

"What is it?" Scotty whispered.

"I dunno, but let's open it and find out." Niki reached up and pulled down the box, then shined the circle of light on its top. They leaned closer and breathlessly read the inscription they saw there.

Not to be opened until January 1, 1912.

"1912!" They gasped simultaneously.

"That was twenty years ago!" Scotty, who was good at math, said in an awed voice.

"And nobody opened it."

"Wonder who put it here?"

"And why they didn't come back?"

"Probably they're *dead*!" whispered Scotty.

Both children shivered.

Then Niki asked, "Should we open it?"

"Seeing that nobody's come to claim it . . . I guess," Scotty answered slowly.

"Let's see if I can get these knots untied," Niki said and, began tugging at them. "I should have got Luc's pocketknife, these are the very dickens!" she said, puffing from the effort.

Just then they heard Cara's voice, "Niki! What are you and Scotty doing up there? Aunt Garnet is opening her presents. Come on down right away."

Startled, Niki dropped the flashlight with a clatter. They had left the sliding door to the hidden room half-opened. Fearful that their snooping about would be discovered and they would be scolded—or worse, that everyone, even Luc and Stewart, would find out about their secret—both girls jumped to their feet.

"We'd better go," hissed Scotty.

"I guess. . . ." Niki was more reluctant to leave their exciting, unexpected treasure unopened.

"Niki, do I have to come up there and get you?" Cara's voice came again.

Niki put down the box and slipped out of the enclosure and ran to the nursery door. "We're coming, Tante. Just a minute," she called.

"Well, hurry up, honey. We're all waiting."

Niki dashed back into the secret room. "We've gotta go. We'll come back another time. Come on."

Scotty shoved the box back where they'd found it. Carefully they pushed the sliding door back in place, and then they left the nursery and ran down the stairway, their patent Mary Janes clattering on the uncarpeted steps.

Cara was standing at the bottom of the stairs. "What on earth kept you?" she asked, frowning. "And what are all these cobwebs in your hair?" She brushed Niki's curls.

They didn't have to answer, because at that moment Jill poked her head out of the drawing room door, saying, "Aunt Garnet's getting impatient. Do come along."

Exchanging a guilty look, the two girls followed Cara back to where the rest of the family was waiting. Neither of them knew just how long it would be before they could safely return to the hidden room and examine the contents of the secret box.

Tonight being such a special occasion, the children were allowed to sit at the table with the grown-ups. Tante had told Niki that in the "olden days," when Montclair was famous for its hospitality and entertaining, it wasn't unusual to have thirty people seated around this table.

Nicole's gaze traveled the length of the table and then back again, taking in everything and everyone. The table looked gorgeous. She had helped Tante set it with the best dishes, the crystal-prismed candleholders, the silver peacocks, whose sweeping tails flanked the centerpiece of flowers Aunt Jill had brought over from the gardens at Cameron Hall. Niki wished they had flower gardens at Montclair, but Tante said she didn't have time to keep a garden. She was too busy with the horses. There were lots of wildflowers, of course, in the meadows and along the drive, and in the spring there were rhododendrons and acres of yellow daffodils.

Among the grown-ups there was much laughter, talk, reminiscing. Tante looked pretty, being all dressed up for a change. She was usually careless about her appearance. She was more comfortable in jodhpurs and riding boots, her hair tied back with whatever happened to be at hand.

Niki glanced at Aunt Kitty and felt a sharp ache in her heart. This morning she had found that Aunt Kitty had moved out to the cottage in the woods to stay. When Niki had asked Tante why, she had received a sharp reply. Of course, Niki knew why. It was because of their terrible quarrel. They were still barely speaking. Aunt Kitty hadn't come up to the house until after Brynie and Gareth arrived.

Niki leaned forward and looked up to the head of the table, where Aunt Garnet sat. In the flattering of candlelight, it was hard to believe she was as old as Tante said. She looked like a queen, Niki thought. Her diamond drop earrings sparkled like little crystal chandeliers, and the glow of the pink candles softened the lines in her face.

The combined Montrose and Cameron families certainly made a crowd, Niki thought. Both families had lived side by side for generations, as far back as when Mayfield was first settled. They had been close friends and neighbors, related for years and years. Niki felt a small pang. It was something she often felt, a kind of longing that had no name, a deep-down wish to really belong.

Just then Scott tapped on his glass with a fork and announced, "Attention, everybody." Conversation stilled momentarily as Cara came in from the kitchen, carrying a cake alight with tiny twisted candles studding the tiered layers of white frosting.

Instantly an expectant hush descended on the table, which had a moment before been a buzz of talk, laughter. Everyone seemed to realize the significance of this celebration. Garnet Cameron Montrose Devlin, born in the last century, represented the history of both families.

As the cake was set in front of her, Garnet forced a smile and murmured, "My goodness! What a lot of candles!"

"Happy Birthday!" came a chorus of voices.

"Well, yes. Thank you," she responded with a tightened

throat. “You do realize, don’t you, that we’re celebrating a few months early?”

“That’s because you’ll be back in England on your *real* birthday, Grandmother,” Scotty explained as if Garnet did not know.

Garnet nodded. Bright child. Both the Cameron twins were. Her eyes rested on the two redheads fondly. Then she lifted her tulip-shaped wine glass and, summoning all her willpower, looked straight ahead, thinking, *Happy Birthday, indeed!*

Her birthday! Could she really be ninety years old? Her gaze moved around the table, looking one by one at each face turned toward her. All of them were illuminated in the glow of candlelight, which shone also on their raised crystal glasses. Behind the chair of each one here, Garnet saw the others who had once gathered around this same table.

For a moment, past and present merged. Then she chastised herself sternly. Only the old, the senile, the demented, saw ghosts ...

Attempting to control the suddenly rapid beating of her heart, the racing pulse in her wrists, Garnet concentrated on the beautifully arranged flower centerpiece. Ninety! It seemed unreal. She still sometimes felt like a young girl mistakenly placed in a body that occasionally betrayed her. She touched her silvery, marcelled hair, which she had stopped tinting years ago. There was no dye on earth that could capture her once glorious gold-bronze hair.

While Cara cut the cake and Kitty handed out the pieces, Garnet glanced around herself with satisfaction. What a handsome group the members of this combined family were. Her sharp-eyed gaze traveled around the table. On one side there was Scott, with his aristocratic, British wife Jill. On the opposite side were Garnet’s three grandchildren—Lynette, with her husband, state senator Frank Maynard, and Gareth and Bryanne. At the other end was Kip Montrose. There Garnet's gaze lingered. Kip was the son of Garnet's cherished foster-son Jonathan. Oh, how many people filled her long life.

Her reverie was interrupted as Scott stood and made a toast. "To Aunt Garnet—above all, a survivor."

Scott's choice of words struck Garnet as being more true than he might realize. She had survived heartbreak, war, pain, despair. From somewhere had come the strength to go on. However, it wasn't until a few years ago, after Faith's death, after her long refusal to accept it, that Garnet had experienced an epiphany. It had been a meaningful, unforgettable experience. At last she had learned not to expect happiness nor to explain its loss. She had realized that we are put on this earth not merely for our own purposes but for reasons beyond our understanding, reasons we may never know—at least, not until eternity.

The incident had lasted only a few minutes, yet its effect had lingered. Garnet could measure her own spiritual renewal from that day alone in Jeff's studio at Avalon.

Thinking of Avalon, Garnet turned her gaze to Gareth. How much he looked like his father, Jeff. Yet he had something of Faith in his expression as well. Her eyes, of course, and there was a sweetness about him in spite of his manly build and strong features. If he would only—but she was not going to regret that he hadn't followed some profession. Gareth seemed to have found what few men find—contentment, his place.

He was certainly not like Kip, who even at forty was still restless, unsettled. Garnet frowned. The beautiful silver, the china, the Battenberg lace tablecloth, the gleaming candelabra, didn't fool her for a second, didn't hide the general shabbiness of Montclair. What was he thinking of, to let the place run down so?

And Bryanne. Garnet glanced at her. She was laughing gaily at something Kip was teasing her about. Her eyes sparkled and her color was high. Her hair looked like gleaming satin in the candlelight. She was really quite lovely. Why didn't Lynette see that her younger sister got out and about more? Certainly she and Frank must know any number of eligible young men they could introduce her to.... Garnet decided she must ask Lynette about that.

The younger children were having fun. It was easy to spot the French in Nicole, the little refugee orphan Cara had brought home after the war. Niki and Scotty were giggling irrepressibly. Niki's flashing dark eyes and dark curls tumbled in ringlets about her merry, rosy face. Her hands, moving rapidly as she talked across the table to Stewart, were making typical Gallic gestures.

Luc, Kip's son by his first marriage, was a handsome boy, though quiet and rather thoughtful. However, now he seemed to be enjoying his adopted sister's vivaciousness.

The Maynard's only child, Cara-Lyn, was watching the others with a rather pensive expression. Sadly, the little girl took after her father instead of her beautiful mother and her lovely grandmother, Faith. Garnet heard she was musical. That was a blessing. If developed, it could be an asset and make up for her lack of beauty.

Garnet glanced around the table again with pride. She was glad she had come, glad she was spending this time with her family. And once she was finished with her business here, she would be equally glad to get home. To Birchfields, the lovely English manor where she and Jeremy and Faith had been so happy.

For now, she would be very glad to get to her bedroom, take off her high-heeled shoes and her jewelry, take down her hair, and get into bed. *Ninety,* for heaven's sake! She deserved a good night's rest.

chapter 5

THE MORNING AFTER Aunt Garnet's party, Niki came back from her early-morning ride. She finished rubbing down her pony, led her into the paddock, slipped the feedbag of oats over the velvety nose, and with a final pat of her neck, left the barn and walked up to the house. When she walked into the kitchen for breakfast, she knew immediately something was dreadfully wrong. Instead of greeting Niki in her usual cheery manner, Tante was standing at the stove, her back to the door, frying bacon. Aunt Kitty, dressed for traveling, was at the sink, looking out the window, sipping a cup of coffee.

The tension was so thick that even Luc, who rarely noticed such things, was aware of it. He was seated at the table, silently spooning cereal. Niki took her place opposite him, poured milk from the pitcher onto her bowl of Rice Krispies, and ate. Then, as if they'd exchanged a secret signal, they both got up, grabbed their jackets, and gathered up their books. Although nothing had been said, they both understood what was happening.

"Wait a minute, you two," Aunt Kitty said, turning around. "No you don't. Not without giving me big hugs."

"Do you have to go?" Niki asked plaintively.

"Yes, sweetie, I do." She squeezed Niki hard, then said in a husky voice, "You too, Luc. You're not too old yet for your auntie to give you a kiss." She laughed but it sounded shaky. "Wait, I'll walk out with you, put my things in the car."

There were more hugs outside, and then Niki and Luc went down the driveway. Neither spoke until they were out of their aunt's hearing.

"I never saw Aunt Kitty so sad," Niki said.

"Aunt Cara too," Luc commented gruffly.

That seemed to say it all. In the distance they saw the yellow school bus round the bend in the road, and they both began to run.

On the long drive back to New York, Kitty went over and over the quarrel she'd had with Cara. She winced, remembering the hurt in her twin's expression when Kitty told her she was moving out to Eden Cottage. Could she have handled it any differently? Probably. But Kitty's feelings were too strong, too near the surface. Listening to Kip and his friends speak so casually of what amounted to preparation for war had brought all those feelings out.

She was sorry it had all erupted like that. On the other hand, she didn't care. It was inconceivable to her that Kip and Cara did not feel the same way she did. Her determination stiffened.

She had to *do* something. If more people knew what war was really like, if they had had her experiences, seen maimed bodies, destroyed nerves, ravaged lungs, battered minds . . . Maybe their knowing would turn her anguish into something positive. She had to pray about it, ask God what she could do. She already had a platform—whenever she read Richard's poetry or was asked to speak somewhere. But something more was needed. What, she wasn't yet sure.

Slowly the idea for a book formed in her head. It would be

written like a diary kept by an army field nurse. She had kept a journal of sorts, and her memories were vivid. She could dig into those long-buried scenes, incidents, and experiences, retell them in such a manner that readers would be brought into them. It would be painful to relive her past, but it would be worth it if she could make people understand what war really meant.

Garnet had to wait for the opportunity to talk to Bryanne. Her granddaughter attended art classes at the university, commuting from Mayfield to Williamsburg three days a week. The time for Garnet to present her plan did not come until the weekend before she was scheduled to leave. She asked Bryanne to accompany her on a stroll through the gardens.

"Well, dearie, at last—a chance to have a nice, private chat with my granddaughter," Garnet began, slipping her hand through Bryanne's arm. "The days have gone by so quickly. It seems I've hardly come, and now I'll be leaving. I wanted so much to discuss your future with you. I wanted to tell you my idea."

Bryanne felt a small inward warning that whatever her grandmother was going to suggest might require some powerful resistance, something she had never been good at.

"What is that, Grandmother?"

"Let's sit in the gazebo, where we can be comfy," Garnet suggested, pointing with her cane to the white, ornately cupolaed little summer house at the end of the garden. "You know, it was my mother who had that built. Or rather, my father who had it built for her. The story is quite romantic, actually. It seems it was in just such a gazebo, in the garden of her Savannah home, that he proposed to her. He absolutely adored her and felt himself the luckiest of men to have wooed and won her. She was a Maitland and quite a belle, and he had to compete with countless suitors to bring her to Cameron Hall as his bride."

They mounted the three steps into the latticed enclosure and sat down on the bench that circled the interior.

"Now, Bryanne, what I'm suggesting is this—that you come to Birchfields this summer. While you're staying with me, I'd like to give you a trip to Italy as a gift, all expenses paid." She paused, eyeing Bryanne for her reaction. "You can take as long as you like—a month, six weeks. That will give you a chance to visit all the great museums, the cathedrals, the galleries, where some of the greatest statuary of the centuries is on exhibit. It will be a source of instruction and inspiration. How does that sound?"

"Oh, Grandmother, that sounds very generous, very wonderful—"

"Do I hear a 'but' in there somewhere?" Garnet asked shrewdly, sensing Bryanne's reluctance. The sweet young face had an expression of distress, and the clear eyes were clouded with uncertainty. Surely the child wasn't going to turn down the invitation? Any young artist would jump at the chance.

"Well, you see, Grandmother—," Bryanne began.

Instinctively Garnet pursed her lips. She suspected this had something to do with Bryanne's father. Garnet always winced a little when she thought about the well-known artist whom her daughter had loved and married, a man Garnet had always had misgivings about. "The idea of going to Italy doesn't appeal to you?"

"Oh no, Grandmother, it's not that. It's just that . . ." Bryanne hesitated. "Father is going to Scotland this summer to see Uncle Jonathan's widow, Phoebe, and Fraser and Fiona. I thought I might go with him. . . ."

Garnet pressed her lips firmly together before asking, "And has he asked you to go with him?"

"No, not exactly. But if I go to England to visit you, I thought maybe Father and I could travel together and then I might go up to Scotland with him."

Poor child, still knocking at a door that's never going to open, was Garnet's immediate reaction. She had seen Bryanne's hopes dashed before. But she also knew better than to discourage her. Bryanne would rush to her father's defense, and it would only stiffen her resistance to accepting Garnet's offer.

"Of course, you must do whatever you think best. The offer holds if you want to take me up on the trip to Italy." Feeling suddenly stiff, Garnet rose with the help of the ivory-handled cane she used at times. "You know you will always be welcome at Birchfields, whatever or whenever. It is, after all, your home, too." She tucked Bryanne's hand through her arm and patted it affectionately. "Come, we'll go inside now. Jill will be wondering where we've got to. Besides, it's teatime. An Englishwoman, no matter where she lives, Virginia or South Africa, serves tea every afternoon. I've found it to be a delightful custom myself, and do so at Birchfields."

Enough had been said at the moment, Garnet decided. She had sowed the seed that she hoped would take root in her granddaughter's mind. Garnet wanted very much for that to happen. The big country estate had become lonelier as the years had gone by. It would be lovely to have a young person around again.

At length it was time for Garnet's return journey to England.

The morning of her departure, she woke with a pervasive melancholy. It was nonsense, of course. Wasn't she going back to her own home, to all the luxuries and comforts she indulged herself in and thoroughly enjoyed? As she finished her last-minute packing, she fought this mood.

However, the fact was that she would probably not make this trip again. Not at her age. And after all, it was only natural for her to feel some sorrow at leaving Cameron Hall, where she had spent her childhood, and Montclair, where she had spent her young womanhood. Almost all the important things in her early life had happened here in Virginia.

The quotation "Farewell: We never do anything consciously for the last time without sadness of heart" sprang into her mind. Where had she read that? Maybe in one of *Grace Comfort's* columns?

She chided herself for feeling sad. Looking back was a sign of old age, a reality she had thus far been successful at keeping at bay.

Besides, she had reason to feel that her visit in Mayfield had been worthwhile. She was satisfied that Gareth was finding his own path and was reasonably happy. If only he could find a wife who would support his ideals, want to live his simple kind of life. Lynette, of course, had married well and was a perfect politician's wife—gracious, charming, outgoing.

It was Bryanne who concerned Garnet. But one could only do so much. Young people today had minds of their own. Combating the child's idealized image of her father was impossible. Jeff Montrose, in his daughter's eyes, was the man she wanted him to be, not the man he really was. Someday Bryanne would find that out. Garnet only hoped it would not break her heart.

A tap came at the bedroom door, and she heard Jill's voice. "The limousine driver is here, Aunt Garnet."

"I'll be right down," Garnet replied, picking up her marten fur piece, adjusting her hat in the mirror. She took a sweeping look around the room to see if she'd forgotten anything, then went downstairs.

Good-byes were said, and Scott assisted her carefully into the sleek, black Chrysler.

"Come again next spring, Aunt Garnet," he said.

"Thank you, dear," she said, smiling, knowing that they both knew it was unlikely she would do so.

As the limousine made its leisurely way down the driveway and through the stone posts of the gate, Garnet turned and looked through the rear window, back to the stately house. She raised one gloved hand in a kind of royal wave. Then she settled back against the cushioned gray velour upholstery, determined to enjoy the trip to Richmond, Washington, New York, and then home to Birchfields.

chapter
6

1934

JEFF MONTROSE'S PLANS to visit Mayfield the previous summer had changed abruptly. He had gone to California to visit his mother, Blythe, before going abroad. While traveling up the coast, he had discovered Carmel, the picturesque art colony south of San Francisco. Awed by its scenic beauty, he had decided to stay there for the winter to paint.

So it wasn't until the following spring that he finally made it to Mayfield. Upon his arrival, he was a bit taken aback to find that Bryanne had booked passage on the same ship, the SS *Mauratania,* on which he was sailing from New York. She told him she had accepted her Grandmother Garnet's invitation to spend a summer with her in England but first wanted to accompany him to Scotland, see Phoebe, and meet her cousins.

If Jeff had thought about it at all, he would have been amazed at what a challenge it had been for his daughter to take such an initiative. True to himself, Jeff simply declared that he was pleased at her coming and acted as if it had been his idea.

However, if Bryanne had expected this sea journey to bring a new relationship with her father, she was disappointed. As soon as the news was out that the well-known painter was on board, he was lionized. Still handsome at fifty, Jeff epitomized the popular image of an artist and played his role to the hilt. Wearing a slouch-brimmed hat and cape, he took his twice-daily strolls on deck, collecting companions along the way. Celebrity always attracted, and Jeff gloried in the attention. For Bryanne, watching this day-to-day drama unfold was a sobering learning experience. Jeff was invited to private parties, was asked to sit at the captain's table, and was eagerly sought after wherever he went about the ship. When they were together, of course, Jeff always introduced Bryanne. However, most of the time he conducted himself as though he were traveling alone.

With only two days left before they were to arrive in England, Bryanne decided to confront her father. Joining him on his morning stroll, she took his arm and said, "Father, I'd really like to talk to you about something—something that's important to me."

He looked surprised but said, "Of course, my dear. Go right ahead."

Not wanting to be interrupted by passing acquaintances, she led him over to the rail. "I'd so hoped, Father, that this trip would bring us closer, that we'd get to know each other better." She began to feel both nervous and hesitant about how to proceed.

"And we are, aren't we? You're enjoying all this, aren't you? There seems to be a fine group of young people on board, lots going on—"

Frustrated, Bryanne shook her head. "That's not what I mean. I mean you and I, Father."

Jeff looked puzzled, then amused. "Well, here I am, darling girl. What you see is what you get. What more do you want?"

"It's just that I grew up hardly knowing you, and I thought this would be our chance."

Jeff's expression changed, a shadow passing over his countenance. "I'm sorry, my dear. Fate dealt us a cruel blow. Losing your mother the way we did changed everything. For me and for you children. We can't go back and undo that." He paused. "It nearly broke me. But I knew I had to go on, make something of the rest of my life. That's what I tried to do. And I think I succeeded in doing it." He sighed. "I know it was hard on you, but you had your grandmothers, both of them, and your brother and sister. It wasn't as though you were left alone."

Just then two fellow passengers strolled by, smiled, and stopped to say good morning.

A casual conversation about the day's posted activities ensued, and Bryanne knew that her time with her father had ended. Unsatisfactorily for her, but maybe that's as far as they would have gone even if they hadn't been interrupted.

What she thought she understood was that her father had had to save his life by plunging himself completely into his art. It had been his response to an intolerable loss. To justify his actions, he rationalized that his children had been well cared for, had not suffered irreparable damage.

Shipboard life was too lively, too full of people, Bryanne told herself. Maybe when they got to Scotland, things would be different. They'd take long walks together, and then there would be quiet times when it might be possible to reach her father.

When they docked in England, they wired ahead news of their arrival, then took the highlander train to Scotland. Phoebe Montrose was there to meet them at the small station. A tall, handsome woman, she was plainly dressed but had the presence of a duchess. Bryanne admired the bone structure of her face, the clarity and color of her eyes. Phoebe's warm smile made her almost beautiful as she greeted them. "So this is little Bryanne.

I'm sure you don't remember me. It's been so long since I was in Virginia. But I knew your mother, and she was one of the loveliest women I've ever met."

She directed them to place their luggage and Jeff's painting equipment on a cart to be delivered later.

"It's only a short walk," she told them, "and I expect you'll welcome a chance to stretch your legs after the long train trip."

As she had said, it was only a small distance through the village to the McPherson Arms, her family's hotel. After her husband's death, Phoebe had moved to Kilgaren to take over its management from her uncle, who wanted to retire.

Kilgaren was a small, quaint town of gray stone houses with slate roofs, built on the hilly, winding streets. They crossed an arched stone bridge and soon were at the hotel. Phoebe's uncle, Gordon McPherson, rangy and big-boned, still hale and hearty at eighty, met them in the front hall, accompanied by two bright-eyed, redheaded children. These were Jeff's nephew and niece, Fraser and Fiona Montrose. They smiled shyly as their mother introduced them.

"Come along and have tea!" urged Uncle Gordie, motioning them forward toward the large lobby, where a fire crackled in a large stone fireplace. "A real *good* Scottish tea," he said with a booming laugh, pronouncing it "gude."

The tea proved not only good but enormous, much more a meal than the tea and sandwiches and cookies Bryanne was used to at home. They sat in front of the fireplace and ate while listening to Uncle Gordie's tall tales about streams jumping with trout and salmon, about spectacular views from the cliffs. Bryanne liked him immediately. He was her idea of a rugged Scot, with his shaggy white hair, his bristling eyebrows, and his blue eyes, which sparkled with wisdom and good humor. Both he and Phoebe put her immediately at ease. Bryanne decided that in terms of its hospitality, Scotland had every bit as much to boast about as Virginia.

Bryanne still did not get the chance to become closer to her father, however, despite the fact that here there were no crowds, no one else vying for his time or attention. Once Jeff started to paint, he was lost in his work and seemed to forget that she existed.

With extraordinary sensitivity, Phoebe seemed to understand the situation. On Bryanne's third day in Kilgaren, Phoebe invited her to have tea alone together in her apartment there at the hotel.

A coal fire glowed in the small fireplace, reflecting its winking lights on the polished brass fender. A low table had been drawn up in front. A starched white cloth covered it, and a teapot with a crocheted cozy, teacups, and a basket of freshly baked currant scones were set out.

"I'm sure it seems dull and rather boring for you here, doesn't it?" Phoebe asked Bryanne as she filled a cup and handed it to her. "There's not much to do if you don't enjoy tromping the hills or fishing." Her eyes twinkled mischievously. "Or painting."

"But I do enjoy all those things. I'd just hoped that my father and I could do them together," Bryanne replied, too honest to pretend otherwise.

Phoebe nodded. "I know. You see, I know your father. I've known him since he was a very young man. Jeff Montrose is the most fascinating man I've ever met. Creative, enthusiastic. Even then he was self-centered and not tactful at all, but he had so much charm, one hardly minded." Phoebe paused. "I knew your mother too. She and Jeff came here several times, did you know that? And Faith was just the wife he needed. She adored him, you see. And understood him. I worried about her when they were here. They had been married only a short time, and she was so lovely, and he left her on her own for hours at a time. I started to feel sorry for her. She would have none of it. She just smiled and told me, 'He'll paint as long as the light lasts. There's no use worrying about him.' You'll have to learn that, too."

"I don't know, Aunt Phoebe," Bryanne said thoughtfully. "Perhaps it's too late. Maybe it would be best for me to go. Then he would be free and wouldn't feel guilty, as he must now. That is"—she smiled ruefully—"*if* he remembers I'm here. My grandmother wants me to visit her. She is giving me a trip to Italy."

"We'd love to have you stay, if that's what you decide," Phoebe said matter-of-factly. "Well, think about it some more, pray about it. Then do what you think is best."

After tea Bryanne took a long walk. It was beautiful country. The river wound like a silver ribbon through the rocky hills. Trees lined the banks, and beyond were the rolling moors, covered with lavender heather and gorse. Above on the blue-gray hills, sheep grazed. The air was so crystal-clear, it almost hurt to breathe. In the distance she saw the small farmhouses in patchwork fields of green and brown. As she made her way along the edges of the fields, there were huge rocks, and every once in a while she stopped to climb upon one or to sit and rest and enjoy the view.

On her way back to the hotel, she crossed over the stone bridge and, hearing the sound of water rushing over the rocks, stopped, leaned on the ledge, and looked down. The water swirled in small eddies, then fell in miniature waterfalls over the black rocks.

Phoebe was right, Bryanne thought. She must do what was

best for herself. It wouldn't matter to her father whether she stayed or went. Once she recognized that, it was an easy decision.

She could wait for the rest of her life, and Jeff Montrose would not change. She had her own future to consider. Her future as an artist, too. From somewhere the passage of James 1:17 came into her mind—"Every good and perfect gift is from above and comes down from the Father of lights, with whom there is no variation or shadow of turning." The words suddenly had a new meaning, a personal meaning. Her talent was a gift, and her grandmother's offer of the trip to Italy was a gift. Gifts should be appreciated and accepted.

When Bryanne told her father, he indeed quite easily accepted her decision to leave. The day she left for London, he was enthusiastically setting off for a day of painting. He gave her a hearty hug and a handful of pound notes and sent his regards to her grandmother. "Tell her I'll be down to Birchfields at the end of the summer, and then we'll have a grand reunion."

On the train, Bryanne thought again about what Phoebe had helped her to understand. She had been harboring a vague image of her father as a hero of a magical childhood. That was fantasy, not reality. She must accept Jeff Montrose as he was or not at all.

By the time she reached Birchfields, she had decided to "put aside childish things" in order to find richness and meaning in her own life.

chapter 7

Birchfields

GARNET LIFTED THE polished silver pot and poured them both a second cup of coffee. Sun shone through the French windows of the dining room as they were breakfasting.

"I wish I were going with you, Bryanne, but I'm just not up to everything that travel involves nowadays. All those foreigners you have to deal with, shouting in languages I don't understand. When Jeremy was alive, he always took care of everything, made it all so easy. He was such a cosmopolitan, a world traveler, you see. He spoke French fluently and could make himself understood in both German and Italian." Garnet made a face. "I'm hopeless without an interpreter." She sighed. "Still, it would be lovely this time of year in Italy—not too hot, as it would be later in the summer. . . ."

Bryanne nodded understandingly. "I know, Grandmother. I'm sorry, too." She touched the thin pile of mail beside her plate, the letter containing her visa, her passport, a letter of credit from Garnet's bank, a letter from Lynette. She looked over at her grandmother affectionately. The sun had created a lovely aura around the perfectly coifed head. Since Garnet's back was to the sun, her face was shadowed, concealing any lines or wrinkles that might have marred the illusion of youth. She was wearing a morning gown of pleated, peach-colored chiffon, lavish with lace, and as usual looked queenly.

Bryanne loved her grandmother dearly, but truthfully she was glad to be going by herself. If Garnet were accompanying her, they would have had to stay at all the best hotels, have first-class accommodations everywhere, dine in elegant restaurants catering to wealthy tourists. This way, on her own, she could experience the country differently. She planned to stay at pensions, eat at neighborhood cafes, walk the streets, visit the countryside, talk to people, wander as long as she liked through the galleries and museums. The thought of such freedom was unbelievable.

"Yes, I do think this is the perfect time for you to go," Garnet said. "Most of the tourists will be gone. Then when you come back, we can have a lovely, leisurely visit. We'll have plenty of time for you to tell me all about everything." Garnet gazed at her granddaughter fondly. "It will be quite an adventure. I rather envy you. In my day, it would be unheard of to allow a young woman to travel alone"—Garnet tipped her head to one side, her eyes twinkling almost mischievously—"and her grandmother would probably go with her, giving her all sorts of advice, admonitions. But seriously, dear, I must caution you. Freedom does have its hazards. For some reason, some Europeans think that all Americans are millionaires, so tourists are fair game. Do hold on to your purse. And don't take any chances. Be careful about accepting help or offers to take you somewhere."

"Of course, Grandmother. I'll be careful. Don't worry," Bryanne reassured her.

"And another thing," Garnet said, laughing and wagging a playful forefinger, "whatever you do, don't talk to strangers."

At last the day came for Bryanne to set out on her great adventure. She left Birchfields, took the train to London, and from there traveled to Dover to take the channel boat to France.

Not until she was on board did Bryanne at last feel it was real. Her first chance to travel completely alone. The days before had been hectic. So much to be done. She listened with patience and as much grace as possible to the advice, the suggestions, the warnings, and received quite gratefully gifts of money to be exchanged for francs.

About twenty minutes into the English Channel, Bryanne had occasion to remember one of her grandmother's admonitions, the one given partially in jest. A tall young man stood a little distance from her, looking down at the choppy water swirling in the wake of the boat.

There was a kind of eagerness about his stance as he leaned against the rail, his thick, tawny hair blowing in the brisk wind. From his expression, he seemed to be enjoying everything—the sea spray in his face, the roll of the deck under his feet, the rough sea. The collar of his tweed jacket was turned up, and he had a camera, its strap slung over one shoulder. He was definitely looking forward to whatever lay ahead on the other shore.

As if aware of being observed, he turned, caught her glance, and smiled. A wonderful, wide smile that lit up his face and caused little crinkles to appear around his clear, gray-blue eyes.

"Great, isn't it?" he asked.

Bryanne nodded. He looked to be in his late twenties, probably about her age, and he too seemed to be traveling alone. When she had first noticed him boarding at Dover, there had been no one with him.

Just then a family, a couple with three children ranging in

age from about eight to fourteen—obviously French, judging by their rapid exchange—came up to the rail and stood there, blocking Bryanne's view of the young man.

For a minute she felt vaguely disappointed. It might have been interesting to exchange a few remarks, find out where he was going and so on. That is, if she were able to initiate the kind of casual conversation fellow travelers sometimes do. Basically, however, Bryanne was shy. She had lived a sheltered existence, had grown up mainly among adults, surrounded mostly by family. She had never acquired the social skills her older sister, Lynette, seemed to have come by so naturally.

Unconsciously Bryanne sighed. Maybe it was just as well that she had begun no conversation with the good-looking young man she was sure must be an Englishman. Bryanne smiled, recalling Garnet's last-minute warning—"Be careful who you strike up conversations with. There are clever rogues on the lookout for vulnerable, inexperienced tourists. Sometimes they just want to get information—such as what hotel you're staying at or what train you're catching—for their own devious reasons."

Privately Bryanne had determined to ignore all those overly cautious travel warnings, to be a free spirit for a change, go where the whims of fate took her. Still, she could not help remembering. She had been too well brought up to feel completely unfettered from convention. Not that the English passenger resembled in the slightest the kind of person her grandmother had warned her about.

Regretfully she turned away from the rail and went below deck to the safety of the passenger salon. There she got a cup of tea and sat down, opened her guidebook, and studied it. She didn't see the young man again until they docked at Calais. He must have remained on deck the whole trip. That might have been much pleasanter than her own experience, she thought. The salon had eventually become crowded, warm, and noisy with people.

At Calais, Bryanne caught a train to Paris. She was tired, because she had been too excited to sleep much the night before. Upon reaching Paris, she decided to take her grandmother's advice and check into the luxury hotel Garnet had recommended and get a good night's rest. In the morning, she would start out for her real destination—Italy, whose wonder and glory awaited her.

She changed trains at the Italian border and found a compartment that was already occupied by a German couple, who ignored her and spoke only to each other. A prosperous-looking businessman of some kind entered, sat, and unfolded a newspaper. He was followed by an elderly woman with a young boy, possibly her grandson, to whom she proceeded to talk in a torrent of Italian. Luckily Bryanne got the window seat, and as soon as the train started to move, she became immersed in the passing views of the countryside. She was so preoccupied with the scenery, she hardly noticed the compartment door sliding open and another passenger entering. Then she looked around and saw the same young man who had been on the boat with her. At the same moment, he met her gaze, and both registered surprise.

He nodded and smiled, raising one hand in a gesture of greeting. "Hello!" he said, speaking across the Italian grandmother and boy. The German couple turned their heads and gave him a hostile stare.

"Hello," Bryanne replied, aware that all the other occupants of the compartment were watching.

"On your way to Rome?" he asked.

"Yes," she nodded. Then she realized that since Rome was this train's destination, his question had been largely unnecessary. The thought made her smile.

He seemed to catch the humor of his question and grinned. "Steven Colby," he announced.

Since he was introducing himself, she could do no less. "Bryanne Montrose," she responded, now very conscious of the German couple's disapproving glances.

"On holiday?" he asked.

"Yes. And you?"

"The same," he said. They smiled at each other again.

Carrying on a conversation was virtually impossible under the circumstances. So Bryanne, feeling rather foolish, returned to looking out the window.

When the train finally pulled into Rome, Steven, who evidently traveled light, offered to help Bryanne with her baggage. He took the larger of the two bags, and they made their way out of the train. For a minute they stood on the platform together amid the wild chaos of the busy terminal.

"Is anyone meeting you?" he asked.

"No, but I have a reservation at a pension. I'll get a taxi."

"Let me help you," he said, shifting her large bag to his other hand. They walked to the station entrance, where rows of taxis were lined, their drivers yelling out the names of hotels in aggressive tones.

"I'm staying—at least temporarily—with some friends of my family," Steven told her. "Then mostly I'm going to be on my own. No itinerary."

Just then a wild-eyed driver shouted, "Here, Signorina!" and motioned toward a car parked with its motor running.

"I'd better take it," Bryanne said breathlessly. The driver was already tugging at her suitcases, and Steven surrendered them.

"Thank you very much for your help," she called over her shoulder as she hurried after her luggage.

"Have a nice holiday!" he shouted.

"You too!" She waved, then ducked into the taxi. When she looked back through the window, Steven Colby was still standing at the edge of the curb.

chapter 8

ARMED WITH A guidebook and a pocket-size English-Italian dictionary, Bryanne started out the next morning. Rome was overwhelming. She hardly knew where to begin. But the first thing on her list of must-sees was the Sistine Chapel.

Although she had seen its beautiful ceiling reproduced in photographs in dozens of art books, viewing it firsthand was an indescribable experience. It was with a sense of awe that Bryanne gazed upon this masterpiece. The entire ceiling beautifully portrayed the biblical stories of the creation of the world, the fall of man, the Flood, all magnificently painted by the artistic genius Michelangelo. It had been begun in 1508 and had taken him four years to complete. Sadly, the original colors were dimmed by dirt and dust. Still, it was breathtaking.

The magnificent statue of David left her awestruck. With her interest in sculpture, Bryanne was most intrigued by this type of art. Even though she had studied the history of Greek and Roman sculpture, viewing these works with her own eyes was absolutely inspiring.

Every day, she went to some other famous landmark. She watched people throw coins into the famous Trevi Fountain. Then she noticed little boys jumping in to scoop them up when the people left. Bryanne was amused, since this seemed to defeat the legend that tossing in a coin would make wishes come true. Perhaps it would for the boys! she thought with a grin.

Bryanne made side trips to Pompeii and Naples and Florence. But it was Rome that had captured her imagination, and after two days in Florence, she took the train back there. Even her visit to the Uffizi and other famous museums filled with art and statuary had not dimmed the inspiration that the Eternal City held for her. She knew she could spend all the rest of her time in Europe there in Rome and still not exhaust its splendor.

She had found a pension that was clean, comfortable, and not too expensive, within easy walking distance of most of the sites she wanted to see. For trips farther afield, she had learned to use the public transportation. Her days took on a certain pattern as she fell more and more under Rome's enchantment. She understood how easy it must have been for the nineteenth-century American expatriots to succumb to the beauty and leisurely pace of this most famous of all Italian cities.

In Italy the stores closed from noon until four for lunch and a siesta, then reopened until ten or so. One afternoon, after checking to see if she had any mail, she wandered into the Borghese Gardens, as she often did. There was a little out-of-doors cafe behind a black iron fence, where a set of small antique statues had been placed at intervals. It was cool and quiet there after the heat of the day. There she would usually order an espresso and sit to read her letters or, more often, just observe the ever interesting "passing parade." Families with children, lovers with arms intertwined, elderly couples walking slowly, devotedly attentive to each other. It was like watching the world go by, Bryanne thought.

"Miss Montrose," a male voice spoke. Startled to hear her

name, Bryanne looked up into the pleased face of Steven Colby. He appeared freshly scrubbed and alert, wearing a fawn linen jacket, an open-necked white shirt. His camera was still slung over his shoulder, and he was holding a notebook.

"What a great surprise!" he exclaimed. "May I join you? Or are you waiting for someone?"

"No. I mean yes. Do sit down."

She was disarmed by his smile, put at ease by his open friendliness. It was somehow heartwarming to see someone familiar in a city of strangers, to be recognized in such an exotic and unfamiliar setting.

As they enjoyed one of the famous Italian delicacies, gelato, her curiosity about him was partially satisfied. She found out his reason for this solo trip to Italy. "I was at Oxford," he said, "when suddenly it all seemed rather a waste of time. I can always go back, and I probably shall. It's just that the time to travel is when you're young and relatively free of responsibilities, before anything happens. . . ."

"My grandmother's given me this trip," Bryanne confided. "And it's a chance to do exactly what I want, see the things I want to see. I've traveled some earlier, but it wasn't the same." She smiled and he thought how beautiful her eyes were, lit up with enthusiasm, excitement. "It's such an adventure."

"I noticed your sketchbook," he said. Then he flushed a little. "Truthfully, a few days ago I thought I saw you sitting near the fountain, sketching—"

"Yes, the children. Italian children are so joyous, so free. No nannies lurking"—she laughed—"or parents keeping them in check. I wanted to capture some of that."

"You're an artist, then?"

"In a way. I sculpt. Oh, I'm nobody famous or anything like that. But I'm learning to turn sketches into figures in clay, and later I'm hoping to learn to cast them in bronze or porcelain. . . ."

Steven was leaning forward, chin resting on his clasped hands, elbows on the table. She realized with a sharp little sense of pleasure that he was really listening, really interested. Bryanne wasn't used to people paying so much attention to what she was saying, and suddenly she felt shy.

She remembered sketching the children as she sat on a row of steps in view of the Trevi Fountain. The baroque sculpture was the grandest of all the fountains of that city of fountains. Drawn by two rearing sea horses led by tritons, the sea god Neptune stood in a huge seashell amid the splashing of rushing water that poured in cascades into the stone bowl.

To think Steven had been there at the same time. Had he been too shy to come up to her and speak? Or was he simply so innately polite that he hadn't wanted to disturb her concentration?

"The fountain is unbelievable," he said. "Have you seen it at night?"

Bryanne shook her head. She had not quite had the nerve to venture too far alone at night.

"Oh, but you should. It's an even lovelier sight. The Palazzo Poli is transformed into a stage setting, lit by street lamps and the lights from the shops surrounding it. The light is reflected on the water—it's truly like a glittering rainbow."

How eloquently Steven was describing it. His command of words was amazing. Yet he didn't seem at all pretentious. Bryanne wondered what was in the notebook he carried. A journal? Notes for a travel book? Sketches?

Suddenly the gardens were empty. Bryanne and Steven seemed to be the only people left. Bryanne gathered up her handbag, stuffed her brochures and guidebooks into it, and stood up, saying, "I guess I'd better be going."

"May I take a picture or two before we go?" Steven asked, pulling his camera out of its case. "It's such a beautiful setting."

He snapped several of her. Then he promised that when they were developed, he'd send her the prints. "I can have them in a day or two. Will you still be here?"

"I'm going to Venice tomorrow," she told him.

He looked disappointed but then asked, "Will you be coming back here?"

"Yes. I haven't seen all I want to in Rome."

He walked with her back to the small hotel where she was staying. At the entrance he said, "Will you be staying here again when you come back to Rome?"

"Yes, that's my plan."

His expression became hopeful. "I can give you the prints then, or at least leave them for you."

"Thank you. That would be nice. My grandmother would be pleased to see them."

They said good-bye somewhat awkwardly, as if they wanted to say more to each other but couldn't find the right words.

Bryanne rose early to catch the first train to Venice. The compartment was already nearly full when she got in, and she squeezed into one corner. Most of the passengers were speaking Italian and eating something—oranges, bread, cheese. They rattled along through the countryside, a colorful landscape in shades of ocher, olive green, golden yellow. It was stuffy and hot, and she wished someone would open a window. She had begun to feel lightheaded and a little queasy by the time the train screeched to a stop.

She gathered her belongings and stepped out onto the platform. She took a long breath, glad to be out of the confines of the crowded compartment. All around was the clamor and noise of the large train station. People swarmed about and Italian voices reverberated in her ears. Beyond was the quay, where the gondoliers were shouting, vying for customers. Should she take a gondola by herself to the hotel? It seemed almost heretical to do so. Gondolas were meant for lovers.

Then she saw some travelers moving in that direction, waving their hands and calling, "Gondola! Gondola!" She decided to follow suit. She moved to the edge of the water and raised her arm to signal a gondolier.

One detached his gondola from the group and steered it toward her. It was a long, graceful boat, the prow pointed. Under a fringed canopy were cushioned velvet seats. It was the romantic vision of her dreams. "Si, Signorina," the handsome, dark-skinned gondolier said from where he stood on the plank in the stern. With his large oars he brought his boat close so she could get in easily. His attire was very picturesque. A man attuned to tourists, Bryanne thought, amused. His costume was just as in pictures she'd seen—a red-and-white striped shirt, black jacket, and a straw hat banded in red ribbons around the crown.

She handed him the paper on which she had written the name of the pension that had been recommended to her. "Do you know this place?"

"Si, Signorina," the gondolier said, nodding and flashing a white smile that revealed one gleaming gold tooth. He leaned forward and took her two bags, then extended his hand to help her get in. The boat had a fragile feel, yet as they maneuvered through the heavy traffic of the canal, it glided with a kind of gentle, undulating sway. The water rippled along the side. The gondoliers spoke and called to each other as their boats drifted along.

They passed under bridges, in and out of sunlight and shadow. On either side of the canal rose tall, balconied houses, some painted yellow, some terra-cotta, their windows decorated with scrolled ironwork. In the background the dome of a church could be seen.

They passed under a great arched bridge of stone. Rialto Bridge? she wondered. Bryanne had seen its photograph in an illustrated book she had studied before leaving England.

Finally the gondola came to a smooth stop in front of steps leading up to a grilled gate. The gondolier announced, "Ecco la Pension Benevista, Signorina."

He lifted out her bags then turned to assist her up and out. He held out his grubby palm.

"Como?" she asked, taking several lire out of her purse. "Enough?"

"Si, Signorina."

From his broad smile, Bryanne guessed that it was probably too much. She hadn't yet mastered Italian money. But it had been a delightful ride. Bryanne felt a surge of excited happiness. She felt she was going to love Venice best of all. It was a place where something special was bound to happen.

After washing up and changing into a fresh blouse, she went out to explore. The streets were edged with shops and galleries, and people milled all around, pushing up to booths—loaded with vegetables, fruit, cheeses—that lined the way toward a curved bridge. The enticing smell of fresh, warm bread came from a bakery, and Bryanne stopped to admire the display of delicious-looking pastries. Gift shops and jewelry stores glittered with wonderful things to buy—elaborately dressed dolls, figurines, varieties of gold jewelry.

She wandered slowly along the line of shops, dazzled by the displays. Then, tired from walking from gallery to gallery, she stopped at a small sidewalk cafe and ordered an espresso. As she waited, she studied her brochure, unaware that moving toward her through the crowd was a tall, tawny-haired Englishman.

"Miss Montrose!" a voice with a decidedly British accent said.

Bryanne looked up. "Steven!" she gasped.

"We're going to have to stop meeting like this," he said, laughing.

"You didn't say you were coming to Venice," she accused, trying to regain some composure and at the same time conceal her absolute delight at seeing him. This couldn't be a coincidence. Not again.

Bryanne's suspicion was immediately confirmed. "I didn't know I was," he said. "What I mean is, it somehow seemed the right thing to do. Suddenly Venice was the *only* place in Italy I wanted to be. I must have missed your train." His smile widened. "I brought you your pictures. They turned out really well." He took out an envelope and handed it to her.

Bryanne could not resist smiling. "You came all this way to bring me the snapshots?"

Steven reddened a little under his tan. "Well, anyway, here we are. So!"

Bryanne opened the package of prints and looked through them. They brought back that lovely, unexpected meeting at the Borghese Gardens. "You're a very good photographer, Steven."

"It's a hobby. But I do enjoy it." He paused. "Now that we're both here, would you like—that is, if you haven't other plans, would you have dinner with me this evening? I know a great little restaurant. I think you'd enjoy it. The food is"—he grinned—"Italian!"

Bryanne hesitated only a split second before accepting. Putting aside all Grandmother Garnet's precautions, she said,

"Thanks, I'd love to." After all, Steven Colby wasn't one of those dark, devious persons she'd been warned against trusting. He was the epitome of a well-bred young Englishman.

The restaurant was empty when they entered. Maybe it was too early for more-sophisticated travelers and Italians. The place was not fancy at all. It was not the kind that Grandmother Garnet would have insisted they dine in. There were small tables, ladder-back chairs, whitewashed walls, and a wooden floor. The small table to which they were shown had a crisp, red-checked tablecloth, gleaming silverware, and thin-stemmed wine glasses that sparkled.

Before they ordered, a waiter brought a basket of bread with brown, twisted crust, and a platter of assorted canapés. A delicious soup followed, then plates heaped with pasta, heavily sprinkled with grated Parmesan cheese, and scalloped veal.

Gradually the room began to fill with couples, families, parties of four or more. Tables were pushed together to accommodate large groups. The noise level began to rise, with voices lifted in friendly conversation, laughter, and warm, good-natured camaraderie. A pair of strolling musicians—one man with an accordion, the other with a tenor voice that Bryanne felt was every bit as thrilling as the legendary Caruso's—began to sing. Each song was greeted by appreciative applause.

"He's wonderful, isn't he?" Bryanne whispered to Steven. "He could sing in an opera."

"All Italians are potential opera singers," Steven agreed. "In Verdi's time they used to learn his lyrics by heart within a few days of the opening performance, and everyone from the baker to the blacksmith sang the arias."

Later Bryanne would remember everything about that evening. She and Steven seemed to have so much to talk about. She found herself telling him about herself—her childhood, her life in Mayfield, her sculpting. It seemed so easy, unlike any other time she had spent with anyone. Odd, because in Mayfield terms Steven was practically a stranger. Yet she was talking to him as though she had known him all her life. The Montroses and Camerons were all so talkative, so articulate. There was always so much being said that was interesting, informative, or fun that Bryanne had usually been a spectator, not a contributor. However, Steven seemed to think that everything she had to say was amusing or interesting.

For his part, Steven seemed just as eager to tell her about himself. He had an older brother who was studying law. His parents lived in a village just south of London, where his father was a country doctor, his mother an avid gardener. "I think you'd like them, and I know they'd love you," he said.

He had gone up to Oxford, he told her, not really sure what he wanted to do, whether to go into medicine and eventually practice with his father or become a lawyer. "That's actually why I decided to take this year off—to think about my options. I'm going on to Sicily, meeting up with some fellows I know from my college. Things don't look all that good for the future for any of us—I don't like to be gloomy, but really all you need to do is read the papers to realize that the fuse is short on whatever is going to happen, with Germany on the move." He stopped, then asked her, "How much longer will you stay in Italy?"

"I have another ten days. Not long enough." She sighed. "I wish there were some way to keep all this fresh. Of course, I have my sketches—"

"And I have my snapshots," Steven said quickly. "I plan to take lots more. I'll be glad to have a second set of prints made and share them."

"Thank you. But there is so much we look at yet don't really see," Bryanne said. "I read something Helen Keller wrote, and I always try to remember it when I take something beautiful for granted."

"What was that?"

"She had such a deep appreciation for everything, even though she had lost her sight and hearing as a very young child. She said something like, 'I who am blind can give one hint to those who see. Use your eyes as if tomorrow you would be stricken blind. Hear the music of voices, the song of birds, the mighty strains of an orchestra, as if you would be stricken deaf tomorrow. Touch each object you want to touch as if tomorrow your tactile sense would fail. Smell the perfume of flowers, taste with relish each morsel, as if tomorrow you could never smell and taste again.'"

"So true. We should all take more heed of the joy of the moment."

They lost track of time, but Bryanne suspected it was very late as they walked back to her pension. Both suddenly fell quiet, aware that the enjoyable evening had come to an end.

At length Steven asked, "And when do you go back to America?"

"First I'll go to my grandmother's home in Kentburne to spend some time with her. I haven't made definite plans or reservations for my trip back to Virginia."

"Then I'll have a chance to see you again," Steven said with obvious relief. His voice became soft, his tone serious. "I don't want to lose you, Bryanne."

Her heart began to beat rapidly. She felt her cheeks get warm. Steven went on. "I'm leaving early in the morning, but I can't leave without telling you—" He halted, hesitated a split second, then leaned down and tipped her chin upward, looked at her for a long moment, and finally kissed her gently. "Arrivederci, Bryanne. Till we meet again, in England."

Why was it that the Italian language was so much more

romantic? she thought dreamily when Steven had gone and she was in the pension bedroom, brushing her hair. Arrivederci sounded so much better than good-bye—so much less final.

Had Steven meant it when he said they would meet again in England?

She had written down her grandmother's name and phone number and the name of the village in which Grandmother Garnet lived. Would he call? Had what happened meant as much to Steven as it had to her? Or was this just a brief interlude gilded with the romantic aura of Italy?

chapter 9

Bryanne had been back at Birchfields a week. Her grandmother was eager to hear all the details of her Italian travels. Bryanne tried to comply, but she could not bring herself to tell Garnet the most important thing that had happened to her—that she had fallen in love.

She had hoped Steven might write a note or even call. But he hadn't, and Bryanne began to feel a little let down. Maybe she had assumed too much, expected too much. Maybe they had merely been two travelers thrown together in a foreign land. She shouldn't count on anything so ephemeral, she told herself. She ought to know better. Still, she couldn't help wondering, hoping, fool that she was.

At the end of the summer, Bryanne's stay with her grandmother was unexpectedly lengthened. Her father was supposed to meet her at Birchfields so they could go back to the States together. However, Jeff Montrose proved himself as unpredictable as ever. His London gallery wanted to exhibit his new Scottish paintings, so he remained there to work out the details. When word came that he had decided to take an extended trip to the Orient, neither Garnet nor Bryanne was too surprised.

He had become increasingly interested in Japanese painting and wanted to view it firsthand.

Although Garnet was vocal about Jeff's lack of consideration for anyone else, she was secretly delighted that she would have her granddaughter's company longer. Bryanne, who was harboring the hope that she might still hear from Steven Colby, was agreeable.

The summer lingered into early fall, and Bryanne began to have some doubts as to whether she'd ever see Steven again. He had talked of going on to Greece and maybe even to Egypt. He had told her he had no real itinerary. Sensibly, Bryanne reminded herself that he had no reason to hurry back to England. Except, her heart teased, to see her again before she went back to America.

One afternoon Bryanne went into the village to mail some letters. Deep in thought, she walked along the winding country road. She and Jill had talked at length on the phone. Over and over Bryanne had asked her, "Do you think it was something like a shipboard romance? Is it just one of those things that happen in a strange place, a romantic environment? Is it too good to be true? Will I ever see him again?" Her own heart had doubts. Maybe he'd already forgotten about her. Someone as attractive as Steven Colby surely had an English girlfriend, perhaps someone he'd known since childhood or someone he'd met at college.

Suddenly Bryanne raised her head for some reason and, looking ahead down the road, saw a tall man approaching. His hands were in the pocket of his jacket and his head was down, so she could not see his face. But his walk had a strange familiarity. Thick, sun-streaked hair fell over his forehead, and he shook it back in a way she recognized. She stopped short. Could it be? Could it really be? It *was* Steven Colby!

Without thinking, Bryanne began to run, calling his name. He lifted his head and a smile broke across his face. There was now no mistaking who he was. "Steven!" she called again, waving as she ran. She stopped about two feet from him. "What in the world are you doing here?"

"It wasn't easy. I had a great mix-up—boats, trains, you name it! It would take too long to tell you. I was afraid that I might have missed you, that you'd gone." He halted. His smile widened. "It's so good to see you. I'm glad you haven't left."

"No, I'm still here," she declared and laughed.

Then they both began to speak at once. Explanations were exchanged, all sounding muddled. At length he told her he'd just returned from Italy a few days ago and had gone first to his parents' home in nearby Burnley-Stoneham. "I told them about you and that I had to find you. I only had the name of the town, Kentburne, but I knew that it probably wasn't too large a place and that I could probably find you—even if I had to knock on every door in town."

"That doesn't matter now, does it? Because it all worked out."

"Because it was meant to be. Just like we kept running into each other in Italy."

Bryanne felt her face get warm. "I was just walking up to the village, to the post office." She put her arm through his. "Come along. You'll have to meet my grandmother. Birchfields isn't far. It's a lovely place—there are tennis courts and a lake dammed up to make a pool at the end of the property."

Suddenly Steven stopped walking. Looking rather anxious, he asked, "Will it be all right? Your grandmother won't mind having a stranger just pop in?"

"Grandmother loves to have company, likes to surround herself with young people. She's marvelous. I think you'll enjoy her, and she you. She's over ninety but seems much younger, and is very alert, quite vivacious."

Bryanne pocketed the letters she was going to mail and took Steven back to Birchfields, continuing to reassure him that Garnet would be happy to have him as a guest.

Garnet was wary at first about this whirlwind romance that had begun on foreign soil under quite unusual circumstances, but she was soon impressed by Steven. His tender attitude toward Bryanne, his attention and genuine caring, brought tears to her eyes. Garnet was perceptive enough to see that the young man had come on a mission and would be restless until he accomplished it.

Bryanne's shining eyes revealed her excitement. Garnet's heart melted. The child was obviously in love. Garnet said a prayer that maybe Steven Colby was the man who would make Bryanne forget her heartbreak, stop her from seeking a father who would always remain elusive, and give her the happiness she deserved. Garnet liked Steven. He was a young man who seemed to appreciate Bryanne. During dinner, observing him closely, engaging him in conversation, seeing his impeccable manners, Garnet was satisfied that he was a well-bred, intelligent, thoughtful man, worthy to court her granddaughter. She was convinced that Steven was a man in whom she could safely place her granddaughter's life and happiness.

Wisely, after dinner Garnet excused herself for her afternoon nap and left the two of them alone. Steven and Bryanne went out into the garden. Now, in early fall, it was still in rampant bloom. A new moon added a lustrous glow, touching flowers and foliage with a silvery sheen. Near the lily pond they sat down on the stone bench. For a minute they were quiet, listening to the evening sounds, the gentle lapping of the water.

Steven reached for Bryanne's hand, saying, "I missed you terribly after Venice."

"I missed you, too, Steven."

"I kept seeing things I wished I were seeing with you. You had a way of looking at things, pointing them out, that made them more . . . more everything." The pressure of his hand on hers tightened. "Bryanne, don't go. Please don't go back to the States. Stay here and marry me."

She drew in her breath in a little gasp. Instinctively she almost said the obvious—*This is so sudden.*

Steven seemed to read her reaction, because he immediately said, "Maybe to you it seems to be sudden and certainly not the kind of thing a well-brought-up Englishman should do, but"—he kissed the hand he was holding and looked into her eyes—"I love you. I think I knew it almost from the first, when I saw you on the boat to France. Then when we kept meeting—it couldn't have been all coincidence, could it?"

"But Steven, we hardly know each other. I mean, *really* know each other. We've seen each other in a kind of out-of-the-ordinary set of circumstances. There's so much you don't know about me."

"Everything I know, I love."

"No, listen, Steven. There's so much more."

For a long time she spoke in a low, intense voice. She told him about her life as a little girl, about the tragedy of her mother's death in the *Titanic* disaster, and about how she had been raised here at Birchfields by her grandmother and a nanny before being sent off to boarding school. She talked honestly about her father and how she felt about him. Then she went on to tell him about how she had discovered the gift of her artistic talent.

"I adored my father, even though I wasn't with him much. I guess I idolized him, built him up into some kind of hero. Maybe I thought that if I was really good at art, he would notice me, love me more. I know that probably sounds strange, but it's how I felt." She took a long breath. "Earlier this summer I traveled with him to Scotland. And I think it was there that I came to terms with our relationship." She shook her head. "I guess I grew up."

"Being in love is a very grown-up thing, Bryanne," Steven said softly.

"I know. And I wouldn't want you to think I was looking for a substitute father or anything like that."

"Haven't you ever been in love, then? Has there never been someone?"

Bryanne thought of Sean, of the spring she had come from England to Mayfield and he had been working for Scott at Cameron Hall, of their rides together through the woods, those first tentative steps toward friendship that grew into affection and then into love. It had all been intensely romantic. She had grown up believing in fairy-tale endings, and Sean was shy and sweet and far from home. They had been so young. . . . Then she remembered the shock of learning of his death. Recalling it now, she shook her head and told Steven, "Yes, there was. But we were just kids. And it was over before it had really begun."

Bryanne sighed. She had been such a dreamer, picturing a thatched cottage in an Irish glen, firelight in a stone hearth, Sean coming home, hair windblown, cheeks ruddy from his ride . . . It had been like a painting in her mind, not real at all. "You see, after Sean died, I never thought I'd marry. I mean, I never planned to. I thought to be an artist—you have to be alone, without other commitments, other obligations. That's the way my father is, you see. That's where I got the idea, I guess."

"Don't you think you can have both, Bryanne? I love who you are, what you do. I'd never interfere in any way with your art. It's part of who you are, and I love you." He looked at her earnestly. "Do you believe me?"

"I want to. More than anything, Steven."

"I'll do everything in my power to see that you'd never regret it."

He put his hands on either side of her face, turning it toward him. The moon slipped behind a cloud and then emerged, illuminating her upturned face. Steven kissed her softly, slowly. Bryanne closed her eyes and sighed a little against his lips. The kiss was sweet, tender, but promised so much more. If only she would believe it, it could mean the end of longing and loneliness.

Moonlight streamed into the bedroom. Bryanne, in her nightgown and robe, sat curled up on the window seat, looking down on the garden where it had all taken place.

Could she trust her heart? Love had never been real to her. Or it had had another name. What she had felt for Sean, the young Irishman, had been an affectionate friendship. They had been too young to understand what love really was. And it had all been over so soon, so tragically. She had read dozens of romantic novels and seen movies that depicted love in various ways, but she had never really known it herself.

She was in a daze. Italy was like a dream. But now here was Steven, stepping out of that dream and into reality, asking her to share his life, be his love. What she felt for Steven wasn't a substitute for anything else. She wasn't looking for a father. She wanted someone her own age, someone with whom she could laugh, be young, travel . . . That's what she wanted. That's what Steven said he wanted, too.

Maybe this was it, and she just needed to recognize it. It was slowly becoming clear, beginning to feel right.

Sunday Steven attended church with them, and afterward Bryanne went with him to see him off on the train to the nearby village where his parents made their home.

"We always seem to be saying good-bye at train stations," he remarked ruefully. "I hope we won't be doing this much longer. Bryanne, I wish I could tell my parents you've said you'll marry me. They'd be so happy, because it would make me happy. I don't want to push. I know this is a big step. But I love you so terribly. I want us to spend the rest of our lives together. We could be so happy. Do you see that, Bryanne?"

They had talked for hours. Steven had kept telling her it would work out if only she'd trust him. He told her about all the places they would go together. Maybe to Greece so Bryanne could see the famous Parthenon, visit the ancient temples, see the statues. Bryanne's heart was lifted. Here was someone who said he loved her, wanted to make her happy. So why did she hesitate? She couldn't doubt the candor in Steven's clear eyes.

The train whistle blew. It was time for Steven to go. He held both her hands in his. His gaze was steady, holding both a plea and a promise. All around them, people were making their farewells, saying good-bye, boarding. They heard compartment doors banging shut, one after the other.

"Bryanne, will you? Can I tell my parents?"

The train whistle shrieked again. "Yes, Steven," Bryanne heard her voice above it. "Yes! I want to. I will."

Steven hugged her, kissed her cheeks. "You won't be sorry, I promise you! I'll come down in a day or so, ask your grandmother formally for your hand." As he made a run for the now-moving train, he shouted, "I love you!"

The expressions of people standing nearby were horrified at this breech of English propriety. Bryanne didn't care. She knew she was smiling as she ran a few steps along the platform, waving to Steven, who had jumped aboard the train and was leaning out to wave good-bye.

Bryanne stood there for a few minutes, looking after the disappearing train, then walked slowly back toward Birchfields.

On her way she passed in front of the small village church and stopped. Ivy clung to its gray stone walls. Adjoining the churchyard was the cemetery, with its ancient, lichen-covered tombstones. Jill had once told her that some of her ancestors were buried there, the Marsh family, who had once owned and occupied Monksmoor Priory, the rambling mansion on the hillside, now a private school.

Bryanne felt an urge to go inside. She needed a time of quiet to think about the weekend, Steven's proposal, before returning to Birchfields, where there would be questions she was not yet ready to answer. She pushed through the gate and walked up the well-worn stone path to the front of the church.

At the entrance there was a small sign written in Gothic letters—"We are always open for prayer. Come in and abide awhile with your Lord." Bryanne pushed open the door and stepped inside. Hardly any light from the sunny day outside penetrated the church's dim, arched interior. Familiar smells wrinkled Bryanne's nose—dust, burnt candle wax, wilted flowers, damp old stones.

She moved slowly up the center aisle and slipped into one of the front pews. Looking around, she recalled coming here as a small child with her nanny. She had not been here for a long time. But somehow she felt that this was the place where she and Steven should be married.

Bryanne knew that once she told her grandmother, Garnet would take over, manage everything. It would become another of her projects. It certainly would not be the quiet wedding Bryanne would prefer. She felt some resistance, then gradually let it go. It would give her grandmother so much pleasure. After all, she and Steven had the rest of their lives.

1935

At first Bryanne and Steven had talked of a Christmas wedding. But neither Lynette nor Jill could leave their families during the holidays. Bryanne had explained to her disappointed fiancé that she couldn't get married without her sister and dearest friend in attendance. Her father was cabled but had already left for an extended tour of the Orient, so Gareth, who was coming in any case, was asked to give the bride away.

He had come in time to spend Christmas and meet Steven, who arrived to be at Birchfields for part of the holidays. The wedding date had been set for the twelfth of January.

Lynette and Jill would be Bryanne's attendants, and Steven's brother, Martin, would be his best man. Bryanne had already visited the Colby home, where she had been warmly welcomed. It had been an immediate and mutual affection. Tom and Vanessa Colby were thrilled that Steven, who had seemed at such loose ends when he left on his European journey, had returned so full of optimism and purpose for the future. That he was happy was an unexpected bonus. He had decided to return to Oxford and complete his education after the honeymoon. He was leaning toward medicine as a career, so his physician father could not have been more pleased. Both parents told Bryanne how delighted they were to be gaining a daughter.

Bryanne was right about her grandmother. Garnet liked nothing better than being in charge. She insisted that Bryanne wear a traditional bridal ensemble. Bryanne chose a princess-style gown of creamy velvet. A short tulle veil was wreathed in white rosebuds intertwined with bright-red berries, in keeping with the festive season. An exquisite bar pin of diamonds and sapphires, which her future mother-in-law had given her, and Steven's engagement ring were Bryanne's only jewelry.

The winter morning of the wedding surprised everyone by being sunny, although it was crisp and cold.

Garnet looked superb in a gray satin redingote with a fluffy fox collar and cuffs, exactly like the ones worn by Queen Mary. Garnet had even placed one of her gemstone brooches at the same angle at which the British monarch wore a crown-shaped diamond pin. And Garnet looked every bit as regal, Bryanne thought in affectionate amusement as she watched her grandmother make a stately entrance into the small church and be escorted to the front pew.

At the back of the church, Lynette arranged Bryanne's headdress for a third time. As they heard the introductory chords of the familiar processional, Jill gave Bryanne a reassuring hug. Gareth held out his arm with a grin. "Ready, little Sis?"

Bryanne nodded. "Ready." Until Steven she had never felt ready or sure. Now she couldn't imagine her life without him, didn't *want* to imagine it without him!

She reached the altar and turned toward Steven, and a sudden stream of sunshine, coming through the narrow arched windows, illuminated her face, appearing almost as much a benediction to the couple as the vicar's words. "To have and to hold, from this day forward . . ."

Bryanne raised her veil to lift her face for her new husband's first wedded kiss. Instead, she found herself staring into his eyes, looking so deeply that she felt she was touching his very soul. She saw in Steven's eyes the pure love she had longed for and searched for most of her life. *Thank you, God, for this gift,* was her heartfelt prayer.

As Steven suggested, they went to the south of France for their honeymoon. They stayed two days in Paris and experienced a sense of frenetic gaiety everywhere they went. It had an unsettling effect on Bryanne, who was particularly sensitive to atmosphere. It was like dancing on the edge of a volcano.

They were happy to leave and head for the small coastal town where they had rented a small villa on a hillside overlooking the sea. The sun felt delightfully warm on Bryanne's upturned face, her bare shoulders and legs, as she stretched out on the chaise on the stone terrace. Through half-closed eyes and sunglasses, she could see the ocean stretching in blue-green stripes to the far horizon, its surface sparkling as if covered with jewels.

Steven stretched out upon the lounge beside her, reached out his arm, covered her hand with his, gave it a gentle squeeze. Holding his hand tightly, Bryanne said softly, "Oh, Steven, I'm so happy. I don't remember ever being this happy."

The long days of sunshine were about to end for the world, but these two were unaware of anything but each other.

chapter 10

New York
1935

READING THE PAPER, Kitty was suddenly overcome. Bold headlines shouted,

> Italy Invades Ethiopia—Mussolini's Troops Sweep into the North-African Country, Slaughtering the Crudely Equipped and Poorly Trained Ethiopian Forces

In the Far East, Japan and China were enmeshed in a fierce territorial struggle. The world was in turmoil. The possibility of another war crept ever closer. Didn't anyone else realize it? Kitty moaned. Horrible memories welled up within her. How, in less than twenty years, could the world let this happen again?

She thought of Richard, of how he had been when she first met him, then later—body broken, gallant heart weakened, bright future blotted out. What might he have accomplished if he had been allowed to live? What might their lives together have been?

They had had nearly four beautiful years together as kindred spirits, soul mates, lovers in the deepest sense of the word. And he had left his legacy of poems. That's the way Richard's valiant spirit, forever young, lived on. She had received dozens of letters from readers who appreciated what he wrote. The most sensitive of them understood the meaning beneath the lines. One fan of Richard's had enclosed a poem by Laurence Binyon, Britain's poet laureate. The words had been written at the end of the war:

> They shall not grow old, as we that are left grow old;
> Age shall not weary them, nor the years condemn.

It was all very well to write poetry in memory of those lost lives, Kitty thought. The truth was harsher. Those young men had been deprived of all that might have been in the future. She thought of children she and Richard might have had together, and felt bitter.

She worried about Luc and others his age—idealistic, patriotic young men who might be misled into thinking that war was something to be glorified. In a few short years they would be old enough to fight. If America was drawn into another European conflict, their lives would be wasted. Kitty let the newspaper drop to the floor, then put her head down on folded arms and wept heartbrokenly.

Over two years ago she had had the idea for a book. Although she had made notes—scribbled on the back of envelopes, on scraps of paper, when she was traveling, or sometimes late at night when she couldn't sleep—the book had never been written. It was all a jumble. She needed to organize her material, see if she really had something important to say. She wouldn't put it off any longer. She would start right away.

Checking her calendar, Kitty saw she had two more scheduled readings at colleges—one in Maryland, the other in Virginia after the first of the year. That gave her over two months to get organized. After her second reading engagement, she would drive on to Mayfield. She could hole up in Eden Cottage and write without interruption.

Montclair
1936

Cara had just come from the barn and was walking up toward the house, when she recognized Kitty's small blue coupe pulling up the driveway. She stood and waited for the car to stop. Kitty opened the door, slipped from under the wheel, and stepped out.

Cara was suddenly conscious of her own baggy knitted sweater, her scuffed boots, her worn riding pants. Kitty looked smart and citified in a coffee-colored bouclé suit and a triangular silk scarf in which orange, rust, and gold mingled like spilled watercolors. Ironically, Cara remembered that she herself used to be the twin who was clothes conscious. Living in New York had changed Kitty's appearance as well as her attitudes.

With a sudden pang, Cara remembered the last time Kitty had been to Montclair. Had Kitty forgotten their awful quarrel? Cara remembered how close they used to be, how they always seemed to think alike. Now they were so different, so far apart. . . . Quickly, Cara pushed aside those troubling thoughts and greeted her twin.

"Kitty! How wonderful! Why didn't you let me know you were coming? Not that it matters! I've got all kinds of empty rooms. Just pick one."

"Thanks, Cara, but I plan to stay at the cottage. I've come to work on my book."

Cara looked puzzled. "What book is that? Some more of Richard's poetry?"

"No, this is my own. A book about my nursing experiences in the war."

Cara started to ask more but decided against it.

"I just came up to let you know I was here. In case you saw lights on and wondered if there was an intruder or something."

"Well, of course you'll stay for supper? I'll send word to Scott. Jill's in England, and he's wandering around Cameron Hall like a lost puppy. We'll have a grand reunion, the three of us."

"I don't think so. Not this evening, Cara. I need to unpack and get settled."

Kitty was being deliberately cool. So she hadn't got over what happened last time. Determined not to let her twin's attitude get to her, Cara said, "Well, come on in and at least have some coffee so we can catch up."

In the kitchen Cara busied herself making coffee, keeping up a lively monologue about Luc and Niki. She was curious about the book Kitty was writing, but instinctively felt it might be better to avoid the subject. She certainly didn't want to bring up a topic that would cause another eruption. It was like tiptoeing around the brink of a smoldering volcano. Kitty's expression did not invite intimate confidences or an easy exchange of ideas.

Cara scrounged in one of the cabinets for something to serve and found an open box of cookies. Her back was turned when Kitty asked, "How is Kip, and what is he up to these days?"

Cara poured their coffee with an unsteady hand. Should she tell Kitty right away that Kip had applied for active status in the military, or should she let him tell her? Better to be the target of her sister's outburst herself than to have Kip bear the brunt of Kitty's hostility. Cara didn't want him to be upset as well.

She brought their cups from the counter, then looked warily at her sister, took a deep breath, and said, "Kitty, Kip's going back into the service as an instructor. There are so few men with the knowledge and skill the government needs—"

Kitty set down the cup she had just lifted to her lips, so hard that the coffee splashed into the saucer. She pushed back her chair and stood up. "I might have known it!" Her eyes flashed. "The peak experience of Kip's life was the war! He couldn't ever settle down after all the excitement was over, could he?"

"The army needs pilots, Kitty. We just have to be prepared, that's all. In case there's another war. We may be drawn in—"

"Of course we will." Kitty's voice shook. "If warmongers and men eager to flaunt their manhood have anything to do with it!"

Kitty's heels clicked on the linoleum floor as she marched to the back door and yanked it open. She let it slam behind her. From the kitchen window, Cara watched her sister walk back to her car and get in. In a few minutes the car disappeared down the drive toward Eden Cottage.

Cara would have given anything if this had not happened. But maybe it had to. Maybe there was nothing she could have done to prevent it. Maybe the chasm between them was already too deep and wide.

Kitty was on a mission. Kitty was as much a casualty of war as Richard had been. What she had been through—the sorrow, the loss—had strengthened her, but it had also hardened her. She was passionately committed to keeping the flame of her obsessive pacifism alive in the memory of Richard's life and death. Nothing else was as important. And anyone who didn't share her views was the enemy.

The next question was, what would Kip say when he learned Kitty was here and how the lines had been drawn?

When Kitty had left so abruptly after Aunt Garnet's birthday party, Kip had passed it off casually. "She'll get over it," he had said. But she hadn't. In fact, Cara felt that Kitty's convictions were stronger than ever. And this time she was determined to act upon them. Kip only saw Kitty from the outside, only saw the part Kitty allowed the world to see. He could not see the deep, stubborn core inside his wife's twin. Cara saw it. Maybe she was the only one who really did. There was a strength, a depth, an almost spiritual fervor, in Kitty's hatred of war. It had been planted there by her experience, and nothing was going to assuage it.

Cara sighed and hugged her arms as a cold shiver passed through her.

Ironically, it had come to a kind of warfare.

Eden Cottage

Kitty's heart was beating fast by the time she went up the flagstone walk. At the blue painted door, she hesitated a moment. Then, taking the key from her pocket, she inserted it in the lock.

The latch lifted easily under her fingers, and the door pushed open without a noise. The arching trellis over the doorway gave off the sweet smell of roses. Memories stirred as she inhaled the fragrance.

Kitty took a few steps inside. Shadows lurked in the corners, yet she hesitated to draw back the flowered chintz curtains and let in the light. In much the same way, she had kept herself closed, not allowing any other man, any other possibility of love, to enter her still-mourning heart.

She walked through the rooms. Gradually she realized that the pain was not going to go away. Not ever. Once she accepted that, she could begin to find a way to bear it, to live with it.

But could she put aside the memories that still dwelled here? Was there too much of the past? Gradually the truth came to her. This was not the place to write her book of horror, devastation, man's inhumanity to man.

Eden Cottage was a place for lovers. She would let it remain so. Someday two others would be happy here, she prayed. The happiness she and Richard had known together here still held its legacy. The cottage was not haunted. It would open its door, its heart, to the next loving couple to live here. It would give them its benediction. The pattern must not change. Eden Cottage must be forever a romantic haven.

To write what she had to write required concentration, not sentiment. It would take all her self-discipline to recall the scenes, the countless incidents that made up the whole terrible picture she wanted to show to warn people that war, for whatever causes old men dreamed up, for whatever reasons they crafted to send young men off to battle, was wrong.

It wouldn't be possible for her to stay here and do what she had set out to do. No, she would have to go back to New York and shut herself in her apartment, where even the noise, the clatter, and the busyness of the city outside would not distract her from her purpose.

"Must you really go?" Cara asked when Kitty came up to the house the following morning. "I promise we'd give you all the privacy you need. We wouldn't bother you, except to bring you nourishment so you wouldn't starve!" She made an attempt at lightness to offset the heavy feeling that hung between them. "I know you, Kitty. When you get involved in something, you don't even remember to eat half the time."

"Yes, I really must go, Cara. It's something I have to do, and I know I can't do it here." Kitty paused. "Not that I don't appreciate your caring."

The stiffness between them lengthened until Kitty made the first move. "Well, I'd better be on my way. I've a long drive ahead." She hesitated a moment, then held out her arms to her twin. "Wish me well?"

"Of course I do," Cara said over the hard lump rising in her throat. The sisters hugged quickly. Then Kitty ran down the porch steps and to her car.

Cara stood watching her drive away, longing for the old warmth, even the tears that used to mark all their partings. The coldness she felt was real, and she shivered. Would things ever be the same between them again?

chapter 11

New York

KITTY LIFTED HER hands from the typewriter keys as the black cloud of horror about which she had been writing dissipated slowly. Remembering had not been that difficult. Forgetting was what was hard. There were images of Richard as he had been when she first met him—straight and tall in his Canadian officer's uniform. Then there were visions of how he had appeared after long weeks in the hospital—pale, haggard, eyes sunken. He had looked old. Even as a trained nurse used to seeing men in *extremis,* Kitty had been heartbroken to see this once vigorous young man so altered, so ravaged, by war.

Although Richard had consistently tried to be cheerful, sometimes at Eden Cottage she would see a look come over his face—a haunted look that chilled her. Nothing she could say or do could erase the memories that brought this tortured expression.

Sometimes at night she would lie awake, trying to think of ways to help him. At other times she would wake before dawn, slip out of the cottage, walk in the woods, and weep alone, away from the house, where he would not hear her sobs.

Kitty shuddered. Determinedly, she dragged herself back to the task at hand. Richard's tale was the terrible climax of the story she was trying to tell. To keep any other couple from enduring what they had suffered was worth the price she was paying in heart-wrenching recall.

Kitty adjusted the lamp on her desk and once more began to type. The pile of pages to the right of her typewriter grew steadily. She read it over, corrected, revised, rewrote.

At last she had over fifty pages of manuscript, enough to submit with a synopsis of her book. But would anyone want to publish it? People wanted to forget the war, wanted to get on with their lives. Never mind the occupied beds in veterans' hospitals, the men languishing there with ruined lungs, missing limbs—and worse, shattered minds.

She constantly asked herself if this was only a personal catharsis, something that her soul needed to cleanse away the stored-up bitterness of the past. She had started her book in a frenzy of need to bring out that which had been so long bottled inside. Now she wasn't sure if it was any good, if it told the story she wanted to tell.

Whatever the reaction, she had to try to get it printed. She would send it to the same company that had published Richard's poems. Before his first volume was released, everyone had told her that a book of poetry would be impossible to sell. However, they were wrong. Richard's book had gone into a second printing, and some of the poems were now printed in anthologies, studied in college English classes. She had to try to get her book published.

The first fifty pages of her manuscript, and a cover letter stating her qualifications as a Red Cross nurse, her personal convictions, and her reasons for writing the book, were finally packaged and addressed. Kitty took the bundle to the post office and, with a kind of resignation and a whispered prayer, mailed it.

1937

Evalee stared out the train window, seeing the landscape they were passing through as if for the first time. Of course, it had been five years. Gradually the scene became more familiar—the blue hills in the distance, the farmhouses set back in groves of ancient oaks or dark-green pines, the pasturelands where cows grazed peacefully, the rolling hillsides where horses ran, the tiny railroad stations whose names struck a dim chord of memory.

Mayfield! Evalee thought. It was the home of her mother's family, the Montroses. But it was not home to Evalee. She was coming here almost as a stranger.

Evalee had never imagined herself coming here at all. Yet none of the things that had happened to her could have been predicted. A slight smile briefly touched her lips as she recalled one of the favorite sayings of her father, Randall Bondurant—"You've got to play the hand you're dealt." That's what she was doing. The only reason she was coming back to Mayfield was because she had no other place to go.

Looking down at the sleeping child curled up on the seat beside her, Evalee smoothed her pale-gold, silky hair, traced the line of her rosy cheek with one finger. How would her decision to come back here affect her daughter? Natasha had been born in France and had lived her entire life there. Evalee whispered her daughter's name softly. What would her Virginia relatives think of a child with such a name? According to Andre's great-aunt, Countess Irina, it was the Oblenskov family's favorite name for girls and had been since the time of Catherine the Great.

Evalee leaned her head back against the green cushioned seat, let her thoughts travel back to Paris. What were Andre's mother and his aunts, uncles, and cousins all doing this minute? Probably sitting in Marushka's shabby apartment, surrounded by photographs and icons, with the spicy scent of Russian tea simmering in the ornate samovar as she and Aunt Thalia played mah-jongg and sighed about the old days of the imperial court.

Being with them in that setting already seemed long ago, even though it had only been a matter of weeks since she left France. She had not told them her plans until she had had everything arranged. It would have been too difficult to put up with the protests, the pleas and mournful tears. Her reluctant announcement came at last, and there were many emotional scenes. To some of Andre's relatives, her decision to go back to the States was considered a betrayal to her husband. Over and over Evalee had had to explain that her mother, Druscilla, was now a widow, that she was her only child, Natasha her only grandchild, and that her mother was alone and wanted them nearby.

Truthfully, Evalee had known she needed to get away, liberate herself from life among the Russian émigrés. It would have been different if only Andre . . . Of course, *everything* would have been different then.

What she would actually do when she got to Virginia, Evalee did not know. Something would present itself, she thought hopefully. She could stay with her mother until she decided what to do.

Had Mayfield changed? The rest of the world had. The war had changed it. Had Virginia undergone the drastic social, economic upheaval of England and France and Russia? She'd heard that the stock market crash in 1929 had plunged the country into the worst financial depression of the century. Evalee didn't know what effect all this would have had on this small, out-of-the-way town a half day's journey from Washington, D.C., in one direction and from Williamsburg in the other. Evalee hadn't kept in touch with anyone in Mayfield but her mother.

Mayfield represented many things to her, none of which she had liked or enjoyed very much. As a child, she had dreaded visits to town with her mother. She had especially disliked being made to go horseback riding. Both Cara and Kitty, her Cameron cousins, had been practically born in a saddle and were excellent horsewomen, while Evalee was frightened of horses and hated riding.

Mayfield meant being surrounded by family. Too much family. Including Kitty and Cara, whom she used to consider rivals. When the auburn-haired twin beauties were popular belles, Evalee, the visitor, had always felt like an outsider. She had existed uncomfortably beyond the edge of a circle of which they were the center. She had often felt jealous and resentful.

To be sure, their charmed lives were over, as was hers. Long over. All three of them were now widows. Of course, Cara had since remarried—her childhood sweetheart, Evalee's cousin Kip Montrose. They now lived at Montclair, the family home. And Kitty had turned her loss into a medal she wore proudly, in the posthumous fame of her husband. Richard Traherne had become famous. His two books of poetry, which Kitty promoted, ranked him among the so-called war poets Rupert Brooks and Joyce Kilmer. Thus Kitty had been able to mourn openly.

Not so with me, Evalee thought. After Andre's death she had not been allowed the luxury of a prolonged, traditional period of mourning. She had to meet what had to be met. The need to support herself and her infant daughter had been desperate. She had had to find a job. Anything to pay the rent, buy food. For someone who had never before worked a day in her life, it had been a terrifying experience.

At first she had taken any work she could get—as a helper in a bakery, as a stock clerk in a shoe store. These jobs hardly paid a living wage. She earned only slightly more than a street sweeper or laundry worker. She finally went to work in a department store. She knew it was her looks that got her the job. The dramatic combination of blond hair and brown eyes was emphasized by the simple black sheaths that the store, La Mode, made their salesclerks wear. Evalee was exactly the image they wanted to project.

It was there that one of those sudden incidents that seemed to mark her life had occurred. A male customer asked her to model a hat he was buying for his wife. A new possibility for earning money was presented to her by a fellow employee, who pointed out that her slim, boyish figure was perfect for styles the French couturier Chanel had made popular.

Encouraged, Evalee had tried a little modeling. However, she had soon discovered that a model's irregular schedule was too demanding for someone with a child. However, through this she landed a job in an exclusive Rue de la Paix shop. Her aloof manner, which really covered her shyness, proved an advantage, because there were no snootier shop girls in the world than the ones in Paris boutiques. The pay was only a few sous higher than the department store, but she was paid a bonus for pushing the most expensive exotic fragrances, the price of an ounce of which would have kept Natasha and her in food and clothing for a year.

It was work that had bored her. A dead-end job. Evalee knew she wanted more for her daughter, more for herself. Finally she decided to go back to America. Surely it was still a land of opportunity for someone with intelligence and ambition.

How all this would work out in Mayfield, she had no idea. Where could she fit in? In a town as provincial as Mayfield, her European experience, her foreign name, might be an asset. After all, she *was* a countess. A meaningless title in a nonexistent court, but nonetheless . . . Perhaps, for whatever it was worth, it might be useful. How? What could she become? A dressmaker? An advisor on women's fashion? A designer or a decorator? An idea began to take shape in her mind as the train roared through the tunnel, up the grade, and over the trestle toward Mayfield.

In the South to which she was returning, family background—who you were related to—was everything. Evalee's mother had been a member of the Montrose family, which was one of the FFVs, the First Families of Virginia. The Montroses had been famous for generations as landowners, tobacco growers, horse breeders, and more recently as soldiers, statesmen, men of power and influence. Cousin Scott Cameron was the editor of the town's weekly newspaper, the *Mayfield Monitor*. Another cousin, Lynette, was married to a state senator. Such family connections might prove as important to Evalee in Virginia now as they had to the Oblenskovs in St. Petersburg before the Revolution.

Evalee knew she was far different from the young woman who had gone gaily off to Europe. Even her mother never knew the true circumstances to which Evalee's marriage had brought her. Tragedy had thrown her to her knees. She had been through so much, had endured so much. Most important, she had learned to trust God.

As a little girl, Evalee used to always declare, after hearing one of her favorite fairy tales, "When I grow up, I'm going to marry a prince and live happily ever after. . . ." Well, her childhood dream had come true. She *had* married a prince—a count, actually. But one without a castle, without even a country.

Later she began to see the fantasy his family lived—they believed that the Romanovs would eventually be restored and that they would all return to Mother Russia in triumph. In a kind of blind illusion, they held stubbornly to this belief while living in futile hope in shabby hotels and run-down apartments, on the brink of dire poverty. Soon it all began to wear thin to Evalee. She saw it for what it was—a vain dream.

Evalee soon tired of the talk, the endless gatherings to discuss rumors that came out from behind the iron curtain the Soviets had imposed, meetings in which strategy for overthrowing the Communists and taking power again was repeatedly revised and reviewed. All the speculation was completely false and groundless. Afterward all the former counts, princes, and generals went off to their jobs as doormen of fancy hotels or maître d's of fine restaurants—in which none of them could afford to stay or eat—or waiters in bistros or chauffeurs.

Much as she loved Andre's family, their living in the past, dreaming of an impossible future, had come to seem pitiful to Evalee. In the end, she knew she had to make a change. That's when she decided to take Natasha and travel back to Virginia, start again, make a new life for herself and her daughter.

Evalee touched the pearls she wore around her neck, remembering with tenderness the woman who had given them to her—Marushka, Andre's mother, whom she would probably never see again. Before Evalee left for America, the countess had given the pearls to her. Evalee knew how precious they were to her mother-in-law, so the gift was even more valuable to her. The pearls were to be kept by Evalee and then given one day to the countess' granddaughter, Natasha.

"Pearls must be worn to retain their lustrous beauty," the countess had instructed her. "Pearls get sick if you shut them away for years in the box. Any jeweler will tell you the same. They need to be lovingly cared for. They need the warmth of soft skin, or they lose their color, become dull and lifeless. They need fresh air, sunlight, and every so often to be steeped in seawater."

She had bidden Marushka good-bye with a sad heart. So much of her life with Andre had been bound up in his mother. But the past was over—the present was reality. Evalee had to face the fact that life was not a fairy tale. There was no money, and she had to support herself and her daughter.

Starting over in the States after her years abroad would not be easy. But she would make it. She was determined. Besides, she had to. She refused to be an object of pity, a poor relation dependent on others.

Evalee twisted the pearls thoughtfully. All that she had to show for her brief marriage were these pearls—and Natasha, of course. She glanced down again at the little girl, who stirred, making small murmuring sounds in her sleep. Something warm, tender, formed in Evalee's heart as she gazed at her. She would find something worthwhile to do in Mayfield, give her child a good life, make a home for the two of them.

The train slowed, and ahead she saw the small yellow station house. The conductor was making his way down the aisle. "Mayfield. Next stop, Mayfield."

"Come on, darling." Evalee gently nudged Natasha. The little girl screwed up her tiny face, reluctant to be awakened. She dug chubby fists into her still-shut eyes. "Wake up," Evalee urged her, pushing the girl's reluctant arms into the sleeves of her coat and starting to button it. "We must hurry. Grandmama Dru will be here to meet us." Evalee slipped on the jacket of her black bouclé suit and adjusted the silver fox ruff that had belonged to Aunt Irina and had been given to Evalee as a farewell gift. Of all Andre's many relatives, Evalee had felt closest to Irina. She now thought of their affectionate parting that cold, chilly night in the train station when Irina had brought her the fur scarf.

"Darlink, wear it with joy!" Irina had told her. "You look like a queen, and you will be treated like one!" Kissing Evalee on both cheeks, her faded eyes bright with tears, she said, "Go, and God go with you!"

Irina had been the only one to support Evalee's decision to leave Paris. "Of course you must go! If I could go home to Russia, I would go like that!" She had snapped her long, graceful fingers. "Ve live in the past here—you and Natasha belong to the future."

Saying good-bye to all of Andre's relatives had been hard. However, Irina's words strengthened her. She could not let the thought that she might never see any of them again distract her from her goal. Irina was right—it was the future she had to think about now, hers and Natasha's.

Evalee peered out the window and saw the tall woman in a gray squirrel coat and a plum-colored velvet cloche walking along the platform. "Look, Natasha, see Grandmama! There she is, darling. Wave to her!" Evalee tapped with her gloved knuckles on the glass to attract her mother's attention.

Dru Bondurant turned and, seeing the two faces she had been searching for, smiled and waved.

Evalee felt her throat tighten with love and longing. So much had happened since she had last seen her mother. She hardly seemed changed. A rush of tender memories flooded through Evalee, memories of being sheltered, indulged, comforted. At the same time, she felt an irrational yearning to be embraced again by that love and to be told that everything was going to be all right.

chapter 12

Mayfield
Dovecote

THE NEXT MORNING, Evalee woke up in the slant-ceilinged bedroom of the small, yellow, eighteenth-century clapboard house that had once belonged to Dru's mother, Dove Montrose, and in which Dru now lived. For a minute she could not remember where she was. Slowly the long journey she had made with her little girl came back to her. She snuggled further down under the downy quilt and let the almost childlike feeling of security flow through her. From downstairs she could hear the murmur of voices, her mother's and Natasha's. The little girl must have awakened earlier and Dru had taken care of her.

After a while Evalee put on her robe and went down the short flight of stairs. In the sunny breakfast nook, Natasha was eating biscuits and honey while her tall, slender grandmother told her some story in her low, sweet voice. Evalee stood there for a minute, observing the scene tenderly.

"Mama!" Natasha exclaimed when she saw her. "Nana is telling me 'bout when *you* were a little girl!"

"Good morning, darling," Dru greeted her. "Come sit down and I'll pour you a nice hot cup of coffee."

Evalee took a seat beside Natasha, and her mother set a steaming cup of coffee before her. "Jill called earlier," Dru told her. "We're invited to Cameron Hall for dinner tonight. Everyone is so anxious to see you."

Evalee looked directly at her mother, wondering, *Were they, actually?* What did they know of her or remember? That she had been a spoiled child, a petulant teenager? Certainly they knew nothing of what she'd since been through, of the woman she'd become. Would she be as much a misfit now in this closed southern society as she had been as a young girl? Only time would tell.

"And of course, this little sweetheart, whom no one has met!" Dru gazed at her small granddaughter fondly before going on. "I'm not sure Cara and Kip will be there this evening, and Kitty is in New York or on one of her book tours, I'm not sure. But I do know Jill is really looking forward to seeing you."

Evalee remembered Jill affectionately. She was the lovely English girl cousin Scott had married. She had always been kind and considerate to Evalee. Perhaps because she too sometimes felt like an outsider?

It was early evening when they took the country road out to Cameron Hall. It was situated well off the main road and was approached through blue iron gates leading up to the house.

Scott Cameron came out onto the brick terrace as Dru's Chevrolet coupe came to a stop in front of the stately brick house. "Welcome, Aunt Dru," he said, assisting her out of the small car. Then he turned to Evalee, smiling. "All grown up, I see."

"That happens," she replied, thinking that the tall cousin she had idolized as a young girl before the war had changed into a mature man. However, he was still handsome, with strong features and a touch of gray at his temples.

"And this is the little Russian countess," he said, bending slightly to Natasha, who stood clinging to her mother's hand.

"Oh, please! She gets enough of that from her Russian relatives," Evalee protested, shifting the fox scarf uneasily, then glancing past Scott. "Where's Jill and the twins?"

"Jill will be along in a minute. She was overseeing the twins' baths," Scott explained. "They were out riding and lost track of the time. They'd been told to be home in plenty of time to welcome their new cousin. They'll all be along in a while. Both Stewart and Scotty are avid horseback riders. Cara's been coaching them, getting ready for the Mayfield County horse show."

"Of course. I should have remembered. We're back in Virginia, horse country." Evalee hoped that she didn't sound sarcastic and that Scott didn't remember the fuss she used to put up about riding. After all, the Cameron stables were famous, and it would only be natural for his children to ride. She glanced at her daughter. If they were going to live here, it would probably be a good thing for Natasha to learn as well.

"Come along inside," Scott invited, offering his arm to his Aunt Druscilla. "How long has it been, anyway?"

Before they reached the top of the steps, a woman in a rose-colored cardigan and a tweed skirt appeared at the front door. Seeing her, Evalee had to conceal her shock. It had been five years, she reminded herself. She remembered Jill as a slender English beauty who had first come to Cameron Hall as a companion to Bryanne Montrose and had stayed to become mistress of this lovely estate. It was the gray hair that had thrown her temporarily. But Jill's smile was radiant, and so was her rose complexion. She held out both hands, welcoming Evalee.

"Evalee, how wonderful to see you again! And what a dear little girl." She leaned down toward Natasha and spoke very softly. "Hello, Natasha. I'm your Auntie Jill. We've been looking forward to meeting you." To Evalee she said, "What a doll!" Then she straightened. "Aunt Dru, I know you're happy to have these two with you. Do come in, all of you. We'll have tea."

Evalee felt a mixture of emotions as she went inside. Cameron Hall had always seemed like a storybook house to her. It seemed even more so to her today. It was a high-ceilinged, magnificent place filled with paintings, antiques, and priceless rugs. And moving about within it were these handsome, well-fed, well-dressed people, expecting to be waited on, being served meals that appeared magically at the appropriate time, accepting the privilege and position, as was their right. Maybe it all struck her anew after years of living in impoverished circumstances.

Evalee was thrust back to the last time she had been a visitor here. It had been at Christmas, and the house had been bright with holiday decorations. She remembered the scent of the six-foot cedar that stood in the curve of the winding stairway. The tang of bayberry candles, of evergreens, mingled with the spicy smells of baking coming from the kitchen. That day had started out as a happy family holiday but had become a time of tension and turmoil and conflict. Cara, of course, had been the cause. Mercurial, high-spirited Cara had a tendency to be reckless and indiscreet and had caused a mild sensation at the annual party. Later she had upset the household with a secret plan to elope, then just as unexpectedly had returned for an impromptu wedding. To a ministerial student, no less! Cara, the family "wild card," as Scott had named her. Her twin sister Kitty was just the opposite.

Jill's voice, which still retained its delightful upper-class

English accent, brought Evalee back to the present. "You must be tired, coming all the way from New York as you did. Your mother said you didn't even take a day or two to rest after the ocean voyage."

Evalee bit her tongue to keep from blurting out the truth. It would never occur to any of these affluent people that her reason was that she couldn't afford to stay even one night in a hotel.

"Let's go into the library," Scott suggested, leading the way.

Evalee followed her cousin into the splendid room, which had walls of built-in bookcases. It was furnished in a blend of cushioned sofas and deep chairs. In the fireplace a fire glowed cheerily, and in front of it was a small tea table, on which a silver tea service was placed.

Dru took over her little granddaughter, settling her on one of the tufted hassocks beside her own chair. Jill poured tea and handed Evalee a cup.

Evalee listened to the conversation between her mother and Scott. At first the cadence of their southern accent sounded strange to her ears, which had become accustomed to French and Russian. The talk was mostly of family and mutual friends. It seemed Scott had a recent letter from Garnet, with instructions for him to carry out while she was away from the scene herself. This brought amused recollections of some of Aunt Garnet's visits, when in a period of weeks she attempted to arrange everyone's lives. It was a family joke that Garnet always created minor whirlwinds in her wake.

Their discussion was interrupted by the arrival of the twins, scrubbed, shiny-faced, and not the least bit shy. They were handsome and well mannered but very much at ease, comfortable with their parents and the visitors.

Stewart immediately marched up to Natasha. "Are you really a countess? Why aren't you wearing a crown?"

Scotty, a pretty little girl, a feminine version of her brother, brushed by him and took Natasha's hand. "Come on, I want to show you my dollhouse."

Over their heads, Jill said to Evalee, "I thought the children would enjoy eating at their own table in the breakfast room." She rose and led the children out of the library. At the door, Natasha turned and looked over her shoulder at Evalee, who smiled encouragingly. Scotty tugged her hand gently, saying, "Come on, Natasha." To Evalee she said, "Don't worry. I'll take care of her." Then the two little girls followed Stewart out of the room.

"They'll be fine. Scotty is a sweet child," Dru assured Evalee.

Dinner was delicious and beautifully served. All the dishes were typical southern cuisine, reminding Evalee of the meal-times of her childhood. Baked ham, sweet potato casserole, green beans, spiced peaches, and lemon meringue pie for dessert.

Afterward the adults took their coffee back into the library. It was then that the opportunity came for Evalee to speak about the plan she had been formulating.

Scott asked, "So, Evalee, will you settle here in Mayfield?"

"I'm not sure."

"Oh, darling, I do so hope so!" Dru exclaimed, giving Evalee an anxious look. "We haven't had a chance to talk about it yet."

Evalee hesitated a moment. Then she decided it was best to just be blunt. "I have to find a job, some way to make a living."

Maybe being that outspoken was not quite proper, but she had learned that it was pointless to be evasive when one was better served by the truth.

Scott gave her an appraising look. "What kind of job? What can you do? What experience have you had?"

She was grateful that he was getting right to the heart of the matter. With his connections, Scott might be able to help. "I've held several kinds of jobs—selling perfume, hats, working in an art gallery. . . The last one I had was as a concierge in the apartment house where we lived."

She saw Dru's shocked expression. Evalee had still not told her mother about the dire financial circumstances into which they had plunged.

"Well, that's wide-ranging enough, I guess," Scott said then. "But what would you like to do?"

"If I had my choice?" Evalee gave a derisive laugh, as though his question amused her. What if she answered that she'd like to sleep till noon, read novels, eat bonbons, have a maid bring tea? But she knew that was not the ideal life. She had proved something to herself in Paris. She was smarter, more capable, more resilient, than she had ever imagined. She was proud of how she'd scrimped and saved to earn enough to buy their tickets to America, working extra hours and weekends. Here she hoped to put some of her newfound abilities to advantage.

She took a deep breath and told Scott, "I'd like to have a shop, a French-type boutique with frivolous, unique, romantic things, the kind of things people buy as gifts for someone special, someone they love . . ."

Jill was immediately enthusiastic. "What a great idea! That would be something really different for Mayfield."

Encouraged by her reaction and Scott's interest, Evalee began to mention a few of the ideas she had. By the end of the hour, she had been given dozens of suggestions as to how such a venture could be started, where the boutique could be located, how it could be advertised.

"By word of mouth or by elegant cards inviting a special few to come! A hundred or so special few!" Jill laughed. "We could all compile a list of names. With all the organizations and clubs the members of this family belong to, the business would be a success immediately."

"Now, Jill, don't get carried away," Scott cautioned. "A lot of planning has to go into an enterprise like this."

Jill ignored Scott and looked directly at Evalee. "I know, but it doesn't hurt to think ahead."

Evalee smiled gratefully at Jill. "Thank you. I think I needed that." It was wonderful to have someone respond so favorably to something that had only been a vague thought floating on the periphery of her mind. She felt Jill would be her ally in her future plans. She hoped she would also be a friend. Suddenly Evalee felt exhausted. She hadn't realized how tense she had been as she was telling them about her plans. She had taken an important step by verbalizing them.

Dru, sensitive to her daughter's fatigue, made the move to leave. "We should be going. I don't like to drive after dark," she said, standing up. "Thank you both for a lovely evening."

"I hope you'll let Natasha come often to play with Scotty. She gets tired of being with boys all the time," Jill said as she walked them to the hall.

There Scott asked Evalee, "So you will be staying at Dovecote with your mother?"

"For the present, yes. Of course, eventually Natasha and I shall want a place of our own."

"Well, you'll have time enough to decide all this, I imagine," he said confidently. "When you are a little more settled in, I may have some more suggestions that would be helpful."

"Thank you. That's very kind."

"Not at all. You're back in the South now, Evalee. That's what kin are for, remember?"

She nodded, thinking, *Just like the Oblenskovs.* Aunt Irina's oft-repeated phrase rang in her ears: "But darlink, of course—what are families for?"

Druscilla's coupe had hardly disappeared down the driveway when Jill turned to Scott. "Couldn't Evalee and Natasha have the gatehouse, now that your mother's living in California?"

Her husband looked at her with a puzzled frown. "Isn't that a little soon to suggest? Besides, we don't know if mother is going to stay permanently in Santa Barbara."

"Buying a house, sending for some of her furniture—sounds pretty permanent to me," Jill replied mildly. "And of course, she can always stay here if she comes back for a visit." She paused. "Evalee said herself she wanted to find a place of her own. It seems to me the gatehouse would be perfect. Mama Blythe remodeled it beautifully and there's plenty of room. Evalee could use the downstairs for her shop or office or whatever she plans to do. The upstairs would be adequate living space for her and Natasha."

Scott raised an eyebrow. "It would be pretty close to us," he said slowly as they walked back into the library. "How would you feel about having them right on our doorstep, so to speak?"

"I'd love it!" she responded. "I love having family around. I love all your family, don't you know that yet? And Scotty would love having Natasha nearby as a playmate. They hit it off immediately, didn't you notice?"

Scott stood at the fireplace, took the poker, and stirred up the remains of the fire. "I wasn't thinking about the children. I was thinking about you, actually. I wouldn't imagine Evalee was much your type."

"And what type am I?" Jill asked archly. "I got the feeling somehow that Evalee—well, there's something about her. In spite of the chic, the sophistication, there's something that touches me. She didn't come back here to be Dru's little girl again. I think the sooner she gets on her own, the better off she'll be. She needs someone to help her attain her independence, her own place. I believe she needs support, a friend. I'd like to be that for her if I can."

Scott looked at his wife with tender amusement. "Ah, Jill, you are so softhearted. As a little girl, you were probably always bringing home lame ducks and homeless kittens, weren't you?"

"I'd hardly call Evalee a stray kitten! Did you see those pearls she was wearing? A king's ransom. And that silver fox? That's high style."

"Well, it's up to you, my darling. Whatever you want to do." Scott laughed. "I know better than to argue when you've got a project in mind. Evalee's your next project, right?"

Jill's expression was already thoughtful. *Gatehouse Gifts,* she was thinking. Evalee's panache would draw customers among the wealthy newcomers who had moved to Virginia, bought up some of the old homes. Even politicians from Washington, D.C., were moving here to get away from the high prices and congestion of the capital. Yes, Evalee might do very well—with a little help. And Jill was determined to give her that help.

chapter 13

THE FOLLOWING WEEK Jill showed Evalee through the gatehouse on the Cameron property. After Scott and Jill's marriage it had been converted into living quarters for his mother, Blythe. However, after Blythe spent a winter in her native California, she had found the climate, the surroundings, and the lifestyle so pleasant that she had decided to make her home there. Since then it had not been used.

Almost as soon as Jill unlocked the front door and Evalee stepped across the threshold, Evalee felt a rising excitement. She saw the possibilities at once. It would be easy enough to turn the downstairs into a shop.

"It needs painting and some fixing up. It's stood empty almost two years, and of course, Blythe had most of the furniture she wanted shipped out to Santa Barbara," Jill told her. "But our attic is full of odds and ends. Between that and what's left here, I'm sure you'd have everything you need."

Evalee walked through the first-floor rooms, stopping every once in a while to glance around as if mentally measuring, placing furniture, hanging curtains.

"Let's go upstairs," Jill suggested.

Evalee followed Jill up the quaint circular staircase to the upper floor. There was a large bedroom with windows on two sides looking out onto the tall oaks surrounding the building.

A dressing room revealed built-in drawers and closets. A large bathroom with pink fixtures and Victorian, rose-patterned wallpaper adjoined a smaller room that looked out over the meadows.

"So what do you think?" Jill asked as they went back down.

"It's perfect, Jill. The downstairs I could use for display purposes and a reception room, with separate space for an office." She smiled. "Tasha will absolutely love having a bedroom to herself—and that bathroom!"

It was an unexpectedly radiant smile. Jill realized that when Evalee was able to relax, she could be almost beautiful. The contrast of pale skin, dark eyes, and blond hair was striking. Jill knew that the young woman had been through a great deal. But maybe now that she was here and had something to look forward to, things would be different. Under Evalee's brittle surface Jill saw someone who was very vulnerable. It strengthened her desire to help. "I'm glad you agree. There is so much that could be done."

"And *will* be done," Evalee added. "Oh, Jill, this was a brilliant idea."

"I think so, too. It will be wonderful to have this place put to such good use. Remember, I want to help you any way I can."

"I'm very grateful. Thank you, Jill," Evalee said and hugged her.

After Scott gave Evalee the key, she went back to look through the gatehouse on her own. As she unlocked and opened the door, she had a strange feeling. She took one step inside. The house was silent, empty. A feeling of loneliness swept over her.

For years her life had been so full of people, she had hardly ever had a moment alone. What she was feeling was totally new. Was it excitement? Expectation? Fear? She wasn't sure.

She took a few steps farther into the large front room, looking around thoughtfully. Her heart began a strange staccato beat.

Suddenly she felt overwhelmed. Evalee took a deep breath and straightened her shoulders, refusing to give in to that momentary feeling of apprehension. She had not come this far for nothing.

She felt the urge to pray for certainty that God was in this decision. She knew this would be a more important kind of prayer than those she'd flung heavenward on the hectic days she'd been on her way to work, hurrying to catch the Metro, worried that the sniffles Natasha had would turn into something worse, that her stockings wouldn't last until next payday, that their cold-eyed landlady would raise the rent again on their flat.

She needed insight, strength, power. The Scripture that had sustained her through all the challenges of the past years came to her now. Shutting her eyes, she repeated the words of Ephesians 3:20—"All praise and glory to him who is able to do exceedingly abundantly above all that we ask or think, according to the power that works in us."

She stood still for a minute. Through the door she had left open behind her, autumn sunshine poured in. She could hear the sounds of birds, the rustle of leaves in the trees that circled the small house. Another sensation began to flow through her, replacing the anxiety. A feeling of promise, of peace.

It was real, as if a great weight were lifting. She realized that what she had felt earlier had simply been that moment of stage fright before the curtain goes up. The second act of her life was about to begin. She was ready to play her role. And who could tell? Perhaps something wonderful was about to happen.

Back at Dovecote that night, Evalee lay sleepless in the high poster bed. As physically tired as she was, her mind was restless and her thoughts roaming. Being in Mayfield, being with her mother and family, was like being in another world, compared with the one she had lived in for the past five years. It was unsettling, disorienting. However, that other life, into which her love for Andre Oblenskov had led her, had once felt just as alien. She recalled the first time Andre had taken her to meet his mother and the other relatives that made up their extended family.

"You'll love them and they'll love you! Don't worry!" he had assured her.

They had only known each other two weeks, and she had yet to meet his family or he hers, but he had already asked her to marry him.

It had been love at first sight—or very nearly so. It had been so immediate an attraction that they had both felt temporarily stunned.

Like so many times in life, there had been no premonition. That night in Paris when they met, she had no idea that her whole existence was about to change drastically.

Dru and Evalee had been in England, visiting Lady Blanding and Mrs. Victor Ridgeway, Dru's stepdaughters and Evalee's older stepsisters. They had gone on to France and were in Paris that spring.

Evalee had been invited to attend an embassy party as the guest of some friends of Aunt Garnet's, Lord and Lady Ainsely. She had been excited, of course, because it was a dazzling affair and she had a new gown to wear. It was with a sense of anticipation that she mounted the steps and entered the reception room, which was glittering with lights from dozens of crystal chandeliers.

She and Andre had seemed to see each other at the same moment. He was standing by the window, tall and slim, dressed in impeccable evening clothes. He had high cheekbones, black curly hair trimmed very short, a thin, arched nose. His eyes were soft and very dark, almost melancholy. At the very second their gaze met, everything—the hum of conversation, the murmur of laughter, the clink of glasses, the background music—seemed to stop. It was as if by the stroke of a conductor's wand, an orchestra had become silent. Everything receded until only the two of them seemed to exist.

In spite of his splendid appearance, he had looked rather lost and awkward in the midst of the laughing, chatting crowd. Her immediate impulse was to go right to him, somehow put him at ease, make him laugh at something witty she might say.

It was such a paralyzing experience that Evalee could not move. She had stood there as one mesmerized, staring into the eyes of the young man across the room. But Lady Ainsley touched her arm to introduce her to some people. And when Evalee turned back, looking over again to where he had stood, he was gone. She felt disappointed, as if she had missed something important.

It was not until she saw him carrying a large tray and stopping among the guests to offer glasses of champagne that the realization had struck. Until then she had had no idea that he was one of the hired waiters.

Later, when she got to know him, she found out that many of the exiled Russians, including Andre's family, had arrived in France practically penniless, escaping with only what they could carry on their person or in their limited luggage. His relatives, like most of the aristocracy, had been trained only how to take their privileged places in life, not how to earn a living.

All that evening Evalee had kept watching him out of the corner of her eyes while she danced, chatted, even flirted, with the half dozen eligible men Lady Ainsley had brought her here to meet. Lady Ainsley had hoped that the young American visitor would have a bevy of escorts to show her around Paris. Strangely distracted, Evalee had not been able to get the waiter with the handsome face and mournful eyes out of her mind.

That night she had found it hard to settle down for sleep. Already she had woven all sorts of romantic tales about him. He had an air of mystery about him, she thought. Inspired by a recent novel she had read about the famous spy Mata Hari, she wondered if he was in disguise. Perhaps he was masquerading as a waiter, working incognito on some daring mission for a foreign country. However, none of her fantasies could have matched Andre's real life story.

Of course, she had not learned that until later.

The next day, after a shopping spree, she and Dru had stopped at one of the sidewalk cafes near the Luxembourg Gardens for a cafe au lait, and there he was, again a waiter. Evalee was surprised, and she was speechless to see him approach their table.

His eyes had sent a message. He recognized her. She felt her face grow warm under his intense gaze. He took their order while she sat silent and astonished.

Later he had slipped a note in with their check before placing it beside Evalee. She reached for it quickly, hiding it in her handbag as she took out her wallet. Outside the cafe, when Dru's attention was diverted by a woman walking past with two adorable poodles on a double leash, Evalee read the note.

I will be off in another twenty minutes. Could we meet by the fountain and talk? My name is Andre Oblenskov.

She had folded the piece of paper and tucked it into her handbag. Dru, tired from shopping, accepted Evalee's explanation that she wanted to walk in the park and would see her mother back at the hotel later.

Evalee's heart had pounded as she waited near the fountain. She had never done anything like this before in her life. It felt daring and exciting. Was it foolish? She knew nothing about this . . . this waiter! Maybe she should leave. But just as she wavered in indecision, she saw Andre hurrying toward her. He was wearing a sweater and baggy corduroy pants. Without his waiter's jacket, he looked like any other casually dressed student. He saw her and quickened his pace. There was such lightness in his step, such happiness glowing in his dark eyes, that Evalee felt as though she were meeting someone she had always known. More to the point, someone she'd been waiting for all her life.

They had spent the rest of the afternoon together. Sitting on one of the benches, unable to take their eyes off one another, they talked. Andre told her all about himself. As he spoke, she felt something unfold within her, something warm, sweet, and very tender, something she had never felt before.

Andre told her he had lived in Paris since he was six years old. He told her of his Russian childhood, describing summers at the seashore and holidays at the family's country estate. Then there had come a night, he said, that changed everything he had known before.

It had been winter, and he had been awakened from his bed by his nurse, hastily dressed, and taken down to where his parents stood in the hallway, talking in low, urgent voices. His mother had on a long, hooded cape trimmed with silver fox fur. To his surprise, his father was dressed in the rough smock, full pants, cap, and boots of a peasant. Outside their carriage waited. Andre was rushed out and placed in it. His mother followed, weeping, and his father kissed him, hugged him hard, then slammed the carriage door. They rode off through the night, his mother holding him so tightly that he could feel the pumping of her heart, and the tears that rolled down her cheeks onto his.

They had never seen his father again. Andre and his mother had joined relatives in Paris and waited—in vain. No word of what had happened had come to them until long after the war. Even then news out of what had become Communist Russia came very slowly and could not always be counted on to be true.

Before they had escaped, his mother had sewn jewels into her corset, into the lining of her cloak, the hem of her dress. They lived for years by selling them, one by one, reluctantly and only out of dire necessity. His mother would not, however, give up her tiara, which was her symbol of having been a countess, or the pearls that had passed down through the family since the time of Catherine the Great.

It wasn't until he started school that Andre had learned about the Bolshevik Revolution and the fate of the tsar and some of Andre's own family who had stayed behind. The family members who had escaped clustered together in Paris, which they had once regarded as a place for vacationing in luxurious hotels. Now they were exiles who could never return to their country, forced to eke out some kind of existence. Andre had at last realized he could never go back to Russia, to the home he remembered.

It was getting dark when Andre walked Evalee back to the hotel. By that time she was in love.

After that first day, they had met every afternoon in the gardens after Andre got off work. He was trying to study at night to get into the university. But the waiting list was long, and natives of France were given first consideration for admittance.

In the meantime he worked at the cafe—and sometimes at special events, such as the embassy party, for extra money. A cousin, who had also been a count in the old days, had connections among the waiters of Paris and was often able to get him extra jobs.

Evalee had known that this would be hard to explain, not only to her mother but also to her two stepsisters and Lady Ainsley. How would she tell them she was in love with an exiled Russian, a waiter? That was hardly the type of suitor they had been trying to arrange for her in England.

But before Evalee had introduced Andre to her family, he insisted on presenting her to his mother, whom he evidently adored. Evalee soon understood why. Countess Marushka Oblenskov was the most courageous woman Evalee had ever met, a woman of strength and faith and fortitude. Strangely enough, she reminded Evalee a little of Aunt Garnet, who had also survived war and great personal tragedy.

Well, I have Montrose blood in my veins, too, Evalee thought drowsily. *Maybe that kind of courage is inherited.* She had already surmounted much. Whatever challenges now lay ahead, Evalee would meet them. *With God's help,* was her last thought as she finally drifted wearily off to sleep.

Moving day came at last. Evalee had all kinds of help. Her cousin Gareth Montrose came to do the heavy lifting and carrying. Jill and Evalee directed positions and placements. Dru kept Natasha happy until it was time for her to inspect her new room. The little girl was delighted with everything. Peeking out one of the dormer windows through the leafy oak branches, she exclaimed, "It's like living in a tree house, Mama!"

Scott joined them later with the twins and a hamper of supper prepared by the Cameron's cook, and they all ate the first meal in Evalee's new dwelling, wishing her great happiness and success in her enterprise.

At last all departed with best wishes and blessings, and a sleepy Natasha was tucked in for the night. Evalee was too excited to sleep. She kept looking all around the house, grateful for her good fortune. There was still much to do, much to plan, before she could get her project underway, but it was a beginning. A wonderful beginning. She was profoundly thankful.

Upstairs in the larger bedroom, Evalee saw in the corner the trunk that had arrived from Paris only a few days ago. It had not yet been unlocked or opened. It contained some of the things from the small Paris flat she and Andre had rented after their marriage, the apartment in which she and Natasha had lived all these years.

She was almost afraid to unpack it, because of all the memories its contents would evoke. It was like all the other things she had kept locked in her heart since the accident, things she did not dare to examine too closely. She was afraid that the feelings she had dammed up out of necessity might burst forth and drown her.

But unless she dealt with those suppressed emotions, she knew, her wounds would never heal.

Resolutely she got out her keys, opened the locks, and lifted the lid. One by one she removed the items. Tablecloths edged with lace crocheted by Aunt Thalia's skilled hands, monogrammed napkins, a few Limoges fruit plates that had been wedding presents. There were piles of Natasha's baby clothes that Evalee had not been able to discard or give away, a christening robe and bonnet, tiny satin shoes. Then, at the very bottom, she took out a square swathed in tissue paper. It felt heavy in her hand, and she knew that was because of the silver frame. Slowly she unwrapped her wedding photo. She had put it away the night of the accident and had never been able to look at it again.

She stared at it for a long moment. Even though the wedding had been preceded by emotional scenes with her stepsisters and concerned talks with her mother, it had been a most beautiful one. But the bride looked like a young girl she did not know.

Studying the picture now, Evalee remembered each detail. Her gown had been a dream of satin, her veil an illusion of lace-trimmed tulle. She had worn the Oblenskov tiara, made of diamonds and amethysts, lent to her by her mother-in-law. When she brought it to Evalee, the countess had recounted the harrowing experience she had had when she smuggled her jewels out of the country, with the Bolsheviks literally at their heels.

"Ve escaped vit only the clothes on our back and our jewels!" she had told Evalee dramatically. But the jewels were worth twenty fortunes, and the large family of émigrés had survived for many years by gradually selling them. There had been just a few of the priceless heirlooms left by 1930.

Evalee's tears blurred the image of Andre. How splendid he had looked in the beribboned uniform of an honorary officer of the White Russian Army. If the Revolution had not happened, he would have automatically been a member of an elite guard.

Their wedding had taken place in the small Russian Orthodox chapel established and attended by the community of Russian refugees living in Paris. It was small and dark, illuminated by dozens of flickering candles set in wrought-iron candelabra before icons—strange, garishly painted wooden images of venerated saints of the church. There were decorated swinging doors, edged in gilt, separating the worshipers from the altar, and the heavy odor of incense was almost suffocating.

Accompanied only by a few members of both families, Evalee and Andre had driven to the chapel together. Andre's hand seemed damp and shaky in hers as they walked solemnly the short distance down the aisle to where the bearded priest, in robes rich with embroidery and gilt trim, waited to perform the marriage ceremony.

Young as she had been that day, dazed as she might have been by the candlelight, by the strange language being spoken, and by her own excitement, Evalee's heart was nevertheless full of thanksgiving. She knew God had brought Andre and her together—she believed that with all her soul. They were meant for each other. Coming together as they had from far-distant lands was God's destiny for them.

And so she had continued to believe, through all the hardships they encountered. The strength of their bond had grown even stronger through the trials they endured. The birth of their child had been a shared joy.

Tears began to stream down Evalee's cheeks. For the first time, she allowed herself to weep for all she had lost. She wept without trying to stop, and it was like the rush of a springtime thaw over frozen land. She had never given in to it before. She had needed to be stoic and resourceful and strong. There was the baby to look after, a living to be earned, Andre's relatives to comfort, the horrible tragedy to face.

Andre, a newly licensed taxi driver, had died instantly in an automobile accident on a stormy night at a rain-slick intersection. He was inexperienced behind the wheel of a car, and he was a man whose mind was more often preoccupied with dreams of glory than focused on traffic. At twenty-eight, all his education, bright dreams, hope for the future, were gone—

leaving a widow and a little daughter, who was, ironically, a countess, heiress to a lost dynasty.

Evalee placed the photograph on the bureau. It all seemed like a story that had happened to someone else. Their marriage had been idyllic and tragically brief.

She stood gazing at the picture a little longer. Having confronted the worst blow of her life, she now had to play the hand she had been dealt.

She would always have the Paris of her youth. What she and Andre had shared—love, pure and true, without hidden purpose or past secrets—would never be completely lost. She and Andre had been each other's first love, and that memory would always remain pristine.

Now she could go on, build a new life, a good life, for herself and Natasha.

With God's help.

chapter 14

EVALEE AND NATASHA had settled in happily. The upstairs apartment of the gatehouse was now very like its tenant—exotic. The treasures Evalee and Jill had gleaned from the attic mingled with others they had discovered while foraging through secondhand stores in nearby towns. In front of the rosewood Victorian sofa, which was piled with petit point pillows produced by the skilled needle of Evalee's grandmother, Dove Montrose, was a low, glass-topped coffee table. On it Evalee had placed a Fabergé box and several lavishly illustrated art books. Nearby, beaded art deco lamps stood on French tables with curved legs. More pillows were scattered at random along the window seats around the two bowed windows overlooking the wooded backyard. Evalee's bedroom, reflecting her own personality, had a luxurious ambiance. The wide bed had a satin coverlet, and beside the bed were lamps with fringed silk shades.

The remodeling of the downstairs took a little longer. Evalee had decided that her enterprise would have a dual focus—it would be both a boutique and an interior-decorating business, and it would be called Gatehouse Interiors. She had definite ideas of how she wanted her new store and office set up. She needed room to display gift items, drapery and upholstery materials, sample furniture, and antiques, and she needed room to do her work—making phone calls, scheduling appointments, creating designs, meeting with customers, keeping records.

It was during this time that Evalee became fully aware of what it meant to be among family, who cared about her and were genuinely interested in her success. Gareth, who was a skilled carpenter as well as a landscape architect, volunteered to do some work for her. And Scott and Jill were particularly helpful. Scott adamantly waived any rent from Evalee until the business showed a profit. "What are families for, if not to lend a hand when needed?"

During these months Jill became Evalee's close friend. Their personalities, although very different, complemented each other, and they were both creative, energetic, and enthusiastic about the project. Jill shared Evalee's European taste, for she had been educated in Switzerland and had vacationed with her family in the south of France. As a result, they found working together a rewarding experience.

At last it was time to open the doors for business. Evalee wanted to do it with a flare. She hoped to immediately get the attention of the clientele she knew she must attract for her enterprise to succeed.

Jill helped her compile a list of potential customers, to whom she sent out invitation cards printed in elegant Gothic lettering that announced an open house at Gatehouse Interiors. Evalee had debated whether to use her royal title with her name on the invitation but concluded that it added to the cosmopolitan image she wanted to project. For the same reason, she decided to modify her first name slightly. It seemed too southern somehow. Countess Eva Oblenskov sounded better.

She planned the opening down to the last tiny detail, thinking, *It's the little things that make the difference.* The tulip-shaped glasses she planned to sell later were set on a table covered with a Battenberg lace cloth. Red roses in crystal vases added a special touch.

Evalee, in a simply cut black velvet dress and wearing the Oblenskov pearls, greeted people at the door. Most were stunned by her soigné appearance—the blond hair swept up from her slender neck, the dark eyes and pale skin. Looking at her, the uninformed might have had the impression that this was someone who had never lifted a finger to work, that this boutique was only the whim of a wealthy woman who used it as a pastime.

Friends of the family, as well as the curious, flocked in. The driveway was crowded with cars as streams of people came to congratulate her and browse, many simply to price the things on display, a few to buy.

Some, Evalee suspected, had come skeptically. Sure enough, she soon overheard predictions that such a store was doomed to fail. "The economy the way it is, who has any money nowadays for such luxuries?" She ignored such comments. She had to remain positive.

Eyes followed Evalee as though she were a rare specimen from some far-off planet, unlike anything that had yet been in Mayfield. They watched her gestures, the graceful movement of her hands with their red-lacquered fingertips, as she chatted vivaciously.

In this small, conservative Virginia town, Evalee stood out like an exotic butterfly among gray, drab moths.

People were intrigued by the unusual. Evalee, with her sharp sense of merchandising, knew that was the key. Even negative attention could be an advantage. She was used to criticism. She had always drawn it. She knew that most likely it was motivated by envy, and she wore her difference like a badge.

Natasha, adorable in a black velvet dress with lace collar and cuffs, was her mother's little shadow, following her among the guests, offering them a small tray of canapés.

Dru looked proud and pleased as she played hostess, refilling cups from the cut-glass punchbowl borrowed from the Cameron collection. Observing her daughter, she prayed that this venture would be successful. She was happy to see that so many people had come. She knew how hard Evalee had worked toward this event, how very important its success was.

Dru wished she could help Evalee more with finances. Her late husband, Randall Bondurant, had been wealthy to an extent, but he had also been a gambler, a high-risk player. In his last years he had played the stock market, and they had suffered heavy losses, as had so many, in the 1929 crash. When he died, there was a mountain of debt that had to be paid off, leaving Dru with only a small annuity that he had resisted borrowing against. Everything had to go—the island home, Hurricane Haven, on the South Carolina coast; the cars; the jewelry. All except the large ring, made of clear amethyst flanked by two baroque pearls, that he had given her as a gift on their twentieth anniversary.

Cara and Kip arrived, too. In spite of all the old antagonism between the cousins, Cara hugged Evalee. She declared, "This is incredible! What a marvelous place. I had no idea you were so talented."

At her somewhat careless remark, a flicker of annoyance crossed Evalee's face. However, she curbed the temptation to respond angrily. Dru, the only one who noticed this incident, had held her breath. Even as a child, Evalee had resented the Cameron girls. Dru was relieved to see that even if Evalee's childhood jealousy could still be aroused, she was able to overcome it.

As the afternoon wore on, people continued to drift in, to linger, to visit among themselves as though at a party. Evalee knew that the grand opening had been successful beyond her wildest dreams. Even though her feet were aching in her high-heeled sandals and her face felt stretched from smiling, her throat dry from talking, she was elated. The business cards she had placed in a small stack on a table near the door were dwindling fast. All had been taken, she hoped, by potential clients.

Outside it grew dark. Evalee turned on two of her prized Tiffany lamps. Shining through the beautiful stained-glass shades, the multicolored light cast a soft glow. At length people began to leave, complimenting and congratulating her and promising to be in touch.

Only a few stayed, mostly family members. It was then that Gareth came up to her, bringing with him a lanky young man. "Here's someone I'd like you to meet, Evalee. Alan Reid, an old friend. We were classmates at Briarwood," he said, naming the prep school both Gareth and his father had attended in Arbordale. "He teaches there now."

Evalee regarded Gareth's companion. He was casually dressed in a corduroy jacket, and his plaid tie was slightly off center. But he had an intelligent expression, eyes that were intensely blue, and the most endearing grin she had ever seen in a male over the age of ten. When he spoke, his drawl was typically Virginian. "I'm happy to meet you"—he hesitated—"Countess."

"Oh, no," she said, laughing. "No titles, especially in front of my cousin here!"

"We just wondered if we might take you out to dinner after everyone clears out," Gareth said. "I know you must be exhausted and certainly won't want to cook or—"

"That's very thoughtful of you, Gareth, but I'll have to say no, with thanks. Natasha has to be fed and put to bed, you see, and after that I shall probably flop. Thanks anyway."

"Another time, then?" Alan asked shyly.

Evalee looked at him. There was something about him—a quiet strength, a clarity in his eyes, a hint of humor in his mouth. He would be someone it might be nice to get to know as a friend.

"Why, yes, thank you. Another time," she said.

Just then a couple came up to say good-bye and ask about a pair of Hitchcock chairs by the window, so Evalee excused herself and left the two young men. As she walked away, Gareth asked Alan in a low voice, "What did I tell you?"

"That was the understatement of the year," Alan replied, smiling. "She's fabulous." Then he shook his head. "But I'm not sure she'd find a schoolmaster good company. She's probably led a pretty glamorous life. Europe, hobnobbing with royalty . . . What could possibly interest her in someone like me?" Even as he spoke, Alan's gaze followed Evalee across the room.

"Maybe it's just what she *does* want," Gareth said. "I think my cousin has had a large enough dose of European nobility. I think some good solid American company is just what she needs." He looked at his friend. "Take a chance, old friend. What have you got to lose?"

New York
1937

Kitty came into the foyer of the apartment building, got her mail out of the box, then took the elevator up to her apartment on the fourth floor. She unlocked her door and went inside, removed her suit jacket and, taking the pile of letters with her, went into the small kitchen. She turned on the electric stove, filled the kettle, and placed it on the burner. While she waited for the water to boil, she sifted through her mail.

It was then that she saw the envelope with the name and address of a publishing firm. It was not the same company that had published Richard's poetry, the one to which she had sent her manuscript. Curious, she opened the envelope, unfolded the letter. Her eyes raced down the page to the signature, which she did not recognize. She began to read.

Dear Mrs. Traherne,

Your manuscript No Cheers, No Glory *was given to me by an editor friend at another publishing firm, to whom you originally submitted it. He was concerned that this book might be too controversial for his company, but he thought I might be interested.*

I must tell you that your name was familiar to me from the two books of poetry by your late husband, Richard Traherne, which you edited and for which you wrote the introductions. Although I understand that this is your first effort at writing, I was impressed by your initial fifty pages. I would very much like to meet with you to discuss this project. Please call my office at your earliest convenience so we can arrange a meeting.

Sincerely,
Craig Cavanaugh

The shrill whistle of the boiling kettle jolted Kitty back to reality. Automatically she turned off the burner. Her hands were shaking as she reread the letter two or three times. The impressive letterhead seemed to indicate that the publishing firm was a prestigious one. And the editor was definitely interested in what she had written. Was this letter the answer to her prayers?

Manhattan Publishers
Editorial Office

The man who rose from behind the desk to greet Kitty was younger than she had pictured him. Shouldn't editors be gray, bifocaled, elderly, pontifical? For a minute she was taken aback.

Craig Cavanaugh was quite tall, well built. Under a tweed jacket he wore a button-down shirt, a knitted tie, a V-necked sweater. He had thick salt-and-pepper hair, and his eyes, clear and very blue, contained a hint of humor, as though he surveyed the world with an amused cynicism. His complexion was ruddy, as if he spent a lot of time outdoors. He looked as if he should be tramping hills somewhere rather than holding down the position of acquisition editor in this handsome office.

"Mrs. Traherne, I'm delighted," he greeted her. "I've been looking forward to meeting you." He politely indicated the chair opposite his desk.

Cavanaugh regarded the young woman as she sat across from him and folded her hands, gloved in gray kid, demurely on her lap. He thought, *So this is Katherine Traherne.* She was not at all what he had expected from the strength of her prose. Not at all. She was dressed with understated elegance in a gray pin-striped suit, not mannish but exquisitely tailored to indicate a slender, small-boned figure. She wore a tiny hat with a veil that just touched the tip of her delicate nose and did not hide her beautiful brown eyes. But her mouth, though nicely shaped, had forgotten to smile. Cavanaugh had the impression that for all her youthful appearance, this woman had known great tragedy, had borne much disappointment and sadness over the years.

"I've read your partial manuscript, Mrs. Traherne. It has received unanimously high marks from others on my editorial staff. I'm interested in discussing with you your reasons for writing this and for taking the stand that you do."

A slight flush swept over her pale face, and she leaned forward a little and said, "Because I think this country is in danger of being drawn into another foreign war, Mr. Cavanaugh. I'm not being paranoid—the signs are everywhere. But most people don't seem to realize what's happening. It's as if they've forgotten the horror of the last war. I want to remind them of the awful price paid by the young men who were made to fight it." Her voice had the soft cadence of a southerner, yet it had the fervor of a zealot. "As you know from my cover letter, I was a field nurse in France for two years. I saw war firsthand. It's madness. And I don't want to see it happen again. I had to do whatever I could to prevent it. That's why I wanted to write this book—"

Suddenly Kitty halted, terrified of seeing glass-eyed boredom on his face. That had happened so many times when she had brought up this subject or when she had been compelled to interject her opinion in a conversation. She knew people felt she had become a fanatic—but she didn't care anymore. This was her chance. She had to make her case, sell Craig Cavanaugh on the idea. She wanted this book published.

"Have you written any more than what you submitted, what I've read?"

Kitty felt her cheeks get warm. She had, on impulse, brought more of the manuscript with her—just in case. It was in a slim leather case she had placed on the floor beside her chair. She drew the case onto her lap, unzipped it, took out fifty more neatly typed pages, and handed them across the desk.

Accepting them, Cavanaugh said, "Fine. I'm spending the weekend out in Long Island. I have a place there, away from phones and other distractions. I will give this my full attention,

I promise. I think I can say that if this"—he tapped a forefinger on the stack of paper—"is as compelling and well written as the first fifty pages, we are definitely interested in working with you."

Kitty felt her heart jump into her throat. She started to say something but couldn't manage it.

"Is there a number at which I can reach you?" he asked, his pen poised above the memo pad on his desk.

She gave him her phone number. She stood up then, carefully smoothing her gloves. "Thank you, Mr. Cavanaugh, for your time."

Cavanaugh rose, too, wishing he could think of something to keep her a little longer. An invitation to lunch, perhaps? No, that would seem too—besides, he had an editorial board meeting at two. She walked toward the office door, and he followed quickly, opening it for her. "It was my pleasure. Good day, Mrs. Traherne. I'll be in touch."

She nodded and left—leaving Craig Cavanaugh strangely let down.

Once out at his beach house, Cavanaugh opened his briefcase and drew out the folder containing Kitty Traherne's manuscript.

He read it at one sitting. He got up once or twice and went into the kitchen to refill his coffee mug, still holding the manuscript, hardly glancing up from the pages. He was caught, held, touched, by the story she told in crisp sentences, graphic descriptions, unbelievably poignant scenes. *No question,* he thought, *Kitty Traherne can write.*

It was getting dark when he finished and put the manuscript aside. He got a sweater and went out to walk on the beach in the last glow of the day, still in the throes of the book's last chapter, "Armistice Day." It was about the end of the war, which had come when the young nurse was beyond caring, and too late for her young patient.

Craig Cavanaugh could not remember when he had been so moved by a piece of writing.

Kitty Traherne's face came back into his mind. He saw the pain in her eyes, heard the urgency in her voice as he recalled the passion with which she had told him her reason for writing this book. Cavanaugh dealt with writers all the time. That was his business. But there was something about Kitty Traherne that touched him in a nonprofessional way.

Before the day she came into his office, he'd only seen her once—in the photograph on the back of Richard Traherne's book of poetry. But when she walked in, he had felt a strange sense of recognition, as though he had met her somewhere before. He had tried to hold on to the sensation, but it was like a photograph that grew faded by too much handling. She seemed so composed, so untouched—and yet Cavanaugh thought he had glimpsed something that lay beneath that surface calm. A quality of commitment, of passion, of intensity for her cause. He felt sure this was a woman with hidden layers, aspects of her personality he would like to discover, explore.

Get ahold of yourself, man, Cavanaugh commanded himself. *Handle this the way you handle interviews with authors every day. She's a total stranger, someone you need to get to know.*

Still, there was that uncanny feeling of having known her before . . .

Maybe it had been the late-afternoon sunlight slanting in through his office window, shadowing her features, giving the impression of sadness, of loneliness and loss.

Whatever it was, Cavanaugh knew he was going to fight to

publish this book—and in so doing, he hoped to get to know Kitty Traherne.

On Monday Cavanaugh phoned Kitty to see if he could come by to discuss the book. Her hesitation at the other end of the line made him realize that she knew this was not the ordinary way an editor interested in a project approached a writer. But she agreed, and four o'clock in the afternoon was set.

Her apartment, when he arrived, seemed curiously impersonal to him. There were no intimate touches, such as framed photographs or curios or mementos, that might indicate the personality, the occupation, or the travels of the resident. However, the flowers had been cut and arranged by someone with a tasteful eye, a thoughtful hand.

Cavanaugh suspected that Kitty Traherne did not actually live here but simply used this apartment as a place to work. He found himself curious to see her true environment. That was the key to a person's personality and character, the things they chose to surround themselves with—the books they cherished, pictures, paintings . . .

"Well?" she prompted.

He was surprised. For all her delicacy of manner, Kitty Traherne got right to the point. But then, perhaps this was the *real* Kitty Traherne, the courageous, incredibly competent nurse. "It's a far cry from the Kitty Traherne on this," he said, picking up the slim volume of Richard's poems and turning it over to reveal her photograph. Then he tapped his forehead with his forefinger. "Or in here."

Ignoring his comment, she asked, "What did you think of it?"

"I was very moved," he said. "It's extremely well written, thoughtful, and . . . explicit and brutal."

"I meant it to be," she said, and her tone was steel-edged.

He stayed and they talked for hours. Kitty made coffee and they continued their discussion. He felt the book should be restructured, with the narrator moving from starry-eyed, patriotic idealist to open-eyed, outspoken pacifist. They talked into early evening, when Cavanaugh suggested they go out for dinner. Instead, Kitty scrambled eggs, made more coffee, and they went through the manuscript page by page.

At length Cavanaugh noticed her pallor, the dark smudges under her eyes. He got to his feet at once, apologizing for how late it was. She walked to the door with him, where he asked bluntly, "When can you have it finished?"

"It depends . . . I'm not sure. The first part went fairly quickly. The rest came harder. I don't know."

"Whatever you did, keep doing it. Write from the heart. Editing is our job. Correcting, polishing, revising. We can discuss all that later."

"I'll try," she said, almost overcome by the enormity of what she had taken on. "I'll do my best."

"I know you will."

Cavanaugh left and Kitty, restless, excited, paced her apartment. She wished she had someone to share this with. Ordinarily she would have called Cara. But that was out of the question. Or if Richard—but then, he would be with her as she finished this book. She knew she was doing this for Richard and all the others, the voiceless ones who had perished. She had picked up the torch their dying hands had dropped. Thank God, she knew this was what she had been called to do, and she would fulfill her mission.

chapter 15

Mayfield
Fall 1937

WITHIN A FEW months, Gatehouse Interiors began to gain a reputation as a place to find unique gifts and collectibles. Evalee's panache and obvious good taste, as well as the lure of dealing with a real countess, brought in customers, and her business began to show a small profit.

However, her cash flow was often nonexistent. The depression hovered uneasily over prospective buyers. Evalee was never sure where she would get the money to keep going. Through it all, she held on to her belief that using her God-given talent was the best way for her to support herself and her child, and that things would work out eventually. Her optimism often ran thin, but her determination to succeed never wavered.

Wealthy northerners, untouched by the country's prevailing economic crisis, had flocked to this rural countryside, buying up large houses that owners could no longer afford and renovating them. Most of the new owners yearned to recapture an authentic antebellum look, and they needed advice. Who better to give such advice than a descendant of one of the FFVs? With the added prestige of her Russian title, Evalee was becoming known as the interior decorator of choice.

In spite of this, Evalee often had bouts of despair. Her business was too new to get a bank loan, particularly in these times, when bank managers, burned by the crash of 1929, were overly cautious. Only Dru knew the financial tightrope her daughter walked, and she tried to help any way she could. A loving grandmother, she was always willing to take care of Natasha so Evalee would be free to attend auctions and estate sales.

One morning early in September, Evalee was at the Mayfield train station to pick up a package from a New York dealer. It was for one of her clients and was due on the next train.

When she pulled up in front of the station house, it appeared deserted. She checked her watch. There was still fifteen minutes until the train from Richmond was due. It was an unusually warm day, too hot to remain in the car, so she got out and went to sit on the bench on the platform outside the ticket office. To make good use of her time, she got out the notebook she always carried in her handbag to jot down random thoughts, ideas, or things she should do. For a few minutes she wrote busily. Her list grew rapidly.

Check date of estate sale at Wemberly.
Pick up fabric swatches for draperies Mrs. Hinton asked about.
Make dentist appointment for Natasha.

At the sound of a powerful motor, her pencil stopped and she looked up to see a sleek silver car of some foreign make pull in beside her secondhand station wagon. The car's convertible top was down. She saw that the driver was a dark-haired man wearing sunglasses. When he got out, she noticed that he was tall, dressed casually but expensively. He wore a butter-colored suede sport jacket over an open-necked blue sports shirt, and beige slacks. He ran briskly up the steps, crossed the platform. As he passed Evalee, he gave her a swift, careless look before going into the station house.

Who is he? she wondered. A man like that would demand notice in any circumstance. In a small town like Mayfield, he stood out like the proverbial sore thumb. The depression had lasted a long time in this part of Virginia. New cars or well-dressed men were rarely seen nowadays.

A few minutes later he reappeared, a package under one arm. He glanced at Evalee again. This time she met his gaze. A slight smile touched his mouth, and his eyes seemed to evaluate her.

Evalee lifted her head coolly and turned away. *Insolent!* she thought, inwardly bristling.

He stood there another half minute, long enough to light a thin, dark cigarette, then went down the steps. Back in his car, he started it with a roar, spun it around, and sped down the road.

Irrationally, Evalee felt annoyed by this stranger. Even his walk irritated her. He had a kind of arrogant grace that shouted supreme self-confidence. She felt that her experience had made her a pretty good judge of human nature. In her clerking jobs in France, she had had to wait on enough such customers—moneyed people who flaunted their wealth ostentatiously, treated store employees like dirt. Of course, by doing so, they showed their own lack of breeding. Obviously he was what the French contemptuously called nouveau riche. Mayfield was old family, old money, old tweeds, not flashy cars, new clothes, swagger. Whoever that man was, he was out of place here, no matter how affluent he was.

The following week Evalee went to the estate sale at Wemberly, which had belonged to one of the oldest families around Mayfield. Once it had been a great plantation, but little by little its acreage had been sold off. Now there was only six acres and the crumbling old house left. The last living member of the Wemberly family was an elderly spinster. The house, with its entire belongings, was up for auction, to pay off the many liens against it.

Evalee was preoccupied as she turned into the long driveway that led up to Wemberly. A sign posted at the entrance announced the time the auction would begin. There was always a preview period set an hour or two beforehand so prospective bidders could browse among the belongings, decide on what they would bid.

It was with a mingling of sadness and anticipation that she found a parking place among the assorted vehicles already in front of the once splendid mansion. Evalee felt sadness that this golden age was dying, that another of these magnificent old homes was on the auction block. Yet she could not deny the tingle she felt as she thought of the treasures she might discover.

She had a list of things some of her clients were hoping she would acquire for their home-decorating plans. She would also be looking for any "gems" to buy for resale in her shop, items that might catch the eye of wealthy customers.

A variety of such items were set out on the sweeping lawn, marked with their starting bid—chairs, tables, lamps, whole sets of china, bric-a-brac, silver teapots, umbrella stands. The accumulation of a lifetime—several lifetimes. The Wemberly family named among their illustrious members, dating back to pre-Revolutionary Virginia, statesmen, soldiers, botanists, a famous writer, a diplomat. To say nothing of outstanding huntsmen, from the look of trophies, horse show cups, and other such mementos of the glories of field and racetrack.

Evalee, notebook and pen in hand, moved about, marking

down the things she might want to bid on. Totally preoccupied, she did not notice the man approaching her. When he spoke she was startled. She was even more surprised when she turned around to see the speaker. It was the same man she had noticed the week before at the train station.

He extended a business card, announcing his name as if she should know it. "Trent MacGowan. And you, I believe," he added with an edge of sarcasm, "are *Countess* Oblenskov of Gatehouse Interiors. Am I correct?"

Evalee glanced at his card, then looked at him again. His features were roughcast in a deeply tanned face. Dark hair waved back from a high forehead, where a V-shaped scar was white against the dark skin. The open-necked denim shirt and its rolled-up sleeves revealed a tan chest and arms. His whole appearance had a studiedly casual air. Phony, Evalee mentally decided.

MacGowan wasted no time on triviality. "I've just closed the deal on the house." He jerked his head toward Wemberly. "It's falling to pieces, of course, after years of neglect. I'm having it completely restored. That will take some time. I'm looking for someone with taste, and experience in dealing with all the people I'll have to hire in order to get the job done. I need someone with a knowledge of the type of decoration used in the eighteenth century, when the house was built. It will be important to have a historical perspective of the period, so that if we cannot obtain the real thing, if antiques are not available, we can have authentic reproductions made. My priority is to bring this house as close to the way it looked when it was newly constructed—wall colors, upholstery, decorations, all that sort of thing."

Evalee was too overwhelmed by this avalanche of information to even comment. And his next statement really stunned her.

"You've been recommended to me as the person to contact.

There are more than twenty rooms that need painting, remodeling . . . Did you know that these old houses don't have closets in the bedrooms? Where did people put their clothes? Worse still, there's only one bathroom in the whole place, and that has vintage-1900 plumbing. So all that has to be done before we get to the decorating. But I like nailing things down to the last detail. I want to have plans for each of the rooms now, or at least before the structural restoration is completed." His dark, uneven eyebrows drew together in a scowl, and he demanded, "Do you think you could do this?"

Evalee was totally taken aback. To delay her reply, she looked down again at his card.

Trent MacGowan, Global Enterprises
New York, London

Although she remained speechless, her mind was busy, calculating, computing, figuring. The job he was proposing was enormous. Could she handle it? The fee would have to be large. She regarded the man, who was piercing her with stiletto eyes. MacGowan didn't look like someone who would balk at expense. And she had seen the asking price on Wemberly. Even in its present condition, the house was costly, as it stood on valuable land with one of the most magnificent views in all of Mayfield County. MacGowan had bought it—evidently without blinking an eye—so he had money. Even so, she was sure he would want to see every invoice, check every order down to the last detail. You didn't get to be that rich without knowing where every penny was spent.

His voice interrupted her thoughts.

"Well, Countess"—again he used her title with an almost imperceptible sneer—"what do you say? Would you be interested in taking on such a project?"

Evalee drew herself up. It wouldn't do to let MacGowan

think she was awed by his presence or at the prospect of such a huge and possibly lucrative assignment.

"I'd certainly consider it, Mr. MacGowan." She paused, realizing it would be wise to play her cards right with this obviously bold entrepreneur. "I'll have to check my schedule to see what jobs I have already scheduled. The due dates for completion on some of them might conflict with yours." She paused again. "How soon do you expect to move in?"

"Not for about nine months. I have an apartment in New York, and I go to my London office frequently. That's why I need to have a commitment—as soon as possible. I want to know that my place is in good hands while I'm away and out of the country. I want to be sure that it will be ready when I come back here to live."

Evalee flipped through her notebook to her appointment calendar. "I think we should discuss this after I've had a chance to look through my files and consider what's involved, if that is all right with you, Mr. MacGowan. Shall we say a week from today? At my office?" She felt it was important to see MacGowan on her own turf. Also, it would give him a chance to see Gatehouse Interiors, get an idea of her taste, the ambiance she created.

"Very well, a week from today. Tuesday, the twentieth," he said. "Time?"

"Two?"

"Two it is." With that he turned and walked to his car, which she recognized. It was parked near the house he had just bought. It seemed strangely out of place in front of the gracious old mansion, just as Trent MacGowan seemed out of place in Mayfield.

Later, back at Gatehouse Interiors, Evalee faced the hard task she had been avoiding for the past few weeks—taking inventory of where her business stood. Before long it became obvious that her unpaid bills and accounts due far outweighed her projected income. Numerous people who had talked to her about remodeling or decorating hadn't called back. Her operating expenses mounted each month. She was embarrassingly late paying Scott this month's rent.

Of course, he would never pressure her for the money, but how long could she take advantage of her relative's generosity? The business should be starting to take off by now.

For a few minutes she felt the same sick sensation she'd lived with constantly in Paris. The panic of being terrified that her paycheck wouldn't last to the end of the week. The fear of being evicted, broke—or worse, destitute. Although she knew that would never happen here, the fear of it was still very real.

The scope of a job like Wemberly was huge. She did not have the confidence she had shown Trent MacGowan. She had neither the experience nor the professional training for the project. Of course, he didn't know that. The facade she had used so often had evidently worked with him. But what if she failed?

Quickly Evalee stuffed the pile of bills into one of the desk drawers. She had to accept the challenge. This could be her big break. Done successfully, it could bring her everything. She had to believe she could do it. *With God's help*, she thought.

The next week on the appointed day, promptly at two, Trent MacGowan arrived at Gatehouse Interiors. At the sound of his car engine, Evalee, in a last minute of nervousness at the coming interview, adjusted the scarf at the neck of her simply styled plum wool dress, touched the amethyst cameo brooch. She had chosen her outfit to make the best possible statement. To a man like Trent MacGowan, image was everything.

He didn't see her at first. But sitting behind the graceful

Sheraton table she used as a desk, which was angled in a corner at the back of the room, she was able to observe him.

He walked in and glanced around, making a sweeping inventory, taking stock of the merchandise on display, the framed paintings, the mahogany breakfront with its glass doors and its blue-and-white Meissen collection.

Knowing he didn't see her and might be offended if she didn't make her presence known, Evalee moved the paperweight on her desk, rustled some papers, and stood up, saying, "Good afternoon, Mr. MacGowan."

If he was startled by her presence, he covered it well. However, there was a slight flush under his deep tan, as if he realized he might have been observed, and didn't like it.

He took a few quick strides toward her and looked her up and down as if evaluating a fine piece of furniture, then asked brusquely, "Well, Countess, have you decided whether you'll undertake the renovation of my house?"

"I've done some research on the original floor plan and read descriptions of the rooms, decorations, other details, and I—"

He interrupted. "Can you do it or not?"

Refusing to let his manner rattle her, Evalee continued. "As I was going to say, Mr. MacGowan, if I could also have a copy of the blueprints—"

"Whatever you need," he said shortly. "Just contact Doris, my secretary. I'll set up an account at the local bank, with your name as cosigner of any checks written in obtaining antiques, rugs, wallpaper, whatever. Doris will countersign and keep dual records. Is it settled, then?"

"Just a minute, Mr. MacGowan. I haven't submitted my proposal yet or—"

"My lawyers will handle all that and draw up the contracts."

"You haven't heard my fee."

"I know this sort of job doesn't come cheap. Let's say I'll put an additional amount in this account as a reasonable advance. You can negotiate the total amount of your fee with my attorneys. Whatever it takes, I want Wemberly restored to its former glory. Fair?"

Momentarily speechless, Evalee stared at him. She usually had to approach the subject of money cautiously, tactfully, always ready to come down on her fee if a client seemed at all reluctant. She saw no such reluctance in Trent MacGowan.

He looked at her almost defiantly. "I think you'll find it difficult to reach the end of my resources, Countess. When I want something, the price is no object."

"I can see that," she murmured, feeling a stir of resentment. This man was flagrantly arrogant. But she controlled herself, knowing that this job could make her reputation. She studied MacGowan, realizing that she knew very little about him. She had no idea what drove the man's ambition, except her suspicion that he was a self-made millionaire who had the outsider's typical hunger to belong.

Beginning to lose patience, MacGowan suddenly lashed out. "Am I to assume that your hesitation to take this job is due to some inborn prejudice against newcomers in this valley? Let me put your mind to ease on that subject. I am far from being a Yankee carpetbagger, as I have been mistakenly called. I was born and raised in the South—albeit in Milltown, on the other side of the tracks from your sainted ancestors. I understand it galls you that someone with no FFV background now owns the Wemberly estate."

Before Evalee could gather herself enough to respond, MacGowan said with a smile that was more a sneer, "I'm just a country boy at heart, one who grew up with the knack of making money."

"Money isn't everything," Evalee snapped. But she thought, *Unless you don't have it.*

He showed no emotion. There was only a slight tightening of his mouth, a deepening of the lines that ran on either side of it. "Money is power. Power to get you what you want in life. I had a mama who drank and a stepfather who beat me. I ran away when I was fifteen and joined the merchant marine. So nostalgia for Mayfield's glory days doesn't move me. I happen to have money, quite a lot of it, and now that I have it, I intend to use it to renovate that house—and the fact is, I need someone to help me do it." He smiled, his eyes cold as steel. "Someone like you, Countess. Want the job?"

Holding back the sharp retort she might have made, Evalee managed to say evenly, "Yes, I do, Mr. MacGowan."

Their transaction had taken place with incredible swiftness. Her mind was already calculating what payment for this project would mean to her—and to Natasha. In spite of Evalee's dislike for this man, the job would get her out of the red, put her business on its feet, provide handsomely for her and her daughter. This job was a gift. Evalee breathed a prayer of thankfulness.

chapter 16

New York

KITTY TORE A page out of the typewriter, crumpled it, and tossed it into the wastebasket. All week she had been revising, rewriting, and still it wasn't right.

She had spent most of the summer shut up in this stuffy place, the windows closed against the city noises, the whir of her electric fan going constantly. The pressure of the approaching deadline was making her tension almost unbearable.

She got up from the desk, went to the window, and looked down on the milling traffic in the street below her apartment. She felt confined, trapped.

Should she call Craig Cavanaugh, tell him she was finding it impossible to complete her book? What she had first written in her rush to tell the story seemed amateurish now. She had rewritten parts of it, and it still didn't seem to say what she hoped to say.

What was she to do? Maybe she was too close to it all and therefore unable to be objective. She longed to have someone else's opinion of the book. Yet she knew it was not ready to be read. Craig Cavanaugh's enthusiasm for the first hundred pages had made her almost too self-conscious.

At last, knowing her deadline was nearing, she was driven to make the call to Cavanaugh's office. They arranged to meet for lunch.

As soon as they ordered, she explained her inability to move ahead on her manuscript. Then she added, "I'm sorry to bother you with this . . . problem."

He smiled. "That's what editors are for, to help authors with their problems. What you're going through is not unusual," he said reassuringly. "Lots of authors experience writer's block."

The waiter came and took their order. After he went away, Cavanaugh leaned his elbows on the table and said, "I'm going abroad next week on a trip combining business and pleasure. I'll be meeting with some authors, agents, booksellers, in England, Ireland, and Sweden. I need to make some publishing arrangements with some of our writers, in case—well, things are looking increasingly bad over there, although England is trying not to see it." He halted. "Anyway, I expect to be gone for a few months. So I have a suggestion. Why not use my beach house? You could work out there undisturbed. A change in atmosphere might be just the thing to loose whatever block you have."

"Oh, I couldn't!" Kitty exclaimed. "That's much too much an imposition—"

"Not at all. I assure you, it's comfortable, quiet but not totally isolated, and there's a phone, a small grocery store nearby, and the train to New York runs every few hours." He chuckled. "There are neighbors who live out there year round, but they will respect your privacy. What do you say?"

"I don't know. It's terribly kind of you, but—"

"Not at all." His eyes twinkled. "I want that book for our fall list. Editors will use all sorts of tactics to get their writers writing."

Kitty regarded him thoughtfully. She was so new at all this.

Maybe it wasn't unusual for writers to get bogged down mid-book or have the psychological block she seemed to have. Perhaps it would be all right to accept his generous offer. What she did not know was that although Craig Cavanaugh was a fine, conscientious editor, he had never before offered his beach house to one of his authors.

"Well, if you really—" she began slowly.

"I do. *Really,* Katherine Traherne," Cavanaugh declared. "And it's settled. I'll be leaving Thursday, and you can move in over the weekend."

Their food came, and they spent the rest of the time discussing Kitty's questions, and Cavanaugh's ideas, about the book. By the time they finished, she felt somewhat better, perhaps ready to work again.

Standing outside the restaurant after lunch, Cavanaugh looked down at Kitty. Her eyes still seemed slightly troubled, her expression a little uncertain. She seemed so fragile, so vulnerable. He knew from her manuscript that she was courageous, a woman of faith and unimaginable endurance—still, he felt the urge to take her into his arms, protect her from anything and everything. The feeling was so sudden, so strong, that he was momentarily shaken.

Quickly he hailed a passing taxi for Kitty and put her in it, saying, "When I come back we can go over the book together. We can debate what to take out and what to leave in."

"Thank you," Kitty said. "For everything."

"I'll leave the key to the house, instructions about where things are, with my secretary," he told her before shutting the cab door.

The little resort town was quiet now. The summer people were gone and the beach was empty.

Cavanaugh's cottage was charming, with weathered paneling,

a Franklin stove in one corner, comfortable wicker furniture cushioned in blue-and-white striped ticking. The wide porch had a spectacular view of the beach and ocean. Everything was spotless. He had left the name of his cleaning woman, telephone numbers Kitty might need, and a note on the shiny kitchen counter.

Welcome. Make yourself at home. I've stocked the kitchen with some basic food items, but you may want to get other groceries. The store is only a few streets away. Or you can order by phone and they'll deliver, if you prefer. I hope the weather holds. Good writing! I'll be in touch when I get back.

Craig

Kitty walked around the small house, thinking how perfect it was. A place that held no disturbing memories for her, a place where she could work. How good of Mr. Cavanaugh to let her come here. What confidence it gave her. He must really believe in her book, what she had to say.

She wouldn't disappoint him, she promised herself.

Mayfield

Before eight o'clock one morning, two weeks after she signed the contracts for the work at Wemberly, Evalee received a call from MacGowan's secretary.

"Countess Oblenskov, Doris Miller here. Mr. MacGowan would like to see you before he leaves for New York later today. Could you come to Wemberly at ten?"

Evalee, still in her bathrobe, drinking her first cup of coffee, shot an anxious look at the kitchen clock. Natasha, in her nightie, sat at the table, spooning cereal into her rosy mouth, eyes brightly interested, wondering who would be phoning her mother this early.

"Is it Nana?" she whispered, hoping it would be Dru, whom she adored.

Evalee shook her head while looking around at the clutter of breakfast makings, mentally calculating how long it would take her to help Natasha dress, get her lunch packed, send her off to catch the school bus at the end of the road, then shower and change into her career-woman outfit and drive out to Wemberly. At what MacGowan was paying her, she did not want him to have any reason to complain. He was paying her what an upscale New York decorator would get. Quickly she replied, "Of course. I'll be there."

"Good," Doris said crisply. "He wants to walk through the house with you, hear some of your ideas."

The click and the buzzing sound that followed signified that the phone at the other end had been put down.

"We're going to have to hurry, baby," Evalee said to Natasha, taking a gulp of coffee before setting the mug down on the counter. "Peanut butter and jelly OK for your sandwich?"

Natasha slipped down from her place at the table, a ring of milk around her sweetly shaped mouth. "OK! And some Oreos too, please. They're good for trading."

Evalee smiled. What would Marushka say if she heard her granddaughter so easily saying OK and liking something as plebeian as peanut butter? What did Russian children eat for lunch? Borscht and caviar? They'd come a long way from Paris and all the Russian aunties. Natasha was becoming a typical little American schoolchild.

Smartly dressed in a black jacket and a pencil-slim red skirt, a red scarf tied around her throat, Evalee was on her way to Wemberly. She was feeling strangely excited, as well as apprehensive. Her encounters with MacGowan seemed to stir her up. He was abrasive, and she was out of practice at being a submissive employee. However, she knew that was what she now was—Trent MacGowan's employee. In spite of that, she was determined not to ever let him see that she was the least bit in awe of him, even though his money did sometimes daunt her.

At Wemberly she braked in front of the columned porch. She looked up at the wonderful transformation that had taken place since the day of the auction. Painters were still at work on scaffolding at either side of the house, but the front seemed to be finished. The Corinthian columns were gleaming white, the front door dark green and polished to a shiny background for the eagle-shaped brass knocker.

The house looked ready to receive the guests who must have flocked here in the olden days, when Wemberly was known for its fabulous parties. However, the minute Evalee stepped inside, that illusion was shattered. The center hall, instead of appearing welcoming, looked like the backstage of a theater just getting ready to begin scenery construction. Ladders were everywhere, torn ribbons of wallpaper hung from the walls, paint had been stripped from all the door frames and wainscoting, and paper strips crisscrossed the once beautiful parquet floors, which were now scarred and scuffed. Buckets, crates, and cardboard cartons were stacked all around, as though everything had been started and then given up in hopeless abandonment.

The only room that was furnished, he had told her, was an office he had set up there so he could be on the scene while the grounds and exterior of the house were being restored.

Doris, seated at a makeshift desk in a cubbyhole to the left of the entrance, rose and came toward Evalee, greeting her. "Good morning, Countess. You can see we're in quite a mess here, except for Mr. MacGowan. He's expecting you."

When Doris showed her into the office, Evalee looked around admiringly, wondering who had designed it. Had MacGowan hired a decorator to do it, then fired the person? And if so, why? It seemed tasteful and perfectly suited to the architecture of the house.

Dark-red leather-bound books filled the floor-to-ceiling bookshelves that lined the walls, surely among them a first edition or two. Did MacGowan actually read any of them, or were they just for show?

Trent MacGowan turned from the windows that overlooked the long stretch of lawn. He was wearing a creamy, roll-necked, cable-knit sweater, gray slacks. "You approve?"

"Indeed I do. It's very fine. I guess I'm wondering why you hired me, when obviously you had someone with very good taste and historical perspective to design this room."

"I had my reasons."

Evalee had a sudden insight that startled her. MacGowan's mocking way of speaking belied how he felt. These were things he cared deeply about. This house and what went into it were important to him.

Seating himself behind the massive desk, MacGowan said, "I called you over here this morning for two purposes. I understand there are some rumors about me circulating around Mayfield, and I'd like to put them to rest. I hope you will help me do that while you act as my representative. Contrary to what you may have heard, Mrs. Oblenskov—or Countess, if you prefer—I did not steal this property, although I'm sure Miss Wemberly will tell quite a different version of our transaction. I paid her market value plus. Not something my business manager or accountant totally approved of, I might add. I certainly didn't swindle a poor, helpless old lady, no matter what the current rumors making the rounds are."

Evalee saw a muscle in MacGowan's cheek tense. If these rumors made him angry, he was suppressing it. He went on matter-of-factly.

"In recent years there have been a great many changes in Mayfield of which you apparently have not been aware. For instance, did you know that Dunning Mills went into receivership? I bought the mill and now run it, along with some other business interests in Virginia. When the Wemberly mansion became available, it seemed appropriate that I purchase it as well. It is halfway between Mayfield and Dunning, an easy commute." He halted and then went on more quietly. "You see, I always loved this house when I was a youngster passing by it in my stepdaddy's pickup truck." The last few words were laced with heavy sarcasm. "You may not understand this, but I believe every man has a dream, one that is often born in boyhood. I was fortunate enough to be able to buy mine."

He took out one of his black Turkish cigarettes from a square silver box on the desk and lit it with a flick of his ornate lighter.

Evalee looked past him, out through the French windows behind his desk. They were open, and she could hear the drone of a lawn mower. He had already hired people to care for the lawns. She had noticed three gardeners at work when she came this morning. One was setting out dozens of bedding plants in the newly spaded circular flower beds, another was meticulously clipping the boxwood, and the third was moving sprinklers constantly to bring the grass to a velvety perfection.

She thought of the Wemberlys, who had lived here for generations. Particularly she thought of old Miss Wemberly, with her papery skin, her sunken cheeks dabbed with two spots of rouge, her wispy hair twisted into a knot at the nape of her thin neck, her stooped, skeletal figure in her faded finery. How she must have hated giving up this house—and to someone like Trent MacGowan—even though it meant she could now live in comfort in some snug little apartment in Arbordale and be assured that her last days would not be spent in dire poverty or in the county home. How her pride must have suffered when she sold this place. She must have detested MacGowan for having the money to do what she longed to do to restore her beloved home and property.

Evalee wondered what it would be like to be a millionaire like Trent MacGowan. How would it feel if there was nothing you couldn't get by snapping your finger or lifting a phone or pushing a button? But then, she knew that what he couldn't buy was belonging, the inherited kind. He could not hunt with the Mayfield Valley Hunt Club. But he didn't need to—he could buy a stable full of thoroughbreds, bring his own friends in to form their own hunt. He had a driving, self-absorbed personality, one that would never be satisfied. There would always be something more to acquire, to control, to run. His main preoccupation was wealth and power and what it could bring him.

MacGowan's voice broke into her thoughts. "Shall we walk through the house now? Then you can get a better idea of what has to be done, where to start."

Evalee had brought a notebook, and as they went into the high-ceilinged, spacious rooms, she could only imagine how beautiful this house must have once been. Could she bring that back, to this man's expectations?

Of course, MacGowan could never have seen the interior in its prime. His only view of the mansion would have been as a barefoot boy looking through the iron gates. Nevertheless, it was a bigger job than Evalee had imagined. Was she up to it? And could it all be done before the deadline MacGowan had set?

Evalee didn't let any of her concerns show. Trent MacGowan

was a man who only respected strength and power. Whether he was mistaken about Evalee or not, he felt she had the ability to transform this wreck of a house into its original state. She didn't dare seem hesitant or uncertain.

MacGowan spoke in his harsh voice. "I'm leaving for New York in the morning. And I may have to be out of the country for a few weeks, but you can always report to me through my secretaries—Doris here and Miss Thompson in the New York office—if you need to get in touch with me urgently." He paused. "I hope you're planning to spend most of your time on Wemberly affairs."

How annoyingly arrogant he was! She felt a rush of irritation. "As I told you, Mr. MacGowan, I have a few other clients I'd begun working with before I took on this assignment. I will certainly give you fair time."

He frowned fiercely. "Maybe I should put you on a retainer so you'd be working exclusively for me. Is that possible?"

"I'm afraid not, Mr. MacGowan. I do have other people who are just as eager to have their decorating done."

"If I paid you enough, you could make it possible," he said flatly.

Evalee had to bite her lip not to snap back at him. With effort she kept her voice calm, cool. "I have a business, Mr. MacGowan, customers I want to keep. I cannot afford to devote myself exclusively to one client."

"Well, just as long as my house is ready by June. I want to give a big housewarming party. That's eight months from now. Do you think you can manage that, Countess?" His tone was baiting.

Mentally gritting her teeth, Evalee replied, "Yes, I'm sure I can, Mr. MacGowan."

"Just as long as we understand each other, Countess," he said. "Well, I think that's all for now."

Evalee felt dismissed, but she tried to leave with some dignity. As he turned to walk back to his office, she went to the front door. She had a strong temptation to slam it as she left.

If it weren't for the fact that she needed the money, she would have gladly, at that point, tossed his commission back at him. The man was insufferable.

chapter 17

Kitty typed the last sentence and gave a sigh of relief. Unbelievable! She was finished. She'd done it. Her book was written at last. She wasn't sure if it was good or bad or what Craig Cavanaugh would think of it. But she'd done what she'd set out to do. It had taken her longer than she thought. However, Cavanaugh was still in England, and his office did not expect him back until the last week in November. He'd given her this gift of time, and she was very grateful.

She stretched out her arms, turned her head from side to side. Her neck ached from bending over the desk all morning. The ocean view from the windows that circled the front of the beach house was tempting. The sea, whipped by the brisk wind into a rippling blue-green, was frosted with whitecaps. She could stop now, take a brisk walk along the ocean, breathe deeply the sea air.

Being near the ocean had always refreshed her. There was something particularly bracing about a sea breeze. Maybe she should try to find a small house by the ocean somewhere. More and more she realized that going back to Eden Cottage was no solution. A place like this was perhaps what she needed, a small house of her own where she could see the ocean, walk along the beach—that might be the answer for her restless spirit.

She knew she would miss this house when she went back to New York. It had proved a haven and also a wellspring for her creativity. The work had gone so much better while she was out here. Some days it had seemed to flow. Even the hard parts, the poignant, heart-wrenching sequences, seemed to have almost written themselves in this quiet, concentrated atmosphere.

As far as she was concerned, she had written her heart out, said all she wanted to say. She had ended her book with Armistice Day, on which she had been in the midst of writing a note to the mother of a young soldier she had nursed until he died. The armistice, when it came, had seemed a hollow victory. Too many had perished, too many lives had been forever changed.

Her book was finished. Kitty felt free now. She had done what she had set out to do, what she had been compelled to do. She felt that Richard would have been proud of her. She hoped Craig Cavanaugh would be pleased with what she'd done.

She had arranged for his cleaning woman to come in after she left, so everything would be as spick-and-span as she had found it. She would restock the kitchen cabinets and leave a thank-you note for Mr. Cavanaugh.

After she packed up to return to the city, Kitty glanced around the beach house, took a last longing look at the blue ocean. She then went out, locked the door behind her, and walked to the small station to wait for the train to New York.

Mayfield
December 1937

With the holidays approaching, Gatehouse Interiors was buzzing with activity. Evalee had more people coming in, searching for unusual gifts for special people on their lists. She was very good at suggesting things, helping customers either find just what they were looking for or select something unique. A small beaded purse, a one-of-a-kind teacup, perhaps a scarf or an ornate Victorian picture frame. She also gift wrapped beautifully, which added to the delight of shopping at Gatehouse. Business became so brisk, she had to ask Jill to help out during the hours her twins were at school. Jill happily complied and added her charm and English grace to assisting customers as they lingered uncertainly over a choice.

Evalee had clients who suddenly wanted their interior decorating done before Christmas. She met with them during the morning, returning to Gatehouse when Jill left for home. Evalee then kept the store open until five-thirty.

Christmas week she was busier than ever. She had decided to close the store on the twenty-third so she could enjoy Christmas Eve with Natasha and her mother, then Christmas Day with the family at Cameron Hall.

The Wemberly commission required a great deal of her time. Trent MacGowan's mandate to get the best, the finest, with price no object, necessitated long-distance calls to New York dealers, trips to estate auctions in Richmond. She tried to sandwich all this in between her store responsibilities and her personal life. However, her days were hectic, every one filled with new challenges concerning MacGowan's mansion. She discovered it was a job that couldn't be left when the store closed. She often worked on Wemberly-related problems and concerns late into the night, after Natasha was asleep. Evalee was often exhausted, and she was looking forward to having time off, time to herself, time to enjoy with her little daughter.

She was also anticipating some pleasant times with Alan Reid. Over the past several months they had seen each other frequently. The more she got to know Gareth's friend, the more she liked him. She realized he was the first male friend she had ever had. She had lived by the commonly accepted adage that there was no such thing as a friendship between a man and a woman. Well, it was the exception that proved the rule. With Alan she could discuss many interests they had in common—such as music, art. And they could laugh together. Alan had a droll sense of humor, full of subtleties and self-deprecation, that she thought delightful. What she found particularly satisfying was that he saw beyond her facade and allowed her to be herself—a self he *liked*.

In the warmth of his acceptance, Evalee was able to talk to him in a way she had never talked to anyone. Best of all, he and Natasha had taken to each other immediately. Alan seemed to love children, and Evalee asked him, "Did you always think you'd be a teacher?"

"No, not at all. It was the last thing I thought of, actually. My mother died when I was nine, and I was sent to Briarwood. After that, four years of college. By that time, I'd been at school most of my life. I felt I had too narrow a view of things. So I took off and traveled all over the country, taking different kinds of jobs. I worked in Montana at a ranch, as a guide in Yosemite, anything that would give me enough money to keep going. I wanted to see the country, meet different people, observe various ways of living. It was a wonderful time." He smiled a little sheepishly. "But the depression was in full force, and jobs weren't too plentiful. I finally realized I had to start making a living. A lot of years and money had been spent on my education. It was payback time. Becoming a teacher seemed a logical choice." Now his smile was a bit rueful. "Ironically, I found I loved teaching. Loved kids. And wanted to share some of my own enthusiasm for learning and life."

"And have you?"

"Well, that was a little ambitious, maybe even a little egotistical. But if you can get one boy, one student, thinking beyond certain limitations—well, that's what I've tried to do. Don't know whether I've succeeded." He paused. "Or if I'll be doing it for the rest of my life. I still have dreams of my own. Plans I haven't yet fully explored."

"I know what you mean. You don't like to be categorized, put into a box and labeled—'He's a teacher.' I don't, either. I hate it when people assume something about me that isn't true."

Warming to her subject, Evalee continued. "I don't really expect anybody to understand me—or the world I've created for myself. Like Gatehouse Interiors. Although nobody actually said so to me, there was a lot of doubt about whether I could pull this off. I wasn't even sure if Mayfield was ready for what I wanted to create here. But I had to try. I know people thought it was different, foreign. But it was my vision of the world. It may seem strange to others, but not to me." She paused, and she felt the sadness of the past come over her. "You see, I've been out there. And I don't like it. It's cruel, heartless, tragic. When I lived in Paris, I found out that in order to survive, I had to get beyond the dirty streets, the indifferent people on the Metro, the rude customers . . . Here I can make my own environment beautiful. I think that life should have style, that we should surround ourselves with what we love, what makes us laugh. Beauty, joy, music—all are important to me. Without it life is boring—or worse, unendurable."

Alan seemed to understand her. She enjoyed his company enormously. Tomorrow he was taking Natasha and her to see the local production of Dickens' *A Christmas Carol.* She knew that the three of them would have a wonderful time.

Just before Christmas, on one of the longest, most tiring days Evalee had ever spent at Gatehouse Interiors, there was a constant stream of customers. As the day lengthened, Evalee waited on them in a kind of haze, being pleasant and helpful, answering questions, figuring up purchases, ringing the cash register, wrapping packages. She longed for the business day to be over, yearned for a long, warm soak in the tub, a cozy dinner by the fireplace.

The last customer finally left, and Evalee had started to close up, when to her dismay Trent MacGowan walked into the shop. What was *he* doing here? Had he come for an accounting? She suddenly felt lightheaded, jittery. She'd had nothing but coffee all day.

It was turning dark outside, and Evalee pulled the cord of the Tiffany lamp on her desk. "Mr. MacGowan," she said a trifle breathlessly, "I didn't expect you. I mean, I didn't know you were back in town." She was annoyed that she suddenly felt like a child caught with her hand in the cookie jar.

He was standing by the small Christmas tree she had decorated in Victorian style—paper cornucopias, gilt cherubs, crocheted lace snowflakes, strings of cranberries and popcorn—examining the fragile, painted glass ornaments. "Well, Countess, I don't always feel it's necessary to announce my arrival. Sometimes I simply take a whim. And I did this time. Wanted to see Virginia in December, my house in the snow. I've brought a photographer from New York to take pictures. Thought it might make an impressive Christmas card next year when I'm in residence at Wemberly. By the way, what progress have you made? How close am I to that possibility?" His gaze moved about the room, taking in everything—the wreaths at the windows, the handmade needlepoint stockings hung on the holly-and-evergreen-bedecked mantle. With a tinge of sarcasm, he added, "Or perhaps you've been preoccupied with playing Christmas fairy?"

Evalee felt herself stiffen. He was challenging her. In spite of herself, she felt indignant. She struggled to make her reply coolly professional. "I've received word that the shipment of

Chippendale chairs for the dining room should be here around the first of the year. As they're coming from England, it's hard to put an exact date on delivery." She added evenly, "I reported all this to Miss Miller, but if you'd like to see the correspondence yourself . . ." She made a move to the file cabinet.

He waved his hand in a negative gesture. "That won't be necessary. I'm a man used to having things done quickly. I'm unfamiliar with something as esoteric as furnishing a house with eighteenth-century antiques. I'll accept your word for it that things are moving along as well as they can. I'm sure I don't need to remind you of the June deadline."

He moved about restlessly, pausing here and there to pick up a porcelain figurine or examine a silver porringer. "There are two reasons I stopped by today, Countess. One was to inform you that I've learned that one of the biggest antique shows in the country takes place in New York shortly after the first of the year. I want you to attend. Buy whatever you think would be suitable for the house. I've let them know you'll be representing me. They'll notify you of the exact date. Of course, all your expenses will be paid."

Evalee drew in her breath. She knew about this sale. It was written up in all the material she read about decorating and antiques. The idea of attending it—and with carte blanche—was dizzying.

MacGowan walked to the door and stood there for a moment before saying, "My second reason was to invite you to a party at the Williamsburg Inn. I've brought some friends down from New York to enjoy a Colonial Christmas. I've reserved several rooms for my guests there. I'd like them to meet my . . . my decorator. They'll be sure to be impressed that she is a Russian countess." His eyes swept over her. "Wear one of your Paris gowns, or shop for something new and charge it to me. A Christmas present from a grateful employer." He opened the door. "I'll send a car and driver for you."

"I couldn't possibly," Evalee protested, taken by surprise.

MacGowan frowned. "Why not?" he demanded.

"I'm sorry, but we're spending Christmas with the Camerons and then going over to Montclair. It's a family tradition—"

MacGowan's eyes hardened as if they'd turned to steel. His lip curled sardonically as an expression that was almost a sneer passed over his face. Curtly he cut off whatever else she was going to say. "Of course. I should have thought of that. The FFVs close ranks at Christmas. Family only." She saw his jaw clench. "Well, so much for that."

He turned and left abruptly, letting the door swing shut behind him. The gold sleigh bells hanging on the door jangled, but the sound echoed hollowly. Evalee stared after MacGowan's rigid figure, watched him get into his sleek silver car and roar off into the winter dusk.

"Scrooge," Evalee murmured to herself. Yet she felt something almost like compassion for him as she went about turning off lights, closing the shop. For all his wealth and power, there was something very lonely about Trent MacGowan. For a minute she had seen a hunger in his eyes. He had no loving family with whom to gather around a sparkling tree this holiday. He had to import people from New York to celebrate with him, had to bribe an employee to come as his guest. For what? To impress these so-called friends? Evalee didn't want to feel sorry for him—he was rude, arrogant, and insensitive—but she couldn't help it.

As she turned off the last light and started upstairs to her warm apartment, to her little girl waiting for her, Evalee breathed a grateful prayer. Maybe her bank account was perilously low, but she was blessed—and very, very rich.

Mayfield
1938

Evalee hadn't realized just how much she enjoyed being with Alan until the week she closed Gatehouse Interiors for Christmas. He had taken a skiing holiday in Connecticut, and she missed him more than she had expected she would. Therefore she was delighted when, the first week in January, he invited her to a piano concert by a well-known artist, held at Briarwood.

It turned out to be a program mainly of Russian music. Some of the pieces brought back sharp memories of the rather squeaky old phonograph on which Marushka played records. During the rendering of Rachmaninoff's concerto, Evalee was quite stirred, and although she tried to wipe her tears surreptitiously, Alan noticed them.

Afterward he was contrite. "I apologize," he told her as they drove home. "I should have realized it might be too nostalgic. It was thoughtless of me."

"No, no, Alan. It was the music that moved me, not sad memories. I don't know a great deal about theory or composition, but there is something of the Russian soul that comes through in their music, and I find that it touches me deeply. I'm glad you asked me to come. Truly." She was impressed with Alan's extraordinary sensitivity.

As they pulled into the circle drive in front of Gatehouse Interiors, Evalee saw that the place was dark. "Oh, I must have forgotten to turn on the light before we left," she remarked. The outside light, in keeping with the exterior of the building, was an old carriage lamp that had been wired for electricity.

"Isn't your mother here?"

"No, Natasha is staying with her at Dovecote."

"Well, I have a flashlight," Alan said, and he leaned over to open the glove compartment.

They walked up the path, his light guiding their way.

"There was really no need for this," he said, switching the flashlight off. "See, the moon's just coming up through the trees."

She looked in the direction Alan was pointing. A pale round globe was moving through the branches of the tall trees surrounding Gatehouse.

"Lovely, isn't it?" she said.

"Not nearly as lovely as you," he replied softly. Surprised, Evalee turned and looked at Alan. The moonlight was now illuminating his face, shadowing hers. They were close yet did not touch. A breath away from each other, neither moved or spoke. The wind stirred in the trees with a quiet sound. Everything seemed still, yet taut with intense feeling.

It had been so long since anyone had held her. Her yearning to be loved, to feel that love expressed, was strong. It would be so easy to give in to that longing. But she knew that once she did, everything would change.

Alan was caught between caution and desire. The woman standing there was the most fascinating he had ever met. Every instinct urged him to take her into his arms, to smooth back her silken hair, taste the sweet promise of her lips, hold her slender body close.

At the point of no return they hesitated. Surely they were adult enough to handle this?

A gentle wind moved through the trees, rustling the stillness. And the moment passed.

Evalee lifted her hand, touched Alan's cheek, leaned forward and kissed him lightly. "Thanks for a wonderful evening," she said in a low voice, then she quickly put her key in the lock, turned it, and went inside, shutting the door firmly.

She leaned against the closed door, her breath shallow. She could still turn, open the door, invite Alan in . . . She bit her lower lip, knowing she wouldn't.

For another few seconds, Alan stood on the doorstep. He raised one hand as if to knock, then put it down and plunged it into his jacket pocket. Sighing, he retraced his steps. At the car he yanked open the door, got in. His hands gripping the steering wheel, he looked back at the house, saw the lights go on downstairs.

Alan knew that what he felt for Evalee was so much more than physical. They had found something of value, something precious. One step more and they would have been over the brink. To change the nature of their relationship meant risking everything else.

He didn't know how she felt about him. What, after all, did he have to offer someone like Evalee, Countess Oblenskov?

chapter 18

THAT SAME MONTH, Evalee received the announcement of the New York antique show. She decided it would be a smart business move to accept MacGowan's offer to go at his expense. However, Natasha came down with chicken pox. Even though Dru promised to stay and take care of her while Evalee was gone, Evalee couldn't be persuaded to leave. "There'll be other auctions," she said. "Besides, most of the rooms at Wemberly are practically finished. You'd be surprised at what I've found not all that far from Mayfield."

"But won't he expect you to go?" Dru asked worriedly.

"Mama, he's given me carte blanche. All he wants is for Wemberly to be furnished as it was in the old days. He'll be satisfied with that. He just wants results."

After the first two feverish days, Natasha was not very sick. But she was prickly and uncomfortable and covered with spots. Evalee wasn't a nurse by nature, and her nerves were on edge. She had given the child a silver bell to ring when she wanted or needed something, and it seemed that the bell rang incessantly. Evalee was sure she had made twenty trips up and down the steps during the day, in between taking phone calls and rearranging her work schedule.

Her patience would have worn very thin if it hadn't been for Alan Reid. When he called to invite Evalee to dinner and a show and learned about the situation, he immediately asked if he could visit. He arrived with balloons, orange and lemon popsicles, coloring books, and a board game. It was a relief to Evalee to have some uninterrupted time to work on her books, catch up on her correspondence, make calls. Often she heard the sound of laughter coming from the little invalid's room upstairs.

Late in the afternoon Alan came down to report that the patient was sleeping. Evalee said, "You're a lifesaver, Alan."

"Not at all. I love kids."

Evalee regarded him with new respect and affection.

His attention to Natasha didn't stop with one visit. During the week, when he was busy teaching, he sent her funny letters and cards in the mail, then showed up the following Saturday. Evalee was surprised and grateful. Most adults would have been bored to death spending that much time with a sick child. Alan was a very special guy.

By the time Natasha was well and up and around again, the two were best pals.

The costs of the Wemberly project were mounting. Special shipping fees, long-distance calls followed by telegrams tracing all kinds of merchandise that had not arrived by the promised delivery dates, and other unexpected expenses added to the price of restoring the old mansion, narrowing Evalee's profit margin according to the terms of the contract she had signed with MacGowan's attorneys.

Every week, Evalee bundled up copies of invoices, contracts she'd made with suppliers, correspondence with fabric and upholstery firms, and mailed them to MacGowan's secretary, Doris. As she did, Evalee began to worry that she was grossly overspending, especially on some of the antiques she had purchased. She had justified their cost because she felt they were perfect for the mansion. Among the many articles were priceless items that had once belonged to Wemberly and had been long missing, which she had been able to acquire at an estate sale of enormous proportions in Maryland. They consisted of two Queen Anne chairs with carved-leaf cabriole legs, a Georgian silver tea service, and a pair of French watercolors.

Evalee felt guilty about not going to the auction MacGowan had specifically asked her to attend, and she hoped he would be well pleased with these purchases. But she wondered whether he would agree with her instincts or think she had run amok with his money. She shuddered, imagining what an angry encounter with him might be like.

Troubles awaited her when she went out to Wemberly to check on progress. Workmen didn't always show up when expected. The tile setters couldn't come until the painters finished. The painters arrived before the electricians and said they couldn't paint until all the wiring was completed. The hand-painted wallpaper MacGowan had insisted be copied from the original in the drawing room had not yet arrived from the one factory in England that produced it.

With all the delays and problems, Evalee wasn't sure Wemberly would be completed by the June deadline MacGowan had set.

MacGowan wasn't her only worry. Other clients had become impatient, because Evalee was tied up with his project and their work was delayed. She had neglected other jobs to stay on top of the Wemberly restoration, and a few clients had finally quit her in anger. Evalee was upset to see once loyal customers take their business elsewhere. And the fact that they didn't pay her for work she'd already done for them was financially devastating.

After agreeing to work for MacGowan, she had used her advance, together with the extra income generated by gift sales in December, to pay off her many business debts and to buy clothes for Natasha and other necessities. She had been counting on the income from her other clients to carry her through until the Wemberly project was complete and she received her payment in full.

Evalee was becoming increasingly nervous. Late one afternoon when the shop was empty, she got out her ledgers and painstakingly went over her accounts. Soon her position became all too clear. She was broke, practically penniless. Less than a hundred dollars remained in her personal bank account. And there were no jobs contracted for after she finished Wemberly.

Suddenly she heard the sound of a car swerving into the gravel parkway in front of the store. A moment later Trent MacGowan was striding into the shop.

She gasped, "It's you! I didn't expect—" Then she wondered if she looked as startled as she sounded.

"Obviously. But it doesn't matter. I didn't let anyone know I was coming. Spur of the moment, actually. A yen to see my house," he said, smiling. "And my decorator. How are you, Countess?"

Evalee got to her feet, clumsily swooping loose bills and scraps of notepaper into her ledger and closing it, thinking, *If Trent MacGowan only knew the true state of my finances. A businessman like MacGowan would have only contempt for someone who couldn't balance a budget.* She struggled for words. MacGowan looked pleasanter and friendlier than she had ever seen him. What was on his mind? And why had he made this unexpected trip? She played for time. "I sent Doris last month's report. Didn't you receive it?"

He brushed that aside and smiled. "Oh, yes. You've been doing quite a bit of gadding about, from the look of things."

He didn't seem upset or the least bit angry. Evalee allowed herself to be a little relieved.

MacGowan walked around the room in his restless way, and all she could do was wait until he chose to tell her why he had come. He seemed to use this tactic deliberately, to throw her off and keep the upper hand. Finally he turned back to her and said, "Just so you don't think you're the only one who goes snooping around antique stores, treasure hunting, I want to show you something."

With that he went back out to his car. When he returned, he was carrying a large, square package wrapped in brown paper and tied with twine. "Got scissors?" he asked.

He held out one hand as Evalee fumbled in her desk drawer for a pair and gave them to him. Quickly MacGowan cut the string. The paper fell away, and Evalee saw that it was a painting of some kind. However, she could only see the back of the canvas. Slowly he turned it around.

It was a portrait of a young woman. From the costume and hairstyle, it had been painted perhaps in the mid-1800s. The shape of the face was oval, but the cheekbones were quite prominent, the chin rather square. She had straight, dark brows over large, dark eyes, in contrast to her fair complexion and pale blond hair.

Evalee came around from behind the desk for a closer look.

"Look like anyone you know?" MacGowan hinted as Evalee continued to stare at the portrait. He propped the painting against the front of the desk and stepped to one side of it.

Evalee was stunned. It was like looking at herself in a mirror. Except that the mirror and the young woman must have existed over a hundred years ago. The painting was exquisitely rendered, in the minutest detail—the earrings, the lace fichu outlining the décolletage, the cameo pin at her breast. Her hair fell in satin ringlets, shimmering with golden light, so it appeared as if one could reach out and touch and feel the silky length. She was a young woman from another century and yet astonishingly real.

"Amazing, isn't it?" MacGowan asked. "It could be you. The minute I saw it, I knew it belonged in my house. I knew I had to have it." He paused. Suddenly there was a different tone in his voice. "Just as when I saw *you* for the first time, I knew I wanted you."

Evalee looked at him and took a step away.

"Don't look so shocked," he said. "Surely you knew I was attracted to you?"

She shook her head.

"How could you not have known? Don't you think I could have had a dozen top-notch, experienced decorators, established professionals well known in New York—or London, for that matter—design my house? I saw something in you none of them had. Class, elegance, breeding and background. The perfect woman for Wemberly."

He moved closer to her, his dark eyes blazing with intensity. "Marry me, and I'll give you everything you've ever dreamed of. What a hostess you'd make in that beautiful place. People would die to be invited there with you as its mistress. Say you will."

Evalee tried to regain her composure. "I can't possibly. I never thought ... I mean, you don't even really know me.... Do you know I have a child? A little girl, six?"

MacGowan's brows drew together. For a minute he looked blank. "Yes, I believe I knew that.... Well, that's another reason for you to consider my proposal. I can provide everything for a child—an education, riding lessons, a horse—whatever Virginia's first families do. You can trust that."

Evalee realized she was shaking. She was unable to speak. This had come out of the blue, totally unexpected.

MacGowan rewrapped the portrait, tied it loosely with the string, then said, "I'll take this up to Wemberly. At least I know *this* will be there to welcome me home." His smile was rueful. He shoved the package under one arm and started toward the door. "I know I tend to be . . . overpowering. I didn't mean to startle you or frighten you. Whatever you're thinking now, we could have a good life. A wonderful life. And so could your child." He was at the door now. He turned, and there was some wistfulness in his voice as he asked, "Will you at least consider what I'm offering?"

Numbly Evalee nodded.

Natasha was spending the night at Dovecote, and when MacGowan left, Evalee was alone. Her knees felt weak, and she went back to her desk and sat down. She stayed there for a few minutes, trying to collect her thoughts. It was all so stunning. She could hardly believe what Trent MacGowan had proposed.

The first thoughts that flashed through her mind were compelling and tempting. No more financial worries, no bills to put off, no tactful reminders to clients who hadn't paid her fee, an unlimited bank account, the best of everything for Natasha . . .

By every rule of heritage and background, Evalee knew she should not be attracted to a man like MacGowan. But even as she repeated to herself the things she disliked about him, she had to admit that the man was maddeningly attractive. He had a marvelous face, even with its brooding expression. It was intriguing to imagine what might be behind the veiled look in his deep-set eyes.

She thought of those traits that had so annoyed her at first—his brusqueness, his arrogance, his high-handed manner. Did he have any qualities that would entice her to accept his offer? What kind of father would he be for Natasha? Just at the ready with his checkbook? Evalee, in spite of all that had happened to her, held a romantic, idealistic idea of what marriage should be. She felt it shouldn't be simply a business arrangement, a mutually beneficial contract.

But was it fair to Natasha to reject MacGowan's proposal out of hand? The most important thing in Evalee's life was her child's future. That's why she had left France, come to America, started her own business, struggled to make it succeed . . . The truth was, it had been more difficult than she had imagined. Now all she could see ahead was years of struggle, the two of them living on the proverbial shoestring. MacGowan was offering Natasha a gilded existence. Shouldn't her mother at least consider it?

Wearily Evalee went upstairs. She was tired but she wasn't sure she could sleep. Her mind churned with all the possibilities. Maybe you only had one great love in your life. Andre had been hers. She never expected to love anyone like that again. It was too much to ask. Still, she didn't want to live the rest of her life without love, without the possibility of owning a home, having other children. But would MacGowan's kind of marriage be enough?

Evalee was awakened by the sharp jangle of the phone by her bed. She reached for it and answered sleepily.

"It's Trent." The brisk voice immediately made her alert. "I called to tell you that I'm leaving for New York. A business emergency. I may have to go on to London." There was a slight hesitation. "I just wanted to let you know that I meant what I said last night. Are you thinking about it?" Not waiting for her to answer, he went on. "You'd never have to worry again, Evalee. Whatever you want to do, I'll back you. You can expand your business or sell it, we can move to a bigger place, whatever. Your child will have the best of everything. The finest schools, in Europe if you want. I'll give her a debutante party like Mayfield's never seen—"

"Please, Trent. Believe me, if I had feelings for you the way you want me to, none of that would be important."

"Then what is important?"

"Love," she said gently.

"Love is a commodity, like everything else," he said bitterly. "It can be bought."

"No, you're wrong, Trent. Some things can be bought, but not love. I like you, I admire what you've done with your life, I'm grateful for the opportunity you've given me. But I don't love you and I can't marry you."

There was silence at the other end of the line.

"I'm not the kind of man who accepts first refusal. Maybe you haven't fully considered my proposal. I won't press you now. I'll be back in the fall. We'll talk again."

The click at the other end of the line meant he'd hung up. Evalee replaced the receiver. She felt sad. She knew Trent was a proud man, and she had wounded him.

Some way or other, she was determined to work herself out of her financial morass. But if she couldn't, was marriage to Trent MacGowan the answer?

chapter 19

DURING THE HECTIC weeks of May, Evalee worked frantically to complete the job at Wemberly—to "connect all the dots," as she facetiously commented to Dru.

"You're working yourself to a frazzle," Dru said worriedly. "I hope it will be worth it when it's finished."

"That depends," Evalee said, then regretted it. She had not told her mother about Trent MacGowan's proposal. She had not mentioned it to anyone. That didn't mean she hadn't thought about it.

It happened mostly when she was physically worn out, at night, after Natasha had been read to and tucked in, when Evalee was alone, sitting at her desk, going over shipping inventories, bills, and invoices. Her drawing account was perilously low. She hadn't wanted to ask Doris for more money, although some of the things she had ordered for Wemberly had cost more than she had originally thought. Some valuable antiques had had to be crated, insured, and shipped from England. All this had added to the totals. Would Trent understand, approve of these purchases? Had he really meant it when he said price was no object? Could anyone but she actually tell the difference between authentic pieces and well-crafted reproductions? And more to the point, did anyone care? Evalee had the feeling that

Trent would resent her if she assumed that he didn't know the difference. But if her costs exceeded what he expected, would he feel justified in subtracting the overrun from her final fee?

Evalee raked her fingers through her hair, got up from her desk, and paced restlessly. She knew that if she accepted Trent's marriage proposal, he wouldn't mind how expensive the finished result was. Trent wanted her, for more reasons than as a "trophy wife."

Evalee couldn't remember a time when money had not been important. Her childhood and girlhood seemed a long time ago. When her father had been alive, they had lived well. It was only since his death that her mother had confided to Evalee the debts left behind, the jewels she had had to sell. And after her marriage to Andre, Evalee had certainly known the pinch of poverty.

But no matter what happened, marriage to Trent MacGowan was not the price she wanted to pay for security. With the Wemberly job done as perfectly as she could do it, Evalee felt sure she was on the brink of success—on her own terms, earned by her own tenacity, talent, and taste. If Trent MacGowan used some excuse that she had not met all the terms of their contract to disapprove of some of the expenditures, that was his problem. He could take it out of her payment. Somehow she did not think he would, but that remained to be seen.

In spite of her brave front, Evalee had many sleepless nights, anxious days, awaiting delivery of some of the last fine antiques. Delayed shipping caused her, she was positive, to spot a few random silver hairs.

At last she could see the light at the end of the tunnel. By the end of the month, the rooms had shaped up beautifully. She had fulfilled her contract, checking every detail, keeping on top of each facet of the work. She had been assertive about promised deliveries and had insisted on quality, even when it meant doing a job over.

Evalee suspected she had earned the reputation of being "one tough lady" among the workmen, dealers, and suppliers. But she had earned her fee. She had nothing to feel guilty about as far as that was concerned.

Then Trent called from New York. "I'll be down next week," he began abruptly. "Is everything ready?"

Having just followed a truck from the train station to oversee the delivery of the last two pieces of furniture out to Wemberly that afternoon, Evalee replied, "Yes" and whispered a grateful prayer.

"So have you made up your mind about my proposal?" was his next question.

"Yes."

"Yes?" She could hear the hope in his voice.

"I mean, no. Yes, I have considered it and no, I can't marry you." There was a pause. Evalee felt her heart pound. "I simply can't."

"Do you want to say why?"

"It would be wrong. For both of us. A marriage without love, a marriage without trust and truth, is impossible for me. You deserve more than that, Trent."

There was another long pause, and then he said crisply, "Well, that's your decision."

Evalee heard the click of the phone being put down. Slowly she replaced her receiver. What repercussions would her decision bring? All she could hope was that Trent would be pleased with his mansion and that he would not exact revenge by withholding full payment of her fee.

Four days before the scheduled housewarming party, she went through every room. Finally satisfied, she sent the last of the bills to Doris and signed off on the project.

Within days she received a check. Depositing it gratefully, Evalee breathed a prayer of thanksgiving. This would keep the business going and take care of her living expenses for the next six months.

Driving out to Wemberly on Saturday evening for MacGowan's housewarming party, Evalee had mixed feelings. She had not heard from him personally since his return from New York. Questions ran through her mind. Was he angry? How would he react when he saw her? Although in some ways she dreaded this night, there was no way she could avoid attending the party. Wemberly, after all, was her triumph. She *had* to be there at its unveiling.

She had spent a considerable amount of time deciding what to wear. The few gowns she had that were appropriate for such an occasion were all part of the elegant trousseau her mother had purchased for her in Paris so many years ago. Were they hopelessly out of fashion? Still, a Parisian designer gown never really lost its style. After uncharacteristic indecision, she had made her choice and got dressed.

Because of this, she was late arriving at Wemberly. Cars were parked up and down the wide, curving driveway. She saw that MacGowan had hired valets. They were standing at the end of the terraced steps, directing traffic and parking the guests' cars. All the cars looked so shiny and new. Hers was shabby, its backseat piled with catalogs, carpet samples, rolls of wallpaper. Embarrassed to have one of the uniformed young men see it, Evalee circled several times, then drove around behind the house and found a place to park near the service entrance.

The gravel bit into her thin-soled high heels as she marched back around to the front of the house. As she went up the terrace steps, she could hear the sound of music, voices, laughter.

The party was in full swing. The place was crowded. She slipped inside unnoticed and looked around.

Milly Kirby, the society editor at the *Monitor,* was at the party, absorbing everything, and would write it up for the Sunday paper, then send a tear sheet of her article to the *Richmond Times,* with the hope that they might reprint it. A reporter and photographer from *PIC,* the popular picture magazine, was everywhere. His flashbulb popped constantly, catching candid shots of guests, all of whom hoped they would appear in the glossy pages.

As her gaze swept the room, Evalee saw that there were not many Mayfielders here. The few she recognized were Tom Oliphant, from the bank, Jed Foster, a realtor—perhaps the one who had negotiated the deal for Wemberly—and two other businessmen she knew by sight. Scott wasn't here. She knew he had been invited—she had seen his name on one of the elegantly calligraphied invitation envelopes. Why hadn't he come? Of course, Jill was in England, but being alone had never prevented Scott from attending important events.

It wasn't hard to spot the host. His broad shoulders, encased in a superbly fitted white dinner jacket, rose above the small group of people encircling him. All were probably sophisticated New Yorkers, friends from his other life. This must be a proud moment for him, she thought. However, as she looked around again, she noticed that few of those present were what one would call old guard. Did MacGowan mind that half his guest list hadn't shown up?

She didn't have long to mull that question, because she was immediately aware that he was staring at her from across the room. It was one of those moments that happen in life—not like the evening she had met Andre but similar in its intensity. She was aware that something important and rather frightening was about to happen. It was like the time she had been out riding with her twin cousins. Cara had been leading, and Evalee's pony had followed. Evalee had been unable to hold the animal back, no matter how tightly she pulled on the reins. The daredevil Cara had headed for a fence. Evalee had known that her short-legged mount could not jump, nor could she stay in the saddle if the pony attempted it. She had felt that wash of cold perspiration, that pounding in her ears, that horrible lurching in her stomach. At this moment she felt that same sensation of fear.

MacGowan crossed the room in a few strides and stood in front of her. In spite of his outer polish, he had the intangible mark of a self-made man, as though he were a bit uncomfortable in his costly, custom-made clothes. His taut aggressiveness contrasted with the comfortable ease of someone like Scott Cameron, who had been born into privilege and casually accepted it as his rightful place, feeling no need to scratch or claw to gain a foothold in society.

There was an enigmatic expression on MacGowan's face, a stubbornness about his mouth, a suspicious glint in his gunmetal gray eyes, as if he were aware of what was going through her mind.

"Good evening, Countess," he said, emphasizing her title as he usually did, as if ridiculing it. "So you came."

"I wouldn't have missed it. I had to see if my work lost anything in translation."

"Have you come to hear your praises sung?" His smile bordered on a sneer. "Everyone is talking about the perfection of the restoration. Minton Prescott, the historian from Washington, D.C., said he could almost hear the swish of taffeta and crinoline hoop skirts on these polished parquet floors. You outdid yourself. You should be very proud."

"It was a labor of love. And you made it easy." She smiled. "With unlimited funds, it was a once-in-a-lifetime opportunity for a decorator."

"You are much more than that. As Prescott said, you've captured the heart of this house, brought it alive again, just as it was when the first Wemberlys moved in." He added sardonically, "I'm sure they must be turning over in their graves to know that someone like me owns their house now."

When he made self-deprecating remarks like that, Evalee never knew whether he was expressing some well-hidden self-doubt or just testing her reaction. "You're too hard on yourself," she said calmly. "I should think they'd be delighted to know that the house they loved has been so lovingly restored."

His eyes narrowed. They seemed to ask if she was being sincere. Like a boxer, MacGowan always kept his gloves up, ready to defend himself. He was always ready to fend off a possible subtle put-down. Strange, Evalee thought. With all his money, he could afford to dismiss any negative opinions and give himself credit for throwing the most extravagant party Mayfield had seen in years. It was too bad that the people he wanted most to impress were not here to see it. But she knew Mayfield was a tight little community of insiders who rarely invited into their ranks anyone new—and then only people with unassailable credentials. Those Trent MacGowan didn't have.

"It's a very posh crowd you've gathered," she said, hoping that the fact that she appreciated the influential guests would please him, make him feel better, in case he realized how few from Mayfield's old families had accepted his invitation.

He started to reply, when one of his guests, a woman with an appearance that must have taken her hours to achieve and a gown the price of which would have supported Evalee for two years, came up to them, put a possessive hand on MacGowan's arm. "Darling, this is a divine place. Do show me around—"

Evalee stepped back, smiled, and moved away to relieve MacGowan of the duty of explaining that she was responsible for most of what the woman was complimenting. He had only signed the checks.

She was glad to get away, glad to shake that weird feeling she'd had when MacGowan saw her. Why should he seem a threat? Hadn't he provided her with a great opportunity, a chance to establish herself? There was just something unnerving about his presence, the way he looked at her . . . Despite the balmy June night, she felt a chill. Suppressing a small shudder, she moved among the crowd, greeting a few people she knew. Just to have something in her hand, she took a glass of champagne from a tray offered by one of the white-coated waiters moving among the crowd. She wished she could leave now that she was able to see that it had all worked out as she had planned. But there was no way she could do that. Dinner had been included in the invitation.

There were name cards at each place setting on the round tables for eight under the green-and-white tent on the lawn. Evalee was seated in sight of where MacGowan sat with some people she did not know. Somehow she managed to keep up a semblance of conversation as the dinner of Maine lobster, new potatoes, asparagus, was served. It looked delicious, but she had suddenly lost her appetite. She kept wondering how soon after the dessert—chocolate cheesecake with raspberry sauce, served with coffee—she could leave. When the orchestra, which had played background music throughout the reception and dinner, began to play dance music, couples began getting up. Evalee decided that this would be a good time to make her escape, and she excused herself from her table.

Her intention was to make a quick exit through the back hall and out to where she had parked her car. She did not think she'd been seen, but as she reached for the doorknob, she heard MacGowan's voice ask harshly, "Just where do you think you're going, Countess?"

She whirled around, surprised and a little startled. "I'm sorry—" She started to use Natasha as her excuse for leaving, but she didn't have a chance.

He shrugged, as if an explanation wasn't necessary, as if it didn't matter. "I didn't get to tell you," he said, his eyes moving over her, "that you're the only one who looks as if she belongs here. You make every other woman here look overdressed."

She thought of the women she'd noticed, all wearing dresses from the most expensive stores in New York, glittering with sequins and beads. She looked down at her own dress. She was wearing a 1930 Chanel, an opalescent chiffon with handkerchief-point hem—and of course, the Oblenskov pearls.

Again he looked at her, this time from the top of her shiny gold hair to the tips of her satin pumps with their marcasite buckles. "You're the most attractive woman here tonight," he said, almost harshly. Then he took her arm. "I don't usually do this. But is there anything that would change your mind? I still want you, and I'm prepared to meet whatever terms you want." He paused, lowered his voice. "This house needs you. *I* need you." Those last words were spoken almost reluctantly. Evalee knew what it cost a proud man like Trent MacGowan to say them.

"I'm sorry. It would never work," was all she could manage.

She saw his face harden. "Well, if that's the way it is, then—"

"Yes," She said quietly. There was an awkward silence, which Evalee finally broke. "I have to go now."

"I suppose that's best."

He escorted her across the foyer, and Evalee realized that there was hardly anything here that she had not personally selected and purchased for the home. The satin draperies hung perfectly at the long windows. The English hunting scenes on the walls were framed in ornate gold. She couldn't help but wonder. Who would finally be mistress at Wemberly?

MacGowan walked her to her car and placed her carefully inside. When she dug into her small evening bag and got out her keys, he leaned into the open window, cupped her chin with one hand, and turned her head toward him. "You're absolutely sure?" he asked.

"Yes," she said quietly. He drew back, stepped away from the car. She turned on the ignition, shifted gears, and started forward. When she looked in her rearview mirror, she saw him still standing there in the driveway.

She drove in a kind of trance. It was only when she turned onto the county road and a car coming in the opposite direction blinked its headlights that she realized with a start that she hadn't turned on her own.

At Gatehouse she parked, got out of the car, and walked toward the house. A silver slice of moon shone through the branches of the trees. On the door an envelope was tucked under the brass knocker.

How about you, Natasha, and me going for a ride in the country to have a picnic? I'll call in the morning after church.

Alan

Evalee read the note, smiled. A picnic with Alan Reid sounded just great.

chapter 20

New York
1938

AFTER A SERIES of readings and book signings for Richard's poetry at two midwestern colleges, Kitty had traveled to Santa Barbara for a long-planned visit with her mother, Blythe. Early in September Kitty returned to New York.

Among her accumulated mail was an advance copy of her book, with a note.

Fresh off the press. Thought you'd like to see this.

Craig

She held it for a minute, admiring the glossy jacket with its photograph of a French cemetery. White crosses marched diagonally across the front cover. On the back was a short author biography (she had insisted that it be brief, that it simply identify her as having been a nurse at the front). There was a small picture of her in her nurse's uniform. Cavanaugh had persuaded her to let him use the photograph. She stared at it now. Had she ever been that young, that optimistic? Richard had taken the picture when they were newly in love. She was standing in front of the gothic chapel, wearing her crisp headband and short veil—which hid the hair she had whacked off impulsively—and her apron with the Red Cross emblem on the front. Behind the chapel was the chateau that had been turned into a field hospital. It all happened so long ago . . . And yet her book had brought it all vividly back to her.

She turned the book over and over. It was real. It was here in print—all the words, the emotions, she had dredged up about that time in her life. And now people would read it. What effect would it have? Her knees felt shaky and she sat down, still holding the book in both hands. This had come out of her very soul. It had been written to in some way vindicate the suffering men she had nursed who had died and could not speak for themselves. She had dedicated the book to Richard. It was not his story, but he had been its inspiration.

Please, God, she prayed, *let it change some minds, chill some hearts, make some people reconsider their views about war.*

Montclair

Cara walked out onto the back porch, took a long breath of the crisp autumn air. At the squeak of the screen door, the old setter sleeping in her wicker bed raised her head. Seeing Cara, she thumped her tail, rose stiffly, and slowly came over to her. Automatically Cara's hand dropped to the dog's head, and she said softly, "Hello, old girl." As she rubbed the silky ears, she said in a low, conversational tone, "There are a hundred things I should be doing here, but I feel so . . . I don't know, at loose ends."

She did not know what was making her so restless. *I need to talk to someone,* she thought finally. Ten minutes later she had saddled her horse and set out upon the woodland path to Cameron Hall. The *Mayfield Monitor* had "gone to bed" the day before, and Scott, having been at the office until midnight, was probably taking the day off at home.

Soon she saw Cameron Hall in the distance. Mellow afternoon sunshine had turned the pink bricks golden. Her heart squeezed a little, as it always did at the sight of her childhood home.

In recent years she looked back on that time with a kind of amazement that she had grown up and accepted without thought all the privilege and position Cameron Hall represented, never having known another kind of life. That had been before the war. After that everything had changed—herself included. Her twin had changed, too. As Cara tethered her horse to the iron hitching post in front of the house, Cara thought about Kitty and the estrangement that existed between them.

The war had traumatized Kitty in a way that nobody realized. Richard's death had been the final blow, and it had galvanized her hatred of war, her vigilant pacifism.

In contrast, somehow she and Kip had been able to come back home, pick up their lives, and go on. Even though both of them had also lost a loved one—Kip, his wartime French bride, Etienette, Luc's mother; Cara, her first love, Owen, an army chaplain. How was it that she and Kip had been able to accept their losses and focus on things that gave life its pleasure—like the children, their work—while Kitty had let the taste of bitterness poison her outlook?

Cara frowned. She needed to talk to her brother. She gave her horse an affectionate pat on the neck, then ran up the front steps, opened the door, and walked inside. In the hallway she noticed a blue-and-white Meissen bowl filled with late hydrangeas on the hall table. She paused a moment, then called, "Hello! Anybody home?"

"In here, Cara," Scott's voice answered.

Cara crossed the hall. As she entered the library, she saw Scott rise from one of the deep leather chairs in the windowed alcove, slipping a marker in the book he was reading. "Sorry to barge in on you uninvited," she said.

"Nonsense. This is still your home as much as ever," Scott protested. "Come in, sit down."

"I don't know for sure why I came." Cara shrugged. "Instinct, maybe? Like a homing pigeon."

"You don't need a reason to come, or an explanation either," Scott said. "Actually, I'm glad you came. I was just thinking about you and Kip, as a matter of fact." He held up the book in his hand. "I wondered if you'd seen this?"

"You know I hardly ever have time to read. What is it?"

"It's an advance copy of Kitty's book. It came to the paper and I brought it home to read. So you haven't got one or heard anything from her?"

Cara frowned. "No, why? You look . . . I don't know. Worried? Concerned? What?"

"It's the introduction. I mean, Kitty has every right to say whatever she wants. We all know her convictions. And the publishers can certainly publish what they want. . . . It's just that in making her point—well, it's very personal. Here." He handed the book to Cara. "Read it yourself."

Cara took it, then sat down in one of the wing chairs. She looked at the cover—*No Cheers, No Glory: A True Account of a Field Nurse in Wartime France* by Katherine Cameron Traherne.

She glanced at Scott, who lifted his eyebrows and made no comment. Cara opened the book to the introduction.

> I make no apology for what this book contains. I hate war. I hate its destruction of men, minds, souls. I nursed soldiers from America, England, France, and Germany. They were horribly

> wounded, and they were all boys. Somebody's son, brother, husband, father. If this book sounds angry, that is no mistake. I am angry. I am angry at people who encourage and glorify war, denying that war is, as a famous Civil War general declared it to be, *hell.* I know it is—I saw it firsthand.

Cara's eyes raced down the page until she came across this paragraph.

> For some, even those who served in the war in whatever capacity, there was something that intoxicated, that somehow blinded them to what was really going on. I can only pity men for whom the war was the peak experience of their lives. For them, nothing that followed has matched the sense of excitement, the thrill of danger, the feeling of accomplishment—that is, if any form of killing, be it from the trenches, from a ship, or from the air, can be called an accomplishment. As a result of that gun being fired, that bomb dropped, someone died! How can they forget that? To give them the benefit of the doubt, perhaps distance has now dimmed the horror. But it is because I cannot forget, and because I want others to remember, that I have written my true account of what I saw in France at a field hospital on the edge of no man's land during the last two years of the war.

Cara looked up from the page.

"So what do you think?" he asked.

Cara let out a long, low whistle. "Well, our Kitty says what she thinks, doesn't she? I had some idea of what she was going to say when she told me she was going to write a book. I was afraid to ask too much about it." She tapped the cover of the book with her forefinger. "I guess I've tried to forget the things I saw in the war. Ambulance drivers were in the middle of things, too, you know." She gave a small shudder.

"How will Kip react to the book? She comes down pretty hard on people who were over there and didn't turn against warfare."

Cara shrugged. "I don't know. I doubt if he'll even read it. Kip knows how Kitty feels. She believes that he should feel the same way she does. Well, he does, in a way. Kip is just going about it differently. He thinks a strong air force is the greatest deterrent to war." Cara closed the book. "I told him that Kitty and I had another quarrel. She had stopped by Montclair and said she was planning to stay at Eden Cottage to write her book. When she found out Kip was training pilots, she left, terribly upset." Cara paused. The memory of the parting with her twin was still raw. That they were still unreconciled was painful. "She hasn't been back, you know."

"Well, she's been traveling, doing her readings and such. Then she had a long visit with Mother in Santa Barbara."

"That's not the reason she's not come to Mayfield, Scott!"

Scott was silent a moment. Then he indicated Kitty's book. "What I've read of this is very good, Cara. She writes exceptionally well, and all her emotion comes through. However, I'm afraid some people will put it down before they finish it. It's pretty explicit stuff. But the ones who do finish it—well, it will have an impact." He paused. "By the way, there's a statement in the back to the effect that all accrued royalties will go to a well-known peace organization. So no one can accuse Kitty of exploitation. And her book is published by a very reputable company." He shrugged. "I think this is an important book. Whether it will accomplish what Kitty hopes, I don't know."

"In a way I admire her. At least she has the courage of her convictions."

"Visionaries are usually without honor in their own country," Scott said, paraphrasing the Scripture. "I'm curious as to how the book will sell."

Talking about her sister had brought up a great deal of emotional turmoil that Cara wasn't prepared to deal with. She handed the book back to her brother and got to her feet, saying, "I'd better be on my way. Thanks for sharing this with me, Scott."

He walked to the front door with her, placed a hand on her shoulder. "I hope this hasn't upset you too much."

"No, I'm glad you showed me the book." She smiled ruefully. "Forewarned is forearmed, right? Now at least I'll be prepared if Kip explodes when he hears about it."

Cara went home by way of the county road and stopped to pick up their mail at the gates of Montclair. Among the bills and circulars was a package. She was sure it was a copy of Kitty's book, as she recognized the publisher's name on the address label.

Thrusting everything into her saddlebag, she remounted and rode slowly back up to the house, wondering if she should show the book to Kip.

chapter 21

September 1938

THAT FALL, EVALEE decided to go to New York and attend a sale at one of the most prestigious auction galleries. She had received the catalog and it looked interesting. She had some new clients, whose decorating needs might be met with some of the items for sale. Several of these commissions had come as a direct result of Wemberly. For that she was very grateful. But she had no regrets about her firm refusal to discuss MacGowan's proposal further.

Evalee prepared for her trip to New York with excitement. Setting out on her own to the big city made her feel like a real professional. Maybe this *was* God's plan for her life.

Natasha would be with Druscilla, and Scotty would come to sleep over at Dovecote. Everyone was delighted with these arrangements. The train trip from Richmond to New York took only four hours, and Evalee relished the feeling of being free and on her own for the first time in years. She spent the time making lists, planning for her days in the city.

It was a whirlwind week. She felt happy and enthusiastic about the things she had purchased for Gatehouse Interiors, and hoped her clients would be just as pleased.

Two days before she was to leave for home, there was a message for her at the hotel desk, giving a number for her to call.

To her amazement, it was Alan who answered the phone. "What are you doing in New York?" she gasped.

"I'm on a quest," he told her, laughing. "I've rented a car and am driving up to Connecticut. The New England foliage is gorgeous this time of year. Would you like to come with me?"

She hesitated. There were still some dealers she might see, and perhaps she should put business before pleasure. But without question Evalee wanted to go with Alan. So before she could change her mind, she said quickly, "Yes. I'd love it."

When Alan picked her up, Evalee was happy to see him. It was good to look into those steady blue eyes, to hear his laugh. He put her in the passenger side, then went around and slid behind the wheel. As he started the car, he asked, "So how has it been?"

"Oh, it's had its moments of splendor. I had a glorious time at the galleries. This was my first swim in the big pond, you know, and I was scared to death half the time. But I must say, I did bid on a few things, and I think they were good choices." She paused, then said sincerely, "I'm really glad you called and suggested this trip. It will give me a chance to touch base with reality."

Alan frowned as if puzzled. "Reality? What have you been doing in New York all week—living in fantasyland?"

"You might say that," she sighed.

"I was afraid you might get dazzled by the bright lights and want to move to the big city."

Surprised, Evalee glanced over at him. Although his remark had sounded casual, his expression, his eyes, seemed worried.

"Not a chance," she said.

"That's good," was his only comment.

The farther from the city they drove, the more spectacular the scenery became. Autumn foliage painted the landscape with vivid scarlet, glimmering bronze, against the dark green of pines, all of it brilliant in the sun of a cloudless blue sky. They passed through storybook towns that looked exactly the way New England villages were supposed to look. Neat town squares, white-steepled churches, shingled saltbox houses with picket fences, behind which bloomed giant blue hydrangeas and bright-red geraniums.

They drove along in the easy companionship of friends who do not need to force conversation, remarking once in a while on something they saw. After spotting a sign for a Howard Johnson's restaurant, Alan said, "Let's stop for lunch."

They pulled off the highway and went inside. After ordering coffee and sandwiches, Alan asked, "Would you like to know the real reason we're doing this?"

"Yes, I guess so. Although I've come to realize you thrive on serendipity." She smiled. "But I'm waiting with bated breath for you to tell me."

"You know so much about me already, Evalee, I don't think you'll be too surprised. I'm up here to check out a job."

"At a New England school?"

"No, it's not a teaching job," Alan said. "It's something else entirely. You know that my hobby is collecting old books. I've been in touch regularly with a book dealer up here for a number of years. He's found me some real gems. Certain authors I particularly like. They're not rare editions or anything too expensive, but it's been a really rewarding friendship. Well, the thing is, I've just learned that he's retiring. His bookstore and its entire inventory is for sale." He paused. "It's an established, successful business, and I have a chance to buy it. That's what

I've come up here for. To look it over. See the place, the town. Decide whether I want to do it."

At first Evalee didn't know what to say. "That is quite a surprise. Not so much that a bookstore might be something that would interest you. But I guess I just assumed you'd stay on at Briarwood until—"

"I became headmaster or another 'Mr. Chips'?" he said, laughing, referring to the fictional English schoolteacher made famous by James Hilton's book. "Well, I never pictured myself like that. I wasn't sure what else I would do, but—well, this would be a dream come true. Actually, I can't think of anything I'd rather do than have a bookstore, be around books, help people find great books to read, to cherish." He added rather shyly, "You might say books are one of my passions."

"I think I did know that."

"But the reason I wanted you to come along with me was"—he hesitated—"because it's important to me for you to see it, give me your opinion."

"I'm flattered."

"You shouldn't be. I have a very high value of your opinion."

Their sandwiches came and Evalee realized how hungry she was. When they finished their lunch and ordered a second cup of coffee, their waitress convinced them to try the famous hot apple pie with cinnamon sauce.

Back in the car, they headed north again. A few miles farther along, Alan pointed to a sign that read, "Burlington Falls." "That's it," he said. "That's where we're going, where the bookstore is. Ben said—that's Ben Swain, the man who owns the bookstore—he said it's hardly a dot on the map but it's a town filled with book lovers."

They took the next turnoff and found themselves on a winding two-lane road along a stretch of peaceful, pastoral scenery.

Every once in a while they saw a farmhouse on the hillside, a rock fence, some children walking home from school. Alan said, "I made reservations for us at a place called the Colonial Arms Inn, just in case. I don't know if it's one of those that boasts that George Washington or Paul Revere slept there, but it came highly recommended."

"Let's just hope it wasn't Benedict Arnold who slept there!" Evalee exclaimed in mock horror.

Alan added quietly, "Separate accommodations, of course."

"Of course," Evalee nodded, suppressing a smile. Alan was always the perfect gentleman.

They came down a slight hill and they were right into Main Street. It was late afternoon, and there were few people on the sidewalk, only three or four cars parked along the curbs. The street itself was lined with small shops—a hardware store, a dress shop, a grocery, a bakery, a cafe. At the very end, on the corner, they saw a wooden sign stating simply, "Books." "There it is!" Alan exclaimed excitedly.

It did not look too inviting, Evalee thought to herself as they pulled over and got out of the car. Ahead of her, Alan cupped his hands and peered through the glass in the door. A faded cardboard sign in the dusty window said that it was closed.

"Ben hasn't been well. Had a slight stroke a few months back. That's why he decided to sell the business, take it easy. I guess he keeps short hours. I've got his home number, so I'll call him later, let him know I'm here."

From what she could see of the place—books piled haphazardly in the window, a general look of disarray—Evalee had a dismayed feeling that it was a business long neglected and rundown. It would take a great deal of energy and optimism to take over such an establishment, especially in a town as small as this. She began to wonder if Ben had been entirely truthful with Alan. But Alan was clearly exhilarated, and she did not want to dampen his enthusiasm.

"Let's go find the inn, have dinner," he suggested. "I'll call Ben, set it up so that we can get together tomorrow. In the meantime we can see a little bit of the town."

Evalee refrained from saying that they'd probably already seen what little town there was. She also reminded herself that a town wasn't buildings—it was people, friendships, community. Mayfield wasn't much to look at lately, but it had a great spirit—supportive, civic-minded people who cared about their town and each other. Burlington Falls just might be the same kind of place. Evalee decided she would reserve judgment about Alan's opportunity.

Alan called Ben Swain from the public phone booth and came back looking happy. "He'll meet us here tomorrow morning at nine."

The Colonial Arms Inn was a gabled, white frame building with dark-green shutters. At each side of its red front door was a row of six rush-seated rocking chairs. A bunch of Indian corn tied with a russet-colored bow hung above a brass knocker. Inside, the owner, Monica Preston, a serene, gray-haired woman, greeted them cordially. First she showed Alan to his room on the main floor, then escorted Evalee upstairs to hers. This was a spacious room with a magnificent view of the wooded hillside. Evalee's trained eye appreciated the fine antique furnishings, the maple armoir, the poster bed with the candlewick bedspread and handmade quilt, the braided rug.

Later they dined in the inn's firelit dining room, at a table set in a bow-windowed alcove with a nice view of the town, which in the autumn dusk looked like a toy village. They were served a delicious New England meal of pot roast, vegetables, and pumpkin pie for dessert.

After dinner, both tired from the long drive, they called it an evening. At the foot of the staircase, Alan covered Evalee's hand as it rested on the wide banister. "I'm glad you came with me, Evalee. This may be the most important decision of my life."

Evalee saw something unspoken in Alan's eyes. A question? Not knowing what to make of it, she simply smiled and said, "I'm glad I came along, too, Alan."

The next morning, after a hearty breakfast of omelettes, currant scones, coffee, they walked down the hill into town. At the door of the bookstore, Ben Swain, a stooped, balding, lean man in his mid sixties, met them. A whimsical sign had appeared in the window—"Browsers Welcome, Buyers Preferred."

To Evalee, for whom orderliness was next to the proverbial godliness, the interior of the bookstore was even worse than its exterior suggested. There were books everywhere. Books were stacked on the floor, crammed into the floor-to-ceiling shelves, spilling out of cardboard cartons, falling out of every conceivable nook and cranny in the long, narrow room. It was so dark that one could hardly read the titles, so crowded that she wondered how customers could make their way through to search for a particular book.

She was amazed at how both Ben and Alan seemed to disregard all this. All they could see was the mountains of books, each one a source of delight, information, and hours of enjoyment for some lucky reader. She could hardly believe the pitch of their voices as they discussed contract terms and payment. She was picking her way through a patchwork puzzle of books to see if she could discover a first edition or even a Victorian children's book she might buy to display in her shop, when Alan said, "Evalee, Ben and I are going over to the bank to sign the deed on this. Do you want to come along or wait for us here?"

So he'd done it. He hadn't really asked her opinion after all. Alan's eyes were shining, and his expression was so happy that she didn't have the heart to ask him if he thought he should think it over a little more. He must have made up his mind about it before they even came up here. Why had he brought her along, then? "I'll wait here," she said, waving them out the door. She watched with a sinking feeling as the two men—one young, vigorous, the other old, faltering—walked down the street, arms linked, both still talking. Kindred spirits, no doubt.

Left alone amid the dusty books and the musty smell of old leather and paper, Evalee realized with a shock what all this meant. Alan would be leaving Briarwood, leaving Mayfield, leaving Virginia! The next thing she realized was that she would miss him terribly. So would Natasha. Evalee's heart gave a small, sharp twinge as she thought of Natasha and Alan together. She recalled how the two of them laughed when he taught her to fish that day they picnicked by the river. She remembered the patient way he helped Natasha learn to balance when the training wheels came off her two-wheeler. With a sudden pang, Evalee realized that if Alan wasn't in it, their life would be very empty.

The drive back to New York that afternoon was a quiet one, at least as far as Evalee was concerned. Wrapped in her ever increasing melancholy, she only half listened to Alan's enthusiastic recounting of his plans for his newly acquired bookstore. She was facing the reality of losing someone she had come to depend on, someone she thought of as a dear friend, maybe even the best friend she ever had. New England was a long way from Virginia. And it was always the one left behind that missed the other the most. Alan would become totally absorbed in his new project, his new surroundings, his new friends in

Burlington Falls. It wouldn't be just a business—it would be an entire life.

In contrast to her silence, Alan was euphoric and talkative. "It will be the kind of bookshop I've always envisioned. I'll have one of those Franklin stoves, and some comfortable chairs, maybe even a rocker, tucked away in a corner near a window. There are two long windows in the back—maybe you didn't see them?" Not waiting for her answer, he went on. "And a cat. I'll have to get a cat, to sleep in the window in front, in the sun. There's something so . . . I don't know . . . just something about a cat in a bookstore." He chuckled. "And of course we're going to have good lighting. I already talked to the man in the hardware store about some ceiling lamps, and he told me there's a local electrician who'd put them in for me. . . ."

Alan's voice went on, enthusiastic, filled with excitement. The more he talked, the more withdrawn Evalee began to feel. She couldn't remember when she had felt like this before. It was a kind of loneliness, a feeling of abandonment. She tried to shake it but it continued to grip her.

The city lights were on as they crossed the bridge and entered Manhattan. Traffic was heavy, so there was little conversation as Alan drove to the hotel.

"When will you be back in Mayfield?" Alan asked as he pulled up to the front entrance.

"I leave the day after tomorrow," she replied. "When will you be going back to Burlington Falls?"

"I turned in my letter of resignation to the headmaster at Briarwood even before I planned this trip. I knew I was going to make a change of some sort. Then when I found out about Ben's bookstore, it seemed to be the answer I'd been praying for. The direction for my future." He paused. "I believe we all have a niche to fill in our lives—a purpose. I really think I've found mine."

For some reason Evalee felt tears stinging into her eyes. Her throat felt tight and terribly sore.

Alan reached for her hand. "Thanks for coming with me, Evalee. It meant a great deal to me. I wanted you to see the town, the bookstore, meet Ben, catch some of what's drawing me there."

Evalee felt as if she might cry. She had to get out of the car quickly, escape, before she broke down. "I'll see you back in Mayfield," she managed to say. Then she pushed open the door, grabbed her overnight case, said a choked good-bye, and ran into the hotel.

All the way back to Mayfield, Evalee gazed out the window of the train, remembering the last time she made this trip, the last time she traveled in this direction over these same tracks. She had been filled with doubt and fear, facing a frightening future, coming back to Mayfield with some bitterness, little hope. Things had turned out much better than she could ever have imagined. God had been very good, had blessed her hard work, her diligence, her goals. Her business was successful, things were working out. Why then did she feel so sad?

She should be happy for Alan. As he said, he had prayed for guidance about his future, and he felt he had found it. Why then had there been that look in his eyes, in his expression, as if he were waiting for something more from her, expecting it, hoping for it?

He could have gone alone to Burlington Falls, could have completed the arrangements, signed the contract on his own. Why had he made it such a point for her to come along?

She thought of the quaint little town, the main street with its row of little stores and shops, the country roads with small farmhouses tucked into the hillside, the breathtaking colors of the fall landscape. It had all looked like one of those "New

England autumn" calendar pictures. Emily Dickinson, Amy Lowell, John Greenleaf Whittier—the poets of her high school English literature classes—had loved New England, had written about it. She thought of all the things Alan planned to do with the store to make his dream come true. She thought of the quiet dignity, the authentic decor, of the Colonial Arms Inn—and she thought of the gray-shingled house with the "For Sale" sign on its sagging fence, which she had seen just as they were driving out of town. . . . .

Oh, this is all foolishness, Evalee told herself sternly. Why was she being sentimental about a town she had visited only briefly?

She had a life of her own to think about. A life with Natasha, a life with a business she had created. Then why this emptiness, this sudden ache of loneliness? People admired her, her taste, her chic, her air of self-confidence.

Yet all that was deceptive, a facade for what was really going on inside. The truth was, she longed for a completion that seemed to have eluded her these past few years. She longed for love—strong, true, devoted love.

Trent MacGowan had offered her everything else, a life of easy elegance. She had been tempted, perhaps, but she had turned it down, knowing that this was not what would fulfill her deepest longings. A real home, a caring husband, a father for Natasha—that was the dream she hardly dared name.

Alan had prayed about his dream and he had received his answer. Had she tried to do it all by herself, afraid to surrender it all to the Source of all good gifts?

Her thoughts drifted. If only someone like Alan . . . What? Loved her? Wanted her and Natasha in his life?

Maybe that's why he had taken her along with him to Burlington Falls. Maybe he had wanted to see her reaction, get her approval, bring her into his dream.

Evalee's heart began to pound. She began to picture the dark, narrow little store. Slowly the image changed. She saw it with proper lighting, a Windsor chair or two, hooked rugs, the potbellied stove Alan had talked about, books arranged by categories, a few good paintings on the walls—and the cat! Yes, of course, a taffy-colored cat curled up in the front window, to be viewed through crystal-clear glass by the welcome browsers. She could do all that for Alan, help make his dream bookstore a reality. And they could live in that gray-shingled house by the side of the road, with nasturtiums climbing the picket fence, which would be all whitewashed and straightened. Natasha could go to school in that little red schoolhouse on the hill, and . . .

Suddenly Evalee couldn't wait for the train to pull into the Mayfield station. She couldn't wait to tell Alan all that was in her heart to tell him. In the deepest part of her soul, she knew that he loved her, that he had been waiting, hoping that she would feel the same way.

chapter 22

Some of Evalee's certainty faded away during the next forty-eight hours. There was much to do when she got home—calls to return, work to be finished on some decorating projects, Natasha to be made ready for the opening of school.

Underneath all this ran the question, should she call Alan? Had she assumed too much? Had she raced ahead of him in her own thoughts? If Alan felt the way she had come to believe he did, why hadn't he spoken while they were in Connecticut, asked her then how she felt? Or hadn't she given him a chance?

She remembered that she had done a lot of the talking. Excited by the experience of attending her first big New York auction, she may have given him the impression that her career was more important than anything else. Maybe he had been put off by that, discouraged inadvertently by her enthusiasm. What could she do to correct that?

Once Alan left for Connecticut, it would be too late. He would never know how she really felt. Did she dare just come right out and tell him?

She prowled Gatehouse like a nervous cat, unable to settle down. Two days passed. Did he know she was home? If so, why hadn't he called? The third morning, Evalee sat staring at the phone on her desk. Dru had come to take Natasha to go shopping for some school clothes, and Evalee was alone.

Briarwood opened later than the Mayfield public schools. Was Alan there? The resident teachers had their own apartments in the dormitory buildings. On the trip, Alan had remarked that moving was going to be a major undertaking. He had accumulated so much "stuff" that it would take a steam shovel to clear it out. Was he over there now, moving out?

Impulsively Evalee reached for the phone. What did she have to lose?

The phone seemed to ring for a long time. She was about to hang up, when Alan came on the line. "Hello."

"Alan? It's Evalee. I just wondered if you were still there."

He sounded very happy to hear her voice. "Yes, I'm here, but I'm practically inundated with cardboard boxes. I'm packing up, getting ready to leave."

"I thought so. I was afraid I might have missed you—"

"I wouldn't have left without coming to say good-bye to you and Natasha." He sounded almost reproachful.

"I'd hoped not. When are you leaving?"

"Day after tomorrow. That is, if I can get all this sorted out."

There was a pause. Then Evalee took a long breath and asked, "Want some help? I'm free. I could drive over. I'm very good at packing."

"You'd do that?" Alan sounded surprised.

"Of course. I can be there in forty-five minutes."

All the way over to Briarwood, Evalee kept asking herself, *What am I doing? What do I expect? What do I want to happen?*

She still hadn't answered those questions when she turned in the gates of Briarwood and drove along the winding roads around the rolling campus greens. Alan's apartment was in Bellamere, one of the dorms. The old brick building was covered with Virginia creeper, its leaves now turning crimson at the edges. She pulled to a stop in front. Before she had even cut her engine, he came running out of the arched doorway. He must have been watching for her.

He looked endearingly boyish. His hair was tousled, and he was wearing a V-necked sweater, rumpled khakis. He was also grinning from ear to ear. "It was great of you to come."

"I couldn't stay away," she said, smiling up at him as he opened the car door and helped her out. They stood there for a long minute, very close. Evalee's heart began to beat very fast. "What I mean is, I couldn't let you go without—"

"Without what?" His hands tightened on hers.

Evalee glanced around. There was no one in sight. The campus was empty.

"Maybe we'd better go inside," she said shyly, feeling her face warm.

They walked into the apartment, which was now bare of furniture, books, pictures. Boxes were everywhere, some already sealed and ready for loading, others standing open. Evalee had hardly stepped over the threshold when Alan prompted, "Now, what couldn't you let me go without doing?"

Evalee might never have had the courage if Alan's eyes and eager expression had not convinced her that she had not come on a fool's errand. She took a deep breath. Although she spoke in a low voice, her words seemed to echo in the empty room. "Alan, I don't want you to go. Not without me. I love you."

She could hardly believe she'd said it.

At first Alan seemed dumbstruck. Then a series of emotions flashed across his face in quick succession—astonishment, relief, joy. "You mean it? You really do?"

"Yes. *Yes!* That's what I came to tell you. I think I knew it even before we went to Connecticut. Then, on the way home—"

Alan never let her finish. He was kissing her and murmuring, "I can hardly believe it. I've wanted it for so long. I didn't think . . . I mean, I wasn't sure you could love me—"

"I do!" She said, holding him, half laughing. "I really do."

For the next hour they sat on packing boxes, holding hands, discussing all that had to be settled. Every so often they stopped to kiss and to declare their love for each other. There was so much to decide upon—the closing of Gatehouse Interiors, a date for the wedding, what arrangements should be made for Evalee and Natasha to travel to Burlington Falls, where Alan promised to see at once about buying the house Evalee wanted.

"We are going to be so happy," Alan said.

"I know." Evalee smiled at him. Her heart was rejoicing. It was as if a hundred bells were ringing.

It was growing dark outside. Since Alan had already packed his desk lamp, the room was soon full of shadows. Reluctantly Evalee stood up, saying, "I'd better go. Mama will be bringing Natasha home soon."

"Will they be happy with our news?" Alan asked anxiously.

"Natasha will be beside herself! She adores you. And Mama will feel content that I have found someone like you." Evalee put her hands on either side of Alan's face, drew it down so she could kiss him. "And I feel very blessed indeed."

New York

The same day her book arrived at the bookstores, a florist's box was delivered to Kitty's apartment. In it there was a note.

May I take you to dinner tomorrow night? I'm at my

office, catching up on a stack of accumulated work. Let me know what time to pick you up. I Look forward to seeing you.

Craig

Under the layers of green tissue paper was a bouquet of flowers—irises, tulips, jonquils. As she lifted them out, their dewy freshness reminded her of spring in Virginia. She felt a twinge of homesickness. Still, she didn't know if she could go back, at least not yet. She wasn't sure what the repercussions would be once Cara and Kip had read her book.

The memory of her last visit to Montclair struck Kitty with a renewed sense of loss. It was not only hard but painful that she and her sister had parted the way they did. She and her twin had always been so close. Too close, Cara had said at times. It was as if they could somehow see inside each other's heart, read each other's mind. It seemed impossible to Kitty that they had reacted so differently to the experience of war.

She put the flowers in a vase and called Craig's office. His voice, when she was put through to him, sounded pleased that she had called. "Are you happy with the book?" he asked eagerly.

"Yes, very. I can hardly believe it."

"You did a great job. I know it was hard work. But it's going to do well."

Craig had another call waiting, so they quickly decided upon a time for him to come for her the next evening. They had not seen each other since her return to New York.

When she opened her apartment door to greet him, she was smiling. He was momentarily stunned. He wasn't used to seeing Kitty smile. The times they'd been together, they had mostly discussed the book, and her expression had usually been serious.

She looks incredible, Craig thought. She was glowing. Everything about her seemed to shine—her hair, her eyes. She was wearing a two-piece bronze velvet suit with satin lapels and cuffs, topaz earrings, and matching beads.

"I must thank you again for letting me use your beach house, Craig," Kitty told him. "I loved it. It was just what I needed. It got me over whatever I was going through, and the work went well out there."

"The book showed it, Kitty. Minimal corrections in the final editing. So how did you like the finished product?"

"It's amazing. Unreal! And yet it's out there. I've seen it, held it, read parts of it here and there. I don't feel so possessive about it anymore. It's got a life of its own." She smiled. "I feel the way a mother must feel when she's sending a child out into the world."

"With her blessing, I hope."

"Fervently that, yes." Her face grew somber. "I want so much for it to succeed, Craig. Not for my sake as much as for Richard's and all the men like him."

They both were silent a moment, remembering. Then Craig held her beaver jacket for her. She slipped into it, and they went out of the apartment together into the city night.

The minute they stepped into the lobby of the famous New York restaurant, Kitty felt a sense of elation. All the months of work were behind her now. Her editor was pleased, and that gave her a wonderful sense of confidence.

The maitre d' recognized Craig and greeted him cordially. They were shown to a corner table, and a waiter soon appeared to take their order. Kitty looked around the elegant room at the pale mauve walls, the muted lighting. It had been ages since she had been so aware of her surroundings. She had been living in a cocoon for months.

They dined leisurely. Their waiter was attentive yet did not hover. Kitty felt relaxed, comfortable, as Craig talked about his trip abroad, mentioning some authors whose names she knew, and shared some interesting anecdotes about them. When their coffee arrived, he leaned back and asked her, "So now what do you plan to do? Write another book?

She shook her head. "No, I don't think so. I'm not a writer, Craig. I had that one story to tell, and I've told it." She paused. "Frankly, I don't know what I'll do. Writing this has absorbed me so completely that I haven't thought of anything, certainly not what's next."

He regarded her thoughtfully for a moment, then leaned forward and said quietly, "Then why not think about marrying me, Kitty?"

Craig's proposal was so unexpected that at first Kitty did not know how to respond. She had never really thought she would marry again. Richard's loss had devastated her. They had been soul mates, so intimate that it was hard to think of achieving that kind of togetherness with someone else.

"I don't intend to press you, Kitty. Take all the time you need to consider. I believe we could have a wonderful life together. I would do everything I knew of to make it so. We have much in common, much we could build on." Craig seemed to deliberately keep his voice from pleading. But his eyes were as anxious as a boy's. "I have come to love you very much, Kitty. The whole of you—the way you think, the way you feel, the way you express the deepest things you cherish." He stopped, then smiled, adding, "To say nothing of the way you look."

She felt a warmth creep into her cheeks. No man had looked at her the way Craig was, not for a very long time, not since Richard.

"I'm flattered, Craig, that you—"

"Nonsense, Kitty. There's no flattery involved here. I admire you for your honesty, your beliefs. Even if you turn me down,

I will feel honored to have known you. But the fact is that I love you. I can't imagine my life without you now."

He took her back to her apartment. At her door she looked up into his kind, strong-featured face, into the eyes searching hers. Slowly he took her into his arms, kissed her. She did not resist. It was a kiss of deep tenderness but also one that stirred fires of passion within her. It awakened in Kitty a longing for the kind of intimacy and fulfillment she had once known. Could she find it again with Craig?

When the kiss ended, she slowly drew away, out of his embrace, but he caught her hands, held them. "Kitty I do love you so. I know we could have a wonderful life together. Promise me you'll think about what I asked you?"

"Yes, I promise, Craig. But you must give me time to think, to consider . . . to pray about this."

"Of course." He leaned forward and kissed her again softly. "Good night, Kitty."

That night Kitty dreamed of Montclair, how it had been when she last saw it, how it must be now with the coming spring.

It happened in her dream just as it did in real life. Every year, with spectacular suddenness, spring burst upon the land, and the lawns stretching down to the curved driveway became golden with daffodils.

In her dream Kitty was running away from the house, not across the meadow to the woodland path or the rustic bridge that led to Eden Cottage but past all that, down to the gates and into the county road. She ran with a kind of lighthearted joyousness and woke up to find herself smiling.

She lay there for a few minutes, thinking about her dream. Kitty was not the least bit superstitious, nor did she put much credence in the meaning of dreams. Yet this one seemed to be saying something important. It came to her that she was running toward something new, something different, to a road that led to a wider world than she had known before.

When Craig called later in the day, she asked him if he would like to meet her in Central Park. Of course he agreed to do so. They strolled the paths and talked at length.

"As I said last night, Kitty, I hadn't meant to speak so quickly of my love. But being with you again . . . well, it happened. I had planned to be completely honest with you before I asked you to marry me. I wanted to tell you the truth about my background, who I am—or more specifically, who I am not."

Puzzled, Kitty stopped walking to look at Craig. What did he mean? She thought she knew him. What she saw was a good-looking, self-assured man in his early forties with an enviable position in a prestigious publishing company.

"I know the kind of background you come from, Kitty, and it couldn't be further from my beginnings. I know you have a list of ancestors a yard long, stretching back to this country's Colonial days. I know you have well-regarded relatives in all kinds of occupations. I don't. I don't know who my parents were, where I was born. I was bundled up in a basket and left under one of the benches in a railroad waiting room." Craig's smile was rueful. "Someone found me. Nobody at the station remembered having seen anyone or knew how I'd come to be there. I was taken to an orphanage. I didn't have a name, so they gave me one. Picked out of a hat, so to speak. The station was on the corner of two streets, Cavanaugh and Craig, so they combined them." Again the half-amused, half-sad expression crossed his face. "I guess I'm lucky they didn't call me New York Central, right?"

They started walking again as Craig continued. "Anyway, they kept me there until I was sixteen. Evidently I wasn't considered adoptable. I'd been taught a trade, printing, and from somewhere I'd developed a love of books. I'd exhausted the orphanage library by the time I was eleven. *Moby Dick, Robinson Crusoe, Huck Finn*—read them over and over. When they opened the door of the orphanage and told me, "Good luck," I knew I was going to need it. Still, I thought I could conquer the world." He paused. "I must say, I'm grateful they did prepare me, give me the tools to earn a living. I worked as a printer and went to school at night. Eventually I got my college degree. Getting into publishing is a long story, though. I'll tell you some other time." They had reached the statue of Hans Christian Anderson, and they stopped there.

Craig reached for Kitty's hand, brought it up to his chest, over his heart. "I wanted you to know all this, Kitty. I know I promised I wouldn't pressure you, but . . . I've never wanted anything in the world so much as for you to say yes."

All the time that Craig had been talking, telling her about himself, pouring out his story, something had been happening within Kitty. The tale of a lonely, "unadoptable" little boy struggling to find his place in a world that had abandoned him touched her deeply. In contrast, her life had been safe, secure, surrounded with loving, caring family—a family from whom she had estranged herself. She had what Craig longed to have, and she had not valued it enough.

"Thank you for being so honest, Craig. Not that it would have made any difference to me if you had a family or not. You are you, and I respect and admire you very much."

"But you're not sure you love me?"

"I had never thought of you in connection with that kind of love . . ."

"Will you think about it now?"

Kitty hesitated. There was so much to consider. "Yes, of course I will. I can't promise anything."

"Is there someone else? Another man?" Craig looked worried.

Kitty shook her head. "No, there's no one. And maybe that's just it. I've been alone for so many years, Craig, I don't know if I could share my life with anyone again."

"I would do everything possible to make you happy, Kitty."

"I know. I just need time—"

"Of course," he said. "I'll be patient. At least, I'll try to be."

They went their separate ways then—Craig to his office, Kitty to walk a little longer in the park. All the things Craig had told her swirled in her mind. So much had happened in a relatively short time that it was hard to put it all in perspective. There were so many unknowns. From her experiences with Richard's poetry books, Kitty knew that now that her war memoirs were published, she would hear from the public. There would be those who agreed with her and those who didn't. Her life as she had lived it was bound to change. If she accepted Craig's proposal, her life would change even more. Was she ready for that? Was she ready to love again?

By the spring, Kitty's book had moved up on the nonfiction best-seller list of the *New York Times*. Her book had been serialized by a leading women's magazine and excerpted in a prestigious weekly. Letters flowed in, forwarded to her by her publisher. Kitty had been asked to speak, sign books, on numerous occasions.

Craig basked in Kitty's success. One evening when they were dining together, he teased, "In all your new celebrity, have you forgotten that I asked you to marry me?" His tone was light but his eyes were serious.

Kitty reached across the table and placed her hand on his. "No, of course I've not forgotten, Craig. I've thought about it a great deal. But before I give you my answer, I have to go to Virginia. I have some unfinished business there—"

She had thought hard about everything they had talked about in Central Park, and she had come to one decision, at least. Just as Craig had felt that he had to empty himself before he could expect an answer to his proposal, Kitty realized that before she could give him that answer, begin a new life, she had to go home, to Mayfield, and make peace with her past.

He frowned. "What does that mean? You told me there was no one else who had to be considered or consulted—"

"It's nothing like that, Craig. I have to see my sister. My twin. I have to do that first. Now that my book is out, I need to see how she feels about it. I told you, she and my brother-in-law—well, we've had a misunderstanding over the way I feel about war. They knew I was writing a book, and of course they got a copy. Still, I have to go there in person."

"To mend fences? I see. I should think they'd be immensely proud of you, no matter what they think of your convictions." He smiled at her. "I know *I* am. Terribly proud."

She saw a look in his eyes that seemed to plead, *Don't make me wait too long, Kitty.*

chapter 23

Mayfield

KITTY DID NOT let anyone know she was coming. This time of year Cara would be busy getting her students ready to compete in the spring horse show.

All along the drive to Virginia, Kitty tried to analyze her feelings for Craig. Almost from the beginning, it had been more than just a good editor-author relationship, although she had not dared to recognize that she felt more than appreciation for his encouragement, admiration for his editorial skills, a growing affection for his consideration and sensitivity. Now he had offered something she had never thought to find again—a rich companionship, understanding, an enduring devotion.

One of the reasons she had wanted to come back to Mayfield, besides reconciliation with Cara, was to face her past. Not to retrieve what she had lost but to find the key to her future. She had to say good-bye to whatever part of herself she had left here. She wanted to be sure she could put the past behind her, open herself to a mature, fulfilling marriage with a man of strength and character like Craig.

Montclair

No one seemed to be at home when she drove up to the house, so Kitty left a note pinned on the screen door.

Cara,

I'm at Eden Cottage. Need to see you alone, to talk. Please come down as soon as you can.

Kitty

In the cottage she got a fire going, unpacked the groceries she had stopped in Mayfield to buy. She looked through the records she and Richard had collected, and selected a favorite to put on the phonograph.

Instead of filling her with melancholy, the little house seemed to welcome her. It had always been a receptive sort of place, and now it seemed to reflect her new happiness.

It was getting dark when Cara walked across the rustic bridge that led to Eden Cottage. She was full of curiosity and apprehension. The last meeting with her sister had ended with resentment and a kind of sorrowful regret. It was a breach that had not been healed. Kitty had not been back since well before her book was published. No letters had been exchanged. A heaviness had lodged painfully in Cara's heart. Now Kitty had come back unexpectedly. Why? Cara hesitated, then rapped lightly on the front door.

Thinking her knock must not have been heard, she opened the door and tentatively called her sister's name. Cara stepped cautiously inside and was greeted with warmth, the glow of a fire in the brick fireplace, and the sound of music playing.

"Kitty?"

"Cara!" Kitty appeared in the alcove between the front room and the kitchen.

For a moment the two stood across the room from each other, the atmosphere tense with all that had been said in the past, all that was in their hearts and minds to say now.

Kitty was the first to speak. "I was just fixing tea. Would you like some?"

"Yes, that would be nice," Cara answered stiffly. Then she offered, "Need some help?"

"No, thanks. It's all ready. I'll just bring it in." Kitty disappeared into the tiny kitchen. In a few minutes she returned, carrying a tray, which she set down on the cobbler's bench table in front of the fireplace. She smiled almost shyly at her sister. "I'm so glad you've come! I'm so happy to see you."

"Why didn't you let anyone know you were coming?"

Kitty's hand shook a little as she poured tea into their cups, then handed one to Cara. "I guess because I wasn't sure how I'd be received." She paused. "I mean here, at Montclair." She stopped and looked at Cara. "Have you read my book?"

"Yes."

"And has Kip?"

Cara took a sip of her tea before answering. "No. But then, Kip hardly reads anything but aeronautic manuals." She put her teacup down. "It was good, Kitty. Very good."

"Thank you. I had to write it, you know." She shrugged. "I don't know what good it will do. One of the major magazines is running it as a book-length feature, though."

"That should reach a lot of people."

"Yes," Kitty sighed. "That means a great deal. But it won't be worth it to me if we—Cara, I'm so sorry we quarreled."

"I am, too. But I think I understand how you feel, Kitty. It's just that I can't fight with Kip over it. He and I—well, maybe we have an unusual marriage, but I don't tell him what he can do or think or say, and neither does he tell me. That's the way it is with us."

"Marriages are always different, depending on the two people. You and Owen had one type of marriage, Richard and I had another." Kitty leaned forward. "Cara, I have something to tell you. Something marvelous. Something unexpected. Something I never thought would happen again to me. I'm in love. And we're going to be married. That's the real reason I came back now. I wanted you to be the first to know, and I wanted things to be right between us again. Do you think that can happen?"

Tears flooded into Cara's eyes. She reached across the table and grasped her twin's hands, squeezing them tightly. "Yes, of course. Now, tell me everything."

During the next hour their estrangement melted away. It was as if they both knew that even as close as twins can be, each had another path to walk, another life to live, apart from each other. Cara rejoiced for Kitty as her sister told her about Craig. "Of course you'll be married here, won't you? You'll let me do the wedding?"

Her eyes misty, Kitty nodded. "I just hope Craig won't be overwhelmed by my hordes of relatives!"

"Nonsense! We're just what an orphan needs–a big, noisy family!" Cara said, laughing gaily.

Before Cara left to go back up to the house, the sisters hugged for a long time.

"I'm so sorry for all the ugly things I said to you, Cara. Will you forgive me?"

"Of course. This year has been horrible. I missed you so much. I missed your letters, your postcards." Cara stepped back, put her hands on Kitty's shoulders, and looked at her directly. "When you were with Mama in Santa Barbara, did you tell her about our quarrel?"

"Yes. She was really upset about it. She repeated what she

used to quote to us all the time at home when we squabbled. Remember?"

Cara frowned. "No, I don't think I do."

"Matthew 5:25—'Settle matters quickly with your adversary, or he may hand you over to the judge.'"

"Who was the judge? Daddy?" Cara asked, laughing.

"I guess in those days." Kitty joined in her laughter. "But seriously, let's let bygones be bygones. No more arguments."

"Not ever," agreed the other, knowing that distance and time apart would probably make that an easy promise to keep.

Cara hurried through the gathering dark. She saw Kip's old car haphazardly parked near the back. He had kept his beloved sports roadster, scuffed, battered, and rattling as it was. She suspected he did so not only because they couldn't afford a new car but because it represented something to him of his former, carefree days.

Cara ran up the back steps. She hoped Niki and Luc were home and that someone had started something for supper. The screen door banged behind her. She stopped, listening for sounds of activity within the house. As she waited, the door opened again and Kip came in. He stood there, and in the shadows she saw something in his face that sped straight to her heart. Without a word she went into his arms. As they enclosed her, Cara thought of her sister awaiting the fulfillment of a new love. Her own was an old love, cherished like an old book of poetry—tattered and worn perhaps, with phrases underlined, writing in the margins, but still intact, having stood the test of time. Childhood, youth, now the middle of life—she and Kip had come a long way together. No matter what anyone else thought, said, or saw, this love had lasted—and would last through all eternity.

A week later Kitty sent Craig a single-word telegram—"Yes."

chapter 24

KITTY INSISTED ON a small ceremony with only family in attendance. "I don't want to overwhelm Craig on his first visit," she told Cara. "Our combined families will be quite enough for someone who grew up practically on his own."

Craig had arrived by train the afternoon before. Kitty met him at the Mayfield station and drove him to Cameron Hall, where he would stay until after their wedding the next day. That evening Jill arranged a lovely buffet supper, and all the family who were in town came to meet Kitty's bridegroom.

It was an enjoyable evening. To Kitty's delight and certainly to her expectation, Craig conducted himself with sophisticated ease. No one could fault him. He seemed as comfortable with the assorted family members as he would have been in a boardroom, in an editorial conference, or at a booksellers' meeting. He conversed as well with Scott on current events as he did with Gareth on gardening, with Dru on the history of Virginia, and with Evalee on antiques. Kitty experienced a quiet pride in the man she had chosen to marry.

The four little girls sat on the stairway steps, balancing plates of food and glasses of punch.

"He's handsome, isn't he?" Niki commented to the others.

"Yes, but old," said Scotty.

"Not too old. Not any older than Uncle Scott," demurred Niki.

"Daddy's not old," bristled Scotty.

"Sort of. Anyway, it doesn't matter. Let's talk about our weddings," Niki said, changing the subject. "I'm going to wear a veil, not a hat like Aunt Kitty's going to wear. A real veil with lace and little pearls."

"Will I be at your wedding, Niki?" asked Natasha.

"Sure you will, Tasha."

"Me too?" echoed Cara-Lyn.

"Yes, of course. All of you will. We'll all be at each other's weddings," Niki declared emphatically.

"Let's promise. We'll each be each other's bridesmaids!" Scotty bounced excitedly. "Promise," she prompted, holding out her hand, the little finger crooked. One by one each child joined hers with the others all around. Satisfied that the promise was sealed, they went back to eating.

Then Niki announced, "I'm going to marry Luc when I grow up."

Scotty looked at her. "You can't! Luc's your *brother.*" She added scornfully, "People don't marry their brothers."

"He's not my *real* brother," retorted Niki.

"He isn't?" Cara-Lyn was surprised. "How come?"

"'Cause I'm 'dopted," Niki told her.

"You mean, Aunt Cara and Uncle Kip aren't your real parents?"

"Nope. Tante 'dopted me."

"That means you're an orphan?" Scotty gasped. "Like Little Orphan Annie in the comics?"

Orphan. The word hung there for a moment. The three other girls stared with new interest at Niki. Under their scrutiny, her spoonful of ice cream slid down her suddenly tight throat. For the first time she could remember, she realized what the word meant. It meant being alone, abandoned, without a mommy and daddy of your own. It meant you didn't belong to anybody.

The next morning, the little chapel on the Montrose property—built by one of the brides of Montclair, Avril—was being decorated for the noon wedding of Kitty Traherne and Craig Cavanaugh.

The little cousins, who were all going to be flower girls, had been put to work, mostly to keep them out of mischief. They carried in the flowers, which had been placed in water buckets the night before to keep them fresh, and helped arrange them in the white wicker baskets set along the altar railing. Cara and Lynette, who were doing the decorating, tried to keep the children busy—anything to prevent them from escaping to romp outside and have to be bathed, shampooed, all over again.

Niki and Scotty were the hardest to keep track of, chasing each other in and out of the open chapel doors, racing up and down the porch steps. Cara-Lyn stood quietly, waiting for instructions and solemnly handing one gladiola after the other to Lynette. Natasha, awestruck to be included in this special occasion, sat in the front pew, alternately watching the ladies decorate and giggling at the antics of her two older cousins.

"Now, I've had about enough of you two scalawags," Cara said at last, whirling around, hands on her hips, glaring at Niki and Scotty as they came laughing and puffing down the center aisle. "Nicole, I'm warning you." She tried to scowl at the pretty little girls with their flushed cheeks, dancing eyes, and tumbled curls. "Now, you and Scotty sit still until we're ready to go back up to the house and get dressed, or you're not going to be in the wedding at all!"

That threat subdued the two culprits, and they sidled into one of the back pews, momentarily quiet.

"Weddings are really fun, aren't they?" Scotty whispered behind one chubby hand.

Niki nodded vigorously. "But I'm going to have a *big* wedding. In a *big* church. Maybe a cathedral in France."

"How can you do that?" demanded Scotty. "We live in Virginia."

"Well, we're not going to live here our entire lives, silly," retorted Niki. "'Sides, I'm French. I'll have to go back someday and see where I was born."

This thought caused Scotty to wrinkle her brow. "My mother's English, but she got married *here*."

"So what?" Niki sniffed. "That's different."

"How is it different?" Scotty persisted.

"Well . . ." Niki drew out the word, prolonging it as she tried to think of how to answer Scotty's question.

As it turned out, she didn't need to, because Cara turned around just then and said, "Come on, girls, let's go. We've only got about an hour and a half to get dressed and ready." She wanted Kitty's wedding to be perfect. She then said to Lynette, "I think we did a good job. The flowers really look lovely."

"Yes, I agree. So then, I'll see you later. You don't mind letting Cara-Lyn tag along with you? It won't be too much to have another one to dress?"

"Not at all. Cara-Lyn's never any bother, are you, sweetie?" She leaned down and patted the child's cheek, then took the little girl's hands. Cara rolled her eyes dramatically. "It's the other two! But they'll all look adorable, and it will be worth the trouble." Her gaze fell on Natasha, who was still seated in the corner of the front pew.

"I'll take them on up to the house, Cara," Lynette said. "I

know you want to stop by Eden Cottage for a minute and see Kitty. Come along, girls."

When Cara let herself in the door, she found Kitty sitting quietly in one of the wing chairs by the window that overlooked the little garden. She was already wearing the gown she had chosen for her wedding, a tea-rose silk dress made with exquisite simplicity. She had yet to put on her lace gloves and her pale-pink, silk-straw hat, which lay on the table beside her. The hat had an upturned brim, and its band was trellised with a ruffle of satin-ribbon roses.

There was such a sweet serenity in Kitty's expression as she turned to greet her that Cara was filled with emotion. More than anything, Cara wanted her adored sister to be happy.

An hour later Cara felt assured of that prayerful wish.

Listening to Craig and Kitty make their vows, her own throat tightened. It reminded her poignantly of what those vows were supposed to mean when taken with a sincere intention to carry them out. The look on both faces left no doubt in Cara's mind that this was truly a marriage of minds, hearts, and souls.

Burlington Falls, Connecticut

From the living room window, where she stood on a stepladder, hanging the new curtains, Evalee saw the delivery truck turn into their driveway. She wondered if this could finally be the lampshades she'd ordered. She got down and hurried to the front door just as the driver was coming up the porch steps, carrying a large, square package.

"Howdy, Mrs. Reid," he greeted her. "I guess you folks get more packages than anyone else in Burlington Falls."

"Wedding presents, mostly!" she said, smiling.

"Well, this is a right heavy one. Better let me take it inside for you. Unless the mister's at home?"

"No, he's down at the bookstore. Thanks. Bring it on in."

He set it down right inside the door and she signed for it. After they had exchanged a few remarks about the garden and the lilac bush by the door just coming into bloom, the delivery man got back in his truck and drove away.

Evalee examined the address label. They'd received gifts from almost everyone they knew in Mayfield. Who could this be from—and what was it?

Should she wait for Alan before opening it? She glanced at her watch. He would be home for lunch in another half hour, so she decided to wait. Having lunch together was one of the happy little rituals of their married life. He usually had some funny anecdote to tell her about a customer or something that had happened that he thought would interest or amuse her. This had become a time that both of them looked forward to and enjoyed.

Evalee went into the kitchen to heat up the homemade soup and warm the rolls. She looked around the sunny room with its alcoved nook that looked out into the backyard, where two gnarled old apple trees were budding and scenting the early spring air with a delightful fragrance. It was wonderful to be so incredibly happy, so very blessed. She thanked God every day for the unexpected happiness her life had become.

At the sound of the front door opening and Alan's voice calling her name, she spun around and hurried out into the hallway to welcome him.

"We've got another wedding present," she told him. "Come and see. It's very mysterious. There's only the address of one of those packaging places—no return address, no name. I haven't a clue as to who it's from."

"Probably one of your secret admirers," Alan said, grinning. "Here, I'll cut it open." He took his penknife out of his pocket and snipped the string. Eagerly, Evalee began to tear off the brown wrapping paper. Underneath the thick corrugated cardboard, she saw an ornate frame and then the portrait. There was a small label on the back of the canvas—Unknown Lady, circa 1840. An envelope was taped to the edge of the frame. She took it, opened it, and read,

This lady evidently does not belong at Wemberly.

It was signed by Trent MacGowan.

"Let me see, honey," Alan said, and she handed him the card. He read it, then studied the painting. "It could be *you*. The eyes, the cheekbones, the coloring. I suppose that's why he sent it. Did you find it for him for Wemberly?"

Evalee shook her head. "No. He found it himself. But he's right. The lady doesn't belong at Wemberly. She belongs right here." She went over, put her arms around Alan, and kissed him. "I think she'll look perfect right over the mantelpiece, don't you?"

Birchfields
September 3, 1939

THAT BRIGHT SEPTEMBER morning, there was not the slightest hint nor premonition of coming disaster. The papers were not delivered until late in the afternoon. An air of absolute tranquillity sheltered the rambling Tudor mansion. Garnet had spent most of the morning happily, supervising her gardener outside.

At noon she reluctantly left to have lunch and take a nap afterward. Much as she hated to admit it, she was feeling a little stiff. Her hip was bothering her again. But she refused to use a cane. Just feeling her age a bit, she decided. A little rest in the afternoon always seemed to revive her, and she had given in to the necessity of one.

After her rest and a bath, she went downstairs to have her tea, an English custom she had long since adopted. She walked into the drawing room, a beautiful, imposing room whose French windows opened onto the terrace. For a moment she stood looking out at the garden, onto its sculptured hedges, its beautifully blooming flower beds. Now purple shadows stretched across the velvety green lawns.

With a sigh she turned back into the room that had been Jeremy's favorite. The big house taunted her with its emptiness. Since its restoration in the early 1920s, her home had retained much of the same elegance it had when she and Jeremy first bought it, shortly after their marriage. They had made it into not only a showplace to entertain but also a home to be enjoyed. Absently she twisted her engagement ring, placed on her finger by Jeremy so long ago—a rich cluster of garnets circled by sparkling diamonds in delicate gold prongs. Dear Jeremy, he had possessed the gift of soothing her anxieties, calming her anger, and making her behave sensibly and rationally when she was apt to fly off on tangents.

Garnet's loneliness met her at every turn, in every room, at every vista viewed from the windows of Birchfields. She remembered the days when it had been filled with company—Jeremy's friends, his business associates. He had liked to entertain, to show off his beautiful American wife, to bask in the surroundings of hearth, home, family. When Faith was alive, young people had made the place merry on weekends with their music, games, and laughter. All that was gone now. The house had a disturbing quiet that sometimes made Garnet uneasy.

Perhaps she should never have come back here to live. But to stay in Virginia was impossible. Her life there was over—had been over for years. Mayfield and Montclair held too many memories, too many regrets, for her to live happily there.

Of course, Bryanne and her nice husband, Steven Colby, came to visit. However, he was completing his studies at Oxford, and Bryanne was pursuing an artistic career as a sculptor, gaining some recognition with her children's figures. So their visits were not all that frequent. Bryanne did phone once a week, and it was always good to hear her sweet voice and her news.

Garnet sighed again. Maybe these bouts of nostalgia were common as one grew older. She considered herself very fortunate. She had her health, thank God, and life went on in spite of loss, suffering, pain. She had at long last come to accept that, take what joy she could find. She had to—nothing was going to change. All she could hope for was to live out the remainder of her life in comparative contentment.

Still, a person had to know what was going on. Garnet settled down in her favorite armchair. On the table beside it was a small radio. In a few minutes she would turn it on for the BBC's six o'clock news. The reports had been bad lately, yet she felt obligated to listen. Surely the European countries would not repeat their mistakes. But one never knew what that madman in Germany and his equally awful colleague in Italy might do next to upset the balance of the world's peace.

In spite of herself, Garnet shuddered. How often had Jeremy halted her trivial worries—not that this was trivial—to say, "Learn to live in the present moment, darling. That is, after all, all that any of us have."

She turned on the radio, adjusted the dial, prepared to listen to the regular commentator. At first she thought she must not be hearing correctly. She had been having trouble with her hearing lately. She twisted the knob to increase the volume as the well-modulated, perfectly calm voice said, "The prime minister's office has officially announced that Great Britain and France have declared war on Germany."

Shakily, Garnet reached for the folded evening paper beside her chair, as if to confirm the truth of the announcement. Her glance moved rapidly over the page, from the banner headline to the detailed article outlining the steps that had led the country to this inevitable fate. Hitler had invaded Poland, in direct opposition to his signed nonaggression pact with England.

Garnet began to shiver. She had known war firsthand. In America as a young girl, it was the War between the States. Less than twenty-five years ago it was the Great War, the one that was to end all wars. It couldn't be happening again!

"I'm too old for this too!" she said aloud, throwing aside the newspaper. She declared, clenching her jeweled hands, "I can't go through it again. It will kill me!"

From the hall she could hear the telephone ringing.

Marsden, her elderly butler, would get it. She heard the low murmur of his voice, and then he entered the room. "It's Miss Bryanne, madam."

Bryanne, of course. By now she would have heard the news, too. And Steven! With a clutching sensation in her heart, Garnet thought, *Steven will have to go.* Steven—thoughtful, intelligent, with his low-key sense of humor and his supportive love for her granddaughter—would surely have to sign up for one of the services. What a waste. Leaning heavily on her cane, feeling suddenly quite stiff, Garnet made her way out to the hall phone.

She talked for several minutes with Bryanne.

"Well, my dear, if or when Steven has to go, you must come here, be with me," Garnet said.

They spoke another few minutes. Then, before she hung up, Bryanne promised to let her grandmother know what they would do.

Garnet felt somewhat comforted after the conversation. England at war with Germany for the second time in her life. Would America eventually be drawn in, like last time?

What could she do at her age? In 1916 she had turned Birchfields into a convalescent home. This war, too, would have its casualties. Could she do it again? Of course, she would need help. She couldn't manage it all on her own, as she had then. But if Bryanne came here, perhaps . . .

Where had she put her old scrapbooks, her photo albums, her account books, the detailed daily record of the time when Birchfields had been a haven for ambulatory patients? She got up, went over to the window again. In a few months the garden would be budding with lovely blossoms, perfuming the air. Yes, it really could happen. Even in a darkening world, Birchfields could again become a healing place, full of hope, promise.

We want to hear from you. Please send your comments about this book to us in care of the address below. Thank you.

ZondervanPublishingHouse
Grand Rapids, Michigan 49530
http://www.zondervan.com